*To all
who wage peace
by
staff or sword*

Other Books by
Ellen Gunderson Traylor

**ELLEN GUNDERSON
TRAYLOR**

JOSHUA

GOD'S WARRIOR

HARVEST HOUSE PUBLISHERS
Eugene, Oregon 97402

JOSHUA, GOD'S WARRIOR

Copyright © 1991 by Harvest House Publishers
Eugene, Oregon 97402

Library of Congress Cataloging-in-Publication Data

Traylor, Ellen Gunderson.
    Joshua, God's warrior / Ellen Gunderson Traylor.
      ISBN 0-89081-853-3
      1. Joshua (Biblical figure)—Fiction.   2. Bible. O.T.—History of Biblical events—
Fiction.   I. Title.
PS3570.R357J65   1991
813'.54—dc20   90-24542
                                                            CIP

Printed in the United States of America.

CONTENTS

A Note to the Reader

PROLOGUE

EPILOGUE

A NOTE TO THE READER

It was hard to walk in Moses's shadow, to miss the calling of prophet and be appointed instead to fulfill a role that seemed less spiritual.

But Joshua needed to learn that all God's callings are holy, and that there are many ways to serve.

As promised in the preface to *Moses: The Deliverer*, *Joshua: God's Warrior* follows the children of Israel from their escape from Egypt to their entrance into the Promised Land. While these chapters continue the saga of Moses, Joshua looms larger with each episode, and earns his place in history not only as right-hand man to the prophet, but as a mighty leader in his own right.

This is the story not only of God's working through prophecy, but of his special ordination of a military general. It reveals the demanding character of Yahweh, as well as his fatherhood, as he prepares Israel for its inheritance. And it lays the sword parallel with the shepherd's staff, as Joshua fulfills his purpose.

But *Joshua: God's Warrior* is also a story of one man's personal journey. The one who knew the lonely path of leadership would be surprised by love, both human and divine. In finding the Promised Land, tradition says, he also found a home for his heart and embraced a Gentile woman as part of his rightful inheritance.

May this book bless you as you pursue your own Promised Land.

Ellen Traylor

PROLOGUE

Joshua knew where Moses was camped. He had followed close beside him all day, this third day of the great exodus from Pharaoh's Egypt. But as the Israelites had settled down for the night, beneath the orange glow of the miraculous fiery pillar, the young man left the prophet to himself.

This was a fearful night, and he knew the man of God wished to be alone. It was the first night on the very edge of the wilderness, and he had sensed a heaviness in Moses as they approached it.

He had rarely been beyond view of the great leader since they had departed Raamses. Only a few days before, Moses had promised him that he could be his servant, that second to Aaron he was his right-hand man. With eager devotion he had seized the role, happily answering to the name Moses had given him.

Father Nun and Grandfather Elishama were having trouble becoming accustomed to the new name. They still called him Hoshea, if they were not careful. But they were old men. Joshua did not correct them.

His friend, Caleb, had taken easily to the name change. Joshua's closest companion since childhood, the young Judahite had stuck with him and with Moses through the dramatic days when they had gone before Pharaoh. He had witnessed the king's resistance, and encouraged the man of God to hold firm.

It was Caleb whom Joshua sought this night, as he wandered through the great camp of the Israelites. Many dark thoughts were his, and he wished to fill someone's ears with them. He knew Caleb would listen.

As he made his way between the staggered rows of tents, he was glad he had no immediate family. Though he often

11

longed for the comfort of wife and children, the sounds of whimpering babies and the sight of young women cradling them against the peculiar cold that always descended upon the nighttime desert troubled him deeply.

The Israelites had borne with four centuries of misery as slaves to Egypt, laboring beneath whip and rod. The ordeal had toughened their bodies and their spirits. Each new generation was hardier than the last, as those who could not survive died off, and those who could gave birth to strong children. Yet these people were accustomed to the mild climate of the Nile Valley and the region of Goshen, most pleasant land on earth. They had never walked through scorching daytime sands, nor had they shivered with the chill of Sinai nights.

How would they survive the journey ahead?

Indeed, the journey itself was a mystery. Never in human history had three million people set out across unknown terrain, in pursuit of an uncertain destiny, and following a leader enigmatic as his demands. Upon their backs were only the clothes they had taken from their former masters. True, they bore layers of heavy golden bracelets and neckchains upon their arms and torsos. In their wagons were clanking silver vessels and boxes full of coins. But what good were such treasures in the lifeless sands about them?

They had enough food in their colossal company to last only a few days, though they had taken as much as they could carry from the anxious Egyptians. "Go! Get out of here!" their terrified masters had urged. "Take what you want, but go, lest your god send another plague upon us!" While the Israelites lived on the memory of Yahweh's saving hand, on the witness of devastations wrought upon Egypt by the rod of Moses, Joshua wondered how long their faith would last when hunger gnawed at their ribs.

Yes, he was glad, just now, that he had no wife or child. But he did have an aging father and an elderly grandfather. In his extended family, there were many young ones, feeble widows, and nursing mothers. Concern for them, and for all the helpless folk of this exodus weighed heavy upon him.

Joshua was a young man, only forty-five years old. He had not attained the status of an elder among his people. But he was already highly respected for his keen mind and obvious leadership abilities. Hundreds greeted him as he walked through the vast crowd this evening.

When he saw Caleb seated beside an evening fire, he eagerly called to him, "Friend, walk with me."

Glad to be singled out, Caleb rose to meet the handsome Joshua, and joined him on his rounds. Each evening the servant of Moses ventured forth among the people, doing what he could to oversee their welfare, and Caleb was happy to assist.

The two of them made a striking pair, both tall and broad-shouldered, with dark hair and bright, black eyes. Many times, as youngsters, people had taken them to be brothers, and though Joshua was seven years Caleb's senior, they had always been best of friends.

Of course, the fact that they had both served the same Egyptian master gave them much in common. When they were children, they had been wrested from service on the chain gangs, and taken to the home of a wealthy man. Trained as valets to his stable of fine Arabian horses, they had risen in the household to the status of indentured servants, capable of eventually earning their freedom. Accustomed to order and refinement in their master's home, they bore themselves with dignity unusual in slaves.

Tonight, as they walked through camp, Joshua's face was pensive. Caleb, who knew Joshua better than anyone, anticipated his need to talk.

"Look," Joshua sighed, passing his hand over the vast company, "there is no order, no arrangement to this huge population!"

Caleb surveyed the rows of tents, which stretched so far they blended with the dark horizon. As closely as possible, families had tried to stay together. But in the mayhem of the flight from Egypt, this had been difficult. And in many cases, family members would not even have known each other, having been separated by the slave system all their lives.

"Leaders are emerging among the people," Joshua acknowledged, "and groups are forming. But there is no clear organization. Already there is squabbling and division. If Moses hopes to manage such a horde, a chain of command and an appointed government will need to be established."

Caleb scanned the sea of faces all around him. Shaking his head, he shrugged his shoulders. "Have you spoken to Moses about it?" he asked. "Surely he is aware of the need."

"Of course he is," Joshua replied. "But he is overwhelmed, and to this point there has been no time for anything but flight. See," he sighed, "again this night we will be allowed only a few hours sleep, and then we will be on the march once more."

Caleb need not be reminded that all three million were fugitives, that the possibility existed that Pharaoh could change his mind and come after them.

Furtively he glanced toward the north, half expecting to see the torches of the king's army lighting the line between earth and sky.

Because Moses had ordered the people to go forth from Egypt in battle array, Joshua and Caleb had come out tonight bearing swords on their thighs. They tried not to be awkward with them, but though they had sometimes polished their Egyptian owner's ceremonial armor, they were not soldiers. As boys they had received sound thrashings if they were caught playing with the master's weapons, and neither of them had been closer to the things of war than any spectator at one of Pharaoh's flashy military parades.

Nor were any of the men who populated this company men of war. They had never been trained in battle, save for a select few who had served in the king's guard. Israelites had never been allowed to bear arms, and they did not know how to use them.

Yet, everywhere in this vast host were weapons to be seen, lying beside campfires, leaning against tent poles, perched inside tent doors. In the feverish despoiling of the Egyptians, the Israelites had taken spears and hatchets, chariots and bucklers. At Moses's command, they had laden themselves with military paraphernalia. But no amount of martial array would make up for ignorance in battle, and few men kept their weapons in their hands.

Not that they had never yearned to rise up against their oppressors. Every boy of the slave villages had dreamed of revolution. Joshua and Caleb were no exception. When they had lived in the ghetto, and when they were allowed an hour of recreation, they had inevitably turned to games of war, taking on their enemies in a more fortunate, imaginary world.

But they were now men, and having been conditioned by a lifetime of subservience, they were unused to bearing arms. Though their latent longings to subdue the Egyptians had risen with the courage of recent days, they did not know how to fight.

Joshua had no intention of visiting Moses this evening, but a circuitous path had brought him and Caleb near the front of the great company. When the prophet's tent appeared before them, Joshua held back.

"Why don't we speak with him?" Caleb suggested.

"Not now," Joshua said. "There will be time enough for questions later on."

Turning aside, he led his friend toward his father's camp. But as he did so, they were obliged to pass by the company's only hallowed station, the guarded coffin of the great patriarch, Joseph.

Overwatched day and night by a dozen armed men, the laquered sarcophagus gleamed in the towering light of the fiery pillar. At Moses's word, the shining box had been wrested from the mammoth Pyramid of Zaphenath-paneah in Avaris, final resting place of the mighty Hebrew prime minister, and named by his Egyptian name. From the moment it had been brought forth, the coffin had been treated with the respect due the revered ancestor. Borne through the desert upon golden poles, it would not be allowed to touch ground until it reached Palestine. Once there, its sacred contents, the bones of Joseph, would be buried in the holy soil. This had been the patriarch's dying request, passed down through the generations, and Moses would not forget it.

Awestruck, Joshua walked around the hallowed coffin. "Isn't it magnificent?" he whispered to Caleb. "I wish I had been chosen for this duty! To guard the bones of Joseph, I would gladly bear a hundred swords and spears!"

Caleb smiled, and placed a hand on Joshua's shoulder. He knew that Joseph was not only the honored patriarch of the Hebrew slaves, but that he was Joshua's direct ancestor. Joshua was an Ephraimite, descendant of Joseph's second son, and Caleb understood the pride his friend took in the fact.

How many generations had passed since the death of that mighty savior, the one who had spared his traitorous brothers from famine and brought Israel safe into the land of plenty? Had it not been for Joseph, no Israelite would have lived to see this day.

"Just think!" Joshua enthused. "Three hundred years have intervened between us and the rule of Joseph. Yet we would gladly give our lives to preserve his powdery bones!"

Caleb pulled his mantle close to his chest and doubtfully stroked the hilt of his sword. "Well," he sighed, "let us hope there will be no need for that. We are not warriors, Joshua."

PART I
The Slave Set Free

1

King Thutmose's physicians hovered over his bed, speaking in anxious whispers, peering at him from beneath their red fish costumes. The fish, Egyptian representative of health and well-being, was a fitting symbol for their profession, and the doctors always donned the glittering, scaly garb, their faces framed by the open mouth, whenever they tended royalty.

But, today, no matter how fervently they chanted to the river god, no matter how much fish oil they spread upon the king's throbbing temples, they could not rouse him from his stupor.

In vain did they massage his wrists, hoping to spur the blood through his body. In vain did they bathe his limbs with Nile water, petitioning heaven for his escape from the land of Lethe.

Thutmose had succumbed to this morbid fever the night the Israelites had fled. He had been a mere shadow of himself for weeks before, but on that night he slipped into this palsied state, and had not rallied.

Dauntless, he had withstood the blows his enemy dealt him. He may have bowed briefly to the Hebrew's onslaughts, giving in to his demands when plague after plague ripped through the land. But always he had revived, refusing, ultimately, to let the slaves go free.

Only the death of his dearly beloved son had at last devastated him. When frogs and insects and dying cattle, boils and hail and locusts had failed to undo him, he had inspired his people, and Egypt had held strong. But with the death of his son, and the death of all the firstborn of Egypt, something in the king had also died.

19

Perhaps it was merciful that he had been unaware of the slaves' mass exodus. Lying upon his bed, his bony frame curled into a fetal position, he had slept through the great escape. He had not seen the millions walk boldly through the streets and highways, heading straight for the borders of the land. He had not heard the frantic cries of his own citizens as they had rushed the slaves out the doors, filling their arms and their wagons with the wealth of the country, and begging that they never return.

Perhaps it had been a mercy that the king had been spared the witness. But his people needed him now. Egypt needed him.

The old priest, Jannes, had been called night after night to add his prayers to the physicians' efforts. Each time his petitions had been fruitless. And tonight he expected another failure.

Deep in his heart, he knew his prayers lacked fervor. Scarcely had he maintained his own faith in the face of Moses's powers. It was all he could do to appear devout, when he doubted the truth of his own teachings.

Nevertheless, he had gone through the motions, saying the right words, mixing the right potions, and trying not to think of Yahweh. Tonight, as he stood over the king's bed, he managed to say a believable prayer, and was stunned when the patient opened his eyes.

Bleary eyes they were, red and filmy, for they had not seen the light for four days. When the lids fluttered, Jannes took a sharp breath.

The priest had no love for Thutmose. His heart had always been devoted to the vanquished prince, Moses. But he did love Egypt, and since he still believed that the fate of Pharaoh was the fate of the land, he was grateful for this sign of life.

Taking Thutmose's hand in his own feeble fingers, he lifted it to his withered lips. "Return to us, Son of Light," he groaned. "Bring the daylight to your people."

When the king spoke his first words in days, all the doctors gathered close about his bed.

"Darkness..." he hissed. "Nothing but darkness..."

Though his eyes were open, he seemed not to see the yellow glow of the lampstands in the room.

"He dreams of the dark plague," one of the physicians guessed, recalling the three days when no light shone in all the land, when a black pall so thick it was tangible had overwhelmed the sun and every candle, every ember, for seventy-two hours.

"Find your way through the night," Jannes pleaded, pressing close to the king's ear. "Return to your children!"

Motioning toward the windows, the priest sent a servant to throw back the blinds, and afternoon sun flooded the chamber.

"See," he urged the king, "it is the Sun, your Majesty. Add your light to the light of Ra!"

Suddenly the king awoke, raising a hand to wipe the film from his hazy vision.

"Return, O King!" Jannes cried, lifting him to a sitting position. Propping him up with pillows, he ordered the physicians aside, that the sun's rays might spill across the bed.

As the light touched the king's face, he seemed to draw energy from it.

"My son," he rasped. "Where is my son?"

When Jannes did not readily answer, the king stared wildly into his averted eyes. Grasping the priest by the collar, he pulled at him with amazing strength. But, just as it seemed he would choke the old man, reality sparked into memory, and his face twitched.

Releasing Jannes, he fell back again into his pillows, a sigh like a death rattle gurgling from his throat.

"The king is well," Jannes whispered, when the doctors reached for him. "Let him be."

In a moment, the ailing monarch again sat up, this time fully aware of himself and his surroundings. His last recollection was of sending word to Moses and Aaron, telling them to leave, and to take the Israelites with them.

Oh, let it not be! Thutmose thought. Turning fevered eyes to the priest, he clutched at his arm. "Where is Moses?" he cried.

Again, the priest hesitated to answer, and the king became enraged. "Send for Moses, now!" he shouted. "This very instant!"

"Of course, you could not know," Jannes stammered, leaving his arm in the king's grasp. "You have not been with us, so you could not know..."

"Know what?" Pharaoh screamed, his voice taking on the shrill tone Jannes had always loathed. "What does he say?" he demanded, turning to the doctors.

"Do not agitate yourself, Your Majesty," one of them advised. But as he ran a cold cloth over the patient's head, Thutmose jerked away.

Taking a deep breath, Pharaoh tried to calm himself. "What is it I do not know?" he asked through gritted teeth.

Trembling, not for fear of Thutmose, but for fear of Yahweh, Jannes at last replied, "Moses is not here, Your Highness. He has not been here for four days."

A sneer crossed the king's face. He had no patience for half-answers.

"Must I strangle the truth from you, Jannes?" he cried. "Where is Moses? Where is Aaron?"

Swallowing hard, the priest answered, "In obedience to Your Majesty, they have left the country...they and all their people."

2

Joshua awoke with a start. A voice, soft but urgent, called to him, and when he sat up he was greeted by the moonstruck silhouette of a man outside his tent wall.

"Come," the voice insisted. "Moses needs you at once!"

"Aaron?" Joshua replied. "Is that you?"

"Hurry. Meet me at my brother's tent."

With this the shadow departed, and Joshua pulled on his tunic. Fumbling for the door, he stepped outside just in time to see Aaron hastening up a staggered row of tents toward the front of the great company.

Joshua glanced above as he tied his sandals. By the moon's position, he judged it must be the middle of the night. What the prophet and his spokesman could want with him at this hour, he could not imagine.

Between the countless lean-tos and goatshair shelters strewn upon the sand, Joshua found his way, once more, to the tent of Moses. Aaron had already entered when he arrived, and when he hesitated outside, the elder poked his head through the tent flap.

"Come!" Aaron spurred him.

Out of respect for Moses, Joshua did not take a seat until Aaron pointed to a cushion on the floor, and for a while none of them said a word.

Moses, who had apparently not slept all night, sat beside a small, smoking lamp, his dark face pensive, and his hands folded quietly in his lap.

When at last the prophet spoke, his two servants were unprepared for his instructions.

"We must tell the people to turn back," he said.

Astonished, the listeners gaped at Moses, then at one another.

"Turn back?" Aaron stammered. "You can't mean it!"

"Retreat?" Joshua marveled. "Into the jaws of the lion?"

Apparently expecting such a response, Moses only nodded. And Aaron objected loudly, "Have you lost your mind, brother? We have come this far, and against such odds, only to turn back?"

"If it is food we need," Joshua challenged, "we should trust Yahweh to supply!"

"Of course!" Aaron echoed. "He has not saved us with many miracles only to see us perish now. We need not turn back for lack of food!"

With a sigh, Moses looked into the faces of his two best friends. "It is not for food that we turn north," he explained. "And it is not to Egypt that we go, but only as far as Yam Suph."

Aaron shook his head. "The Reed Sea?" he laughed, interpreting the name. "But we have already passed by there. It has nothing to offer but bulrushes. What would we find at Yam Suph?"

"A foil for Pharaoh," was Moses's gentle reply.

Bewildered, the two servants pondered the words. Was the prophet saying that the king of Egypt had had a change of heart? Would he come after the fleeing Israelites?

Aaron and Joshua would have asked the question directly, but Moses was speaking again, his face uplifted to the ceiling and his tone reminiscent of the many times he had spoken for the Lord.

"'Tell the children of Israel to go back and camp before Pihahiroth, between Migdol and the sea. You shall camp in front of Baal-zephon, opposite it, by the sea. For Pharaoh will say of the children of Israel, "They are wandering aimlessly in the land; the wilderness has shut them in." So I will harden the heart of Pharaoh, and he will chase after them. And I will be honored through

Pharaoh and all his army, and the Egyptians will know that I am the Lord.'"

So, it was true. Pharaoh would indeed come after them! Fearfully, Aaron and Joshua turned the phrases over in their minds.

Joshua had not known Moses long. It had been only a few weeks since the holy man had appeared in Egypt, preaching liberty. It was clear, however, that he was a man of God, not only because of the miracles wrought at his word, but because of the spirit of authority with which he spoke.

Still, tonight's instruction did not sit well with Joshua. He had not been trained in war, but he did have common sense. And he had not been called to this little council to hold his peace.

Swallowing hard, he dared to question.

"Sir," he croaked, "though we far outnumber Pharaoh's armies, we are children when it comes to fighting. Can Yahweh truly mean for us to go to war?"

Moses gazed fondly on his young friend. But his reply was unsatisfying. "I wish I knew," he sighed. "In this matter, I have no leading."

Joshua's face reddened. "Very well," he managed. "But, if we *are* to face Pharaoh's men would we not do better with our backs to the open wilderness? To be hemmed in by a marshy sea is suicidal!"

Out of the corner of his eye, Joshua saw Aaron nod in agreement, and he privately commended himself for his courage.

But when Moses also agreed, he was deflated.

"So it would seem," the prophet replied.

Would he say nothing more than this? Joshua bit his tongue, choking on frustration.

"We have the word of the Lord. And sometimes his word is a mystery," Moses concluded.

Silence hung in the council tent as the two servants digested the truth.

Taking a deep breath, Joshua assented weakly. "We turn back tomorrow?"

"Tomorrow," Moses replied.

3

Barely stronger than a rag doll, Pharaoh Thutmose gripped the side of his two-wheeled chariot and peered across the open desert. His driver, armed from head to toe, avoided the ruts and stones of the ancient highway that stretched out from Raamses east toward the wilderness. Thutmose, sensing his protective hesitancy, growled at him.

"Am I a babe-in-arms that you drive like an old woman? Whip your horses, fool!"

Chagrined, the charioteer complied, and the gilded chariot leapt forward. Following the king's lead, all the vast host of the Egyptian army picked up speed, the ten thousand other chariots whose columns stretched for two miles behind him, the twenty thousand horsemen who followed them, and the nine hundred thousand foot soldiers who marched on their heels.

Nearly a million strong was the army of Pharaoh. And this was only the best of his fighting forces. Others occupied his many tributaries or waged war in rebellious provinces. The best he had brought with him to retrieve his fleeing slaves.

Scarcely now could he believe that he had been so foolish as to let the people go. True, the awful plagues brought upon the land had tested him. The puny god of Israel had somehow cowed the "greatest of the Pharaohs." But was not Thutmose also the greatest of the gods, incarnaton of Ra himself? What could he have been thinking, to let the mainstay of the Egyptian economy and the foundation of its social order flee the country?

Well, he reasoned, he had *not* been thinking. Some infernal voodoo had twisted his head.

Not for long, though. Thutmose had regained himself. With the help of Ra, invoked by the holy priests, he had emerged from his living grave, and like the Morning Sun, he shone forth now upon the valley of the sacred Nile.

Through Goshen tramped the mighty million. The shepherd country, ancestral home of the fleeing Israelites, was vacant now. No slave towns filled the green hollows. Not one sheep or goat was left upon the hills, as the slaves had taken every creature of worth from Egypt's delta country. Ahead stretched the lifeless desert, and soon Pharaoh would be returning this way, the slaves and all their booty in tow. Within days, the Goshen hills would be full again of tended flocks, and the slaves would have forgotten their rebellion.

As the king surveyed the bleak wilderness beyond, he wondered how far three million Hebrews could have gotten. Only four days had passed since he had fallen into his swoon, since Moses had wrested his possessions from him and the defiant rabble had looted the land. Surely, with women and children, flocks and herds, old people and laden wagons, they could not have gotten far.

Straining his vision across the hot sands, he gripped the rim of the chariot tighter and remembered his younger days. He had been a mighty warrior, once upon a time. He had led many valiant armies, conquered countless foes. Under the command of this Pharaoh, Egypt had risen to her greatest military glory.

He doubted, however, that there would be need for fighting this time. In reality, the tramping horde behind him was for show, more than for war. It would take no more than a *show* of force to bring the Hebrews to their knees. Why, the very sight of the dust cloud raised by the Egyptians' marching feet should be enough to bow them to the ground!

It was reported that the Hebrews had gone forth in battle array. Stealing weapons and chariots from their masters, they had left Egypt "prepared" to fight. Pharaoh smirked to himself, as he imagined how silly they must have looked, like little children dressed in daddy's armor, swaggering and bumbling.

Glancing behind him again, he commended himself on the proud demeanor of his six hundred most select charioteers, the captains of his host. Looking neither to the right nor the left, chins held high, they peered straight ahead from beneath the brims of their brass helmets, standing upright and arrow-sure in the spurs of their magnificent vehicles. Upon the hubs of their wheels revolved sharp-honed blades, capable of cutting the legs off man or beast that came too near, or of chewing the wheels off enemy chariots. The very appearance of the six hundred commanders and their steeds would cause Moses and his foolish followers to pray for mercy!

But who would hear their prayers? Yahweh had led them to slaughter when he seduced them from Egypt's protective embrace.

Emulating his captains, Thutmose struck a noble pose in the spur of his own vehicle and cast his gaze again toward the wilderness. The three million could not have traveled more than a few miles out. Within a day or two, he would see them upon the horizon.

And when he came upon them, they would be face down in the sand, making obeisance and pleading for forgiveness.

4

What Pharaoh did not know was that the Hebrews had been traveling by night as well as day. Moses allowed them a few hours respite each evening, but beyond this, they did not sleep, following the fiery pillar in the dark hours, and its counterpart, the colossal pillar of cloud, by day.

When a full three days had passed, and Pharaoh still had not found them, his soul began to shiver. The same spiritual dread which had descended upon him with each devastating plague hovered over him once more.

He might have turned back, he and all his men, thinking that the wizardry of Moses had lifted the entire nation of Israel from the face of the earth, had he not reached Yam Suph, or Lake Timsah, called the Reed Sea, by the third night. And had it not been nearing dusk when he came upon the three million camped there, he might have thought a mirage tricked his eyes.

But at twilight there were no mirages.

Leaning over the rim of his chariot, he nudged the driver in the ribs.

"Yes, Your Majesty. I see them," the charioteer confirmed. "The great company has come to rest on the shore of Yam Suph."

A catlike grin stretched the king's face. Throwing back his shoulders, he raised a fist to the air, signaling his captains that the time had come.

Like a tidal wave, the fearsome million poured down the desert slope toward Lake Timsah.

* * *

Long before Pharaoh laid eyes on the Israelites, those on the northernmost edge of the encampment saw the dust cloud raised by the sprawling army. Moses was notified of their approach, and stood on a sandy cliff beside the lake, trying to calm his frightened people.

Joshua, who stood alongside him, tried to calm his own fears. Had not Yahweh spoken through Moses until now? Surely the man of God had not led them astray.

Yet the young Hebrew sympathized with the frantic millions who heard the threatening drums of Pharaoh's hosts, and the awesome tramping of their feet.

"What have you done?" the Israelites cried out to their leader. "Is it because we had no graves in Egypt that you have taken us away to die in the wilderness?"

"What is this?" they shouted. "Why did you bring us out of Egypt?"

Desperately did the women weep and the little children scream. Men slumped to their knees, quaking uselessly behind their shields.

"Did we not tell you to leave us alone?" they accused him. "You should have left us to serve the Egyptians! We were better off serving them, than dying in the wilderness!"

Only Aaron and Joshua stood between the prophet and his manic followers. Trying to be heard above the din, the two servants demanded quiet.

But it was no use. Some of the people already lifted stones in their hands, ready to pummel the man of God. Women spit at his feet and clawed at the limestone cliff, ready to pull him down.

Throwing his arms wide, Moses called above the throng. Over and over his authoritative voice pierced the sky, until those nearest grew silent.

"Do not fear!" he commanded. "Stand still and see the salvation of the Lord!"

When he had repeated these words again and again, they somehow pricked the hearts of the people. Little by little, quiet spread through the crowd.

"Do not fear!" he insisted. "See what the Lord will accomplish for you today! The Egyptians whom you see today, you will never see again, *forever!*"

"But Moses," the men objected, "we cannot fight so great a host! We have not been trained in war!"

Joshua clenched his teeth. That had been his very objection to this venture! Why, oh why, had Moses not led them further south? If they had not turned back, Pharaoh might never have found them.

But as he watched his mentor, who stood boldly before the unbelieving masses, he was reminded of the first day he had seen him in the marketplace. He remembered how Moses and Aaron had mounted the storage crates in the middle of Raamses Square, and he remembered how dauntless Moses had been in the face of his mockers and beneath the leveled weapons of Pharaoh's guards.

Once again, the prophet was proving himself worthy of his calling. It did not matter who opposed him. He declared the words of Yahweh, come what may.

"The Lord knows your weakness!" Moses cried out. "He will fight *for* you, while you keep silent!"

Against this, what could anyone say? A shudder of compliance swept through the crowd, as the Israelites recalled the many times God had saved them by a miracle.

Indeed, the fact that three million could keep silent for any length of time was a miracle in itself. But so they did, until the Egyptians drew so near that their hearts nearly broke for fear.

"God save us!" they pleaded. Pushing down the shore, they began to retreat the way they had come.

But Moses would have none of it. "This way!" he commanded, pointing toward the sea.

Was he lunatic? Would he direct them to march into the miry waters of the Reed Sea?

Yes, it appeared this was his intention, as he stretched his rod out over Lake Timsah and cried, "Go forward!"

At that one instant in eternity, the descending troops of Pharaoh so close upon them they could feel their breath, and the marshy waves of Yam Suph licking at their toes, three million souls made a decision. Knowing they could drown, knowing they should never survive, they moved forward at Moses's command.

But the moment they made their first childlike steps toward the water, the earth began to shake. It was not the tramping of Pharaoh's army that shook it, nor the quaking of the fearful Israelites. It was the sigh of Yahweh, sweeping over the desert floor, sloshing the waters of Timsah back and forth like wine in a goblet.

Suddenly, the waters moved back from themselves, parting like hair is parted as a comb runs through it. Where the waters left a void, the lake bottom saw the sky. Earth water-soaked for thousands of years was suddenly drained dry, as though sucked clean by subterranean lips.

The Hebrews, who teetered upon the shore, rushed forward, pushed by fear, pulled by the pathway stretched before them.

Surging past the cliff where Moses and his servants stood watch, the three million fled across the seabed, between walls of standing water. Barely a soul looked back, as the stampeding horde raced for the eastern shore.

Only Moses, Joshua, and Aaron witnessed the next miracle with a clear view. As the escaping slaves made their desperate course, the cloudy pillar that had led them thus far suddenly lifted higher, and whisked back toward the oncoming army.

Spiraling downward, it spread out between the sea and

Pharaoh's million, obscuring their path and blocking their vision.

Like circus clowns, the troops collided into one another, and the chariots careened to a halt.

Foggy darkness descended upon the confounded army, causing the soldiers to grope for direction.

It was the Egyptians' turn to cry for help. And their fear was greater than any Israel had known.

5

The next morning, there was a great party on the eastern bank of Yam Suph. So great a celebration there had never been in all of human history!

Not only did it involve the largest number of people ever to celebrate together, but there had never been a more worthy cause to celebrate.

Pharaoh and his army, to the last man and beast, were dead.

It had taken the whole night for all three million Israelites to safely pass through the sea's narrow corridor. During that time, the pillar of cloud had kept the Egyptians from pursuing them.

When morning came, the pillar had risen again into the sky, and Pharaoh's men once more took up the chase.

Any fear this inspired in the Israelites, as they watched from the far shore, was quickly quelled. As though rattled by the hand of a giant child, the king's toylike chariots stuttered across the seabed, their wheels swerving and their horses stumbling over invisible obstacles. While the walls of water still stood firm to either side, the army began to cry out in confusion, many of the men turning back and fleeing the unseen challenger.

"Go back!" they cried to their companions. "Flee from Israel! Their god is fighting for them!"

While the amazed Israelites looked on, Moses again stretched his rod over the sea, and the waters closed in upon themselves. Panicking, the Egyptians fled directly into the tumbling walls, their chariots capsizing, and their horses being thrown head-down beneath the overwhelming tide.

Within an hour, there was no sign of the vanquished host. Swallowed alive, they had disappeared beneath the bubbling waves.

By midmorning, the only evidence that such a company had chased after Israel was a few corpses, washed up on the shore.

So now it was time to celebrate! Singing and dancing broke out among the Israelites. Up and down the beach they ran, laughing and pulling more booty from the soldiers' bloated bodies.

Gathering around Moses, Aaron, and Joshua were a thousand maidens, tossing their dark locks and swaying to tambourines and flutes.

Taking Moses by the hands they swung him about, and passed him from girl to girl. Joyous, the prophet laughed with them, while Aaron and Joshua, likewise, were spun around.

Then, emerging from the crowd, came Miriam, Moses's beloved sister. As though she were not a very old woman, she also danced, clapping a tambourine high above her hoary head, and directing all the women of Israel to follow her.

Within moments, a serpentine line of swaying, singing women was winding through the midst of the congregation, thousands upon thousands of them, pounding on hand drums, rattling cymbals and fingerbells, shimmying timbrels against their thighs.

During 400 years of slavery, the Hebrews had developed a knack for spontaneous chorus. Their slave songs had helped them work more easily together, and while often cast in sad, haunting harmony, they had helped to keep the Israelites' spirits from withering.

Today, however, the song was joyous. It mattered not who composed the words. It became a merry chant, voice answering voice, men calling to women, and women to men, African and Egyptian rhythms contributing to a gay symphony of sound:

I will sing unto the Lord, for he is highly
    exalted;
  the horse and its rider he has thrown
    into the sea!
The Lord is my strength and song,
    and he has become my salvation.
He is my God, and I will praise him;
    my father's God, and I will exalt him!
The Lord is a warrior;
    the Lord is His name!

On and on the song went, and Joshua danced and sang along with the others, laughing with his friend, Caleb, who cavorted beside him.

His heart had never been so free. He had seen the miracles of Moses in the plagues and in the exodus. He had been released from chains of slavery, and had followed the fiery pillar, the cloudy pillar, leaving the land of bondage.

But it was not only this that gave his soul wings, and set his feet to dancing.

He had been afraid of war, and the Lord had fought for him. He had feared taking up the shield and sword. But Yahweh had spared him.

Just as the song said, the Lord was the warrior. Israel had not needed to fight.

PART II
The Reluctant Warrior

6

South along the Gulf of Suez, along the western edge of the Sinai Peninsula, the people traveled, until they had gone out from Raamses a hundred and fifty miles. It was slow going. What would have taken a family two weeks to cover had taken the three million three times that long.

It was the fifteenth day of the second month after their departure from Egypt when they entered the wilderness called Sin. It was a bleak wasteland they traversed. With each passing day, the people became more restive.

They were running dangerously low on food. Moses had miraculously provided them with drinking water some days before, when they found the wells of one oasis bitter to the taste. And they had next arrived at Elim, a pleasant respite from their journey, full of a dozen sweet springs and a luscious date grove. Now, however, they were on the brink of Sinai's most lifeless tract. And they saw no prospect for sustenance should they venture further.

This evening, Joshua sat with his father, Nun, and grandfather, Elishama, beside the family stewpot. An uncomfortable hush had descended upon the Israelite camp. None of the three men commented on it, but as Joshua studied the firelit faces of the two elders, he knew they were thinking his thoughts.

The people were hungry. Likely, every family in the mammoth camp had sat down tonight to a paltry supper. The ominous quiet denoted growing desperation.

As Joshua dipped the ladle into his father's pot, it thudded against the bottom, and he scraped the last of a red porridge from the kettle. He would have offered it to

Elishama, but just as he called for his bowl, the old man shook his head.

Beside the family tent stood a small boy, son of a widowed relative. His dark eyes round and large, he watched the three men eat, and wistfully gazed upon the ladle in Joshua's hand.

In his own hands was an empty soup bowl.

"Give it to him, Hoshea," Elishama directed, bowing his head so that his long beard swept across his lap.

"But...Grandfather..." Joshua hesitated.

"Do as he says," Nun whispered.

Elishama was not well. He was frail, and might not make the journey across the desert. Still, the child's beseeching eyes tugged at Joshua's heart as well, and with a sigh, he called him close.

Pouring the last of the stew into the boy's bowl, he patted him on the head and sent him away.

Joshua, like everyone else, was becoming familiar with hunger. Holding his arm firm against his growling stomach, he asked to be excused, and left his father's campfire.

In recent days, as his energy had ebbed, the glory of past miracles was hard to recall. Despite the miseries of slavery, in Egypt he had never gone hungry, and it was difficult not to be bitter as his strength dwindled.

As he passed through camp, heading for Moses's tent, the quiet oppressed him. He could feel the people's eyes following him, steely eyes, accusing eyes. Tomorrow, or the next day, the camp might not be so still. When the people sat down to empty bowls and another hungry night, they would begin to make demands.

In fact, it might not take that long before they rebelled.

"We should have died in Egypt!" someone spat as he walked by.

"Yes!" another grumbled. "There we had plenty of meat, and we ate our fill of bread!"

"Do you go to see Moses?" a young mother cried. "Ask him why he brought us into this place? Does he hope to kill us all with hunger?"

As Joshua grew accustomed to his role as Moses's servant, he was also becoming more bold. Tonight, as he approached the holy man's tent, he did not announce himself, but walked right in.

"Master, the people have no food," he said.

In the lamplight, Moses sat reading a scroll full of Egyptian hieroglyphs. Joshua recognized it as one on which his mentor had been laboring for many days. The handwriting was Moses's own, and Joshua had often been curious as to the scroll's mysterious contents.

The prophet did not look up. "Do you remember when we came to Marah?" he asked.

"Of course," Joshua replied. Marah, meaning "bitter," was the name the Israelites had given to the oasis where the water was undrinkable.

"Why do you think the water was so useless?" the prophet inquired.

Joshua thought a moment. "It was standing water, not a spring," he answered. "Standing water can become rank."

"Yes," Moses nodded, "but that oasis has been used for years, by countless travelers. When I worked the shepherd route for my father-in-law, I went there many times."

Joshua shrugged. "Then I cannot say," he admitted. "It does seem strange that it was rancid."

"Not so strange," Moses replied, leaning back and looking at Joshua. "It was the people's ignorance that caused the problem. Don't you know that they fouled the waters themselves?"

Joshua pondered this. He remembered that the people had eagerly used the waters as a bathing pool. When millions of sweaty bodies had entered and left, the waters had indeed been murky.

"Not only did they swim there, but they relieved themselves there," Moses explained. "God, in his patience, showed me the way to purge the waters, but our people must learn new laws of cleanliness. The ways of the slave camps will not do here."

Joshua vividly recalled Moses's strange command that several shittah trees be chopped down, and thrown into the huge pool. Within a few hours, the waters had cleared and become drinkable.

On that day, Moses had strictly forbidden the people to enter the water. From his scroll he had read to them an edict, instructing them, furthermore, to relieve themselves outside the camp.

"'If you will give earnest heed to the voice of the Lord your God, and do what is right in his sight, and give ear to his commandments, and keep all his statutes, I will put none of the diseases on you which I have put on the Egyptians,'" the prophet had pronounced, "'for I, the Lord, am your healer!'"

At the time, Joshua had seen no connection between the ordinance Moses gave, and the problem of the waters. The Egyptians paid little heed to such matters, and the moving waters of the Nile suffered little for it. Still, from time to time strange ailments did sweep through the land of Egypt, especially through the hovel-lined alleys of the slave camps. Life in this enormous company was even more precarious, and the people must learn a new set of standards to survive.

"So," Joshua wondered, passing his eyes over the open scroll, "has the Lord given you more rules for us to follow?"

Moses reverently lifted the parchment to the lamplight, and scanned it quickly. Then, rolling it up, he placed it in a leather wrapper, and tucked it beneath his pillow.

"Every day God speaks to me, Joshua," Moses answered. "His words are wonderful. I do not understand them all.

But they always pierce my heart like shafts of light. In time I will share them with you."

Joshua bowed respectfully before the prophet. "I shall be honored," he said. But then, clearing his throat, he pressed him. "Sir, what about the present problem? The people are becoming disillusioned. They cry out for food, and soon there will be none at all!"

Nodding, Moses drew out the leather folder once again, stroking it gently. "On that matter," he said, "the Lord has revealed himself this night. Bring the people before me in the morning, and I will calm their fears."

7

The next night, the great congregation slept soundly, having no enemy to fear, and their stomachs full.

Just as Moses had promised, the Lord had taken care of them.

Early that day, the prophet had called the people to him, speaking words of comfort, and rebuke.

"Come near before the Lord," he had cried out, "for he has heard your grumblings!"

In that moment, as the people looked toward the wilderness, the cloudy pillar began to glow and throb, streaks of lightning flashing through it.

Falling back, the crowd gasped, and Moses shouted, "Your grumblings are not against me, but against the Lord! Thus says the Lord, 'I have heard the grumblings of the children of Israel. At twilight you shall eat meat, and in the morning you shall be filled with bread. Behold, I will rain bread from heaven for you, and you shall know that I am the Lord your God!'"

Suddenly, from the midst of the pillar, a smaller, darker cloud emerged, heading straight for the camp.

Covering their heads, the people ducked as the strange configuration swept over them.

Not knowing what to expect, they could barely believe their ears when the cloud swooped toward the ground, shuddering and squawking.

For this cloud had wings, and countless, feathered bodies! It was a gigantic flock of quail that descended from the flashing pillar, and the quail now skittered across the ground, pecking at the lifeless sand and surprising the feet of the bewildered Israelites.

With a shout of hilarity, the people scooped them up in their hands. That night there was meat in the stewpots of Israel, more meat than they could eat.

Next morning, Joshua, having had the best night of sleep since leaving Egypt, awoke to a peculiar sound.

In fact, it was not sound, but the lack of sound that roused him, and as he opened his eyes, the light entering his tent seemed unusually bright.

Sitting up, he cocked his head and listened to the shining stillness. He had never seen snow, but he had heard travelers tell of the bright dawns in mountain countries, and of the peculiar quiet that always came with a snowfall. If it had only been cold this morning, he would have expected to see a frozen landscape when he opened his tent door.

What met his eyes, when he did step forth, was far stranger.

It seemed a fine frost mantled the earth, but when Joshua reached down to touch it, it did not melt.

When he stepped forth, it crumbled into large flakes beneath his feet, but was not cold against his skin.

It was very early, but the sunlight glancing off the white ground was waking the whole camp. As news spread of the strange phenomenon, people cautiously studied the flaky substance, lifting hunks to their noses and smelling its subtle aroma. Like sweet honey, it melted in their mouths, and soon they were gathering it up in handfuls, eating it eagerly and laughing together.

"What is it?" Caleb asked, running to Joshua with a handful.

"It must be the bread the Lord promised," Joshua replied. And sampling it for himself, he shrugged. "Whatever it is, it is very good!"

8

For each of the children of Israel, through all their years of bondage in Egypt, there had been a dualism to life that was unique to their race. While the cultures of other enslaved tribes and nations had been absorbed into the Egytian system, losing their identity over time, the Hebrews had maintained their integrity. No matter how oppressed, the Israelite was first a son or daughter of Jacob, and second a slave.

Though their racial imprint might have been obliterated by intermarriage and by the cares of the world, it somehow survived, passed on by word of mouth, by stories of the patriarchs told around evening fires, by cradle songs, and by stubborn tradition. Their identity, more than anyone else's, was preserved by an ancient and persistent faith. Challenged though it had been, that childlike ideology had endured the ravages of persecution, and the encroachment of other teachings.

A few select names from their national genealogy served to give them a sense of solidarity. For four hundred years the names of Abraham, Isaac, and Jacob had helped the Israelites see themselves in one another.

For Joshua, his ancestral link to Joseph had been a proud distinction.

Blessed with a godly father and grandfather, he had been raised on the legends of Joseph and his brothers. Early on, the longing for freedom and the longing for his people to achieve their true potential had been planted deep within his heart.

Thus it was that while many of his fellow Israelites had scorned Moses when he first returned to Egypt, Joshua had not. Trained up on the truth, he had recognized it when it was spoken. And he had quickly identified Moses as a man of God.

As for the character of God himself, Joshua and all the people were only beginning to know him. They realized he was their protector and their savior, for they had witnessed his miracles on their behalf. But in many ways his dealings with them were mystifying, and the requirements he made of them were difficult to comprehend.

The days following the first provision of the quail and the manna were illustrative of the Lord's strict commands. According to the words of Moses, the men were to gather enough manna each day for the number of people in each household; no more, no less. They were not to have leftovers, for if they left it overnight, the manna bred worms and became foul. If they did not comply with the command to gather the manna before noon, they went hungry, for the strange substance melted in the sun.

The miraculous nature of the peculiar foodstuff was borne out in the fact that it never appeared upon the ground on the seventh day of the week. The Israelites were told that they must gather enough for two days upon the sixth day, and that the amount set aside for the seventh day would not spoil.

"The seventh day is a sabbath observance," Moses explained to them, "a holy sabbath to the Lord. On that day you will not find manna in the field. The Lord has given you the sabbath. Remain in your places on that day, and rest. No one should go forth on the seventh day."

Little by little, Moses was imposing such regulations on the people. And while they were strange laws, they did serve to bind the people together, bringing some sense of order to their lives.

Not that the concept of sabbath was entirely foreign to them. The idea of a "day of rest" was common to many cultures, and the word "sabbath" itself was Babylonian.

Always the Hebrews had maintained that the last day of the week was special, because the Lord God had rested from his work of creation on that day.

But the restrictions on work were new to them, as they had been forced to serve their Egyptian masters regardless of the day.

With the provision of food and the institution of the sabbath, the journey became more relaxed. There was no more Pharaoh to dread, no looking back in fear of his pursuit, and there was one day a week of sheer rest.

In safety and in peace did the people at last come in view of Mount Horeb, or Mount Sinai, the holy mountain where their leader, Moses, had first encountered the Lord.

Four days of travel across the sands had brought them from the Wilderness of Sin to the grazing land of Rephidim, just ten miles west of the sacred site. It was nearing noon when the vast company caught its first glimpse of the mountain's three craggy pinnacles.

Joshua was walking beside Moses, at the head of the congregation, when Horeb appeared on the horizon. As the prophet gazed upon it, a look of awe and reverence lit his face, and Joshua knew he was remembering the hallowed day when the angel had spoken to him from the burning bush.

Truly, the mountain would have inspired awe in anyone coming upon it. For centuries it had been a legendary landmark, lifting the thoughts of passersby toward the heavens. For it was the solitary feature of a barren landscape. In an otherwise drab, flat terrain, it seemed to have no reason for being, other than to take the mind to higher things.

Guardian of the wilderness, it had also guarded the souls of shepherds who walked in its shadow, and merchants who skirted its caverns. To many tribes and tongues it was known as a holy place.

But for Moses and for the children of Israel, it represented more. It was the birthplace of their liberty. Moses's experience there had fathered their freedom.

As the three million made camp at Rephidim, every man, woman, and child scanned Horeb's distant, hazy slopes, hoping for a glimpse of Yahweh himself.

What would the Lord teach them there? they wondered. He had taught them much already. But this was his home, and they were entering holy ground.

As Moses and Joshua made camp at Rephidim, the master was increasingly private.

At last, his servant dared to speak.

"Was it high on the mountain that the Lord appeared to you?" he asked.

Moses smiled and shook his head.

"No, my son," he replied. "Shepherds do not climb Horeb. They tend their flocks in the lowlands."

"So the Lord appeared to you at the foot of the mount?" Joshua deduced.

"Yes," Moses answered. "He did not wait for me to find him, but met me where I was."

9

Joshua rode through the oasis of Rephidim, where the Israelites were resting. Tomorrow they would set foot in the shadow of the sacred mount, and spirits were high in the camp.

People greeted the young Hebrew with smiles and cheers, for though he was only Moses's servant, they respected the regard their leader had for him.

Though Joshua returned their greetings, he shook his head at their inconsistency. Just yesterday, when they had first entered this place, rebellion had once again nearly broken out.

It would have been so easy to slip the last miles toward Sinai on feet of faith. All had been going smoothly since the children of Israel had left the Wilderness of Sin, where they had first received the manna. But it seemed Yahweh would not allow them to enter the holy mountain before they were again tested.

In years past, and during the time of Moses's stay in this region, the wells of Rephidim had always provided respite from heat and thirst. And a great hill which sheltered the wayside gave good shade against the sun. The Rock of Horeb, it was called, being in view of the sacred mount.

What the Israelites found here, however, was dismaying. It had been only a few months since Moses had watered his father-in-law's flocks at this very site, but the wells had now gone dry. Although the people had brought water from Marah, their jugs and flasks were nearly empty. And though it was only a matter of miles before they reached the pasturing land of Sinai, they might not survive the journey in between.

Yahweh had once again proven that he was with Moses by delivering the people through a miracle. From the midst of the Rock of Horeb could still be heard the sound of gushing water. When Moses had, at God's instruction, struck the giant monolith with his staff, it had split asunder, sending a pristine river across the sand.

But this had not happened before insurrection threatened to undo the progress the people had made toward unity.

Reigning his horse along the border of the camp, Joshua dropped in on various families, checking as to their welfare this last night before entering Sinai. Would they forever prove themselves to be fickle under pressure? he wondered. If only they could believe once and for all that God was with them!

Venturing into the night desert, he marveled that anyone could doubt. They had been spared from Pharaoh, from the waters of the Reed Sea, and from hunger. When the reassuring billows of the cloudy pillar dissipated each night, the glow of the fiery pillar was always with them.

Even now, as Joshua headed out from camp, the spiraling watchtower lit the ground.

It was wonderful to be so free, to have the liberty to race across the sands and to return at will! Never in Egypt had he known such freedom. He was still not used to it.

When he heard someone call to him from behind, he sighed. He was not ready to go back. He wanted time to savor the desert quiet.

Turning about, he saw that the one who hailed him came not from camp, but from the direction of Sinai. Dressed in heavy, dark robes, he appeared to be a bedo, a nomadic tribesman, and he rode a galloping camel.

At every wayside along the wilderness route, the Israelites had encountered bedouin clans and caravans of many nationalities. Thus far their exchanges had been friendly, for what could small companies do against so great a horde of people?

But this bedo hailed Joshua with great urgency, and as he drew near, his face was full of fear.

Though Joshua was unfamiliar with the man's native tongue, the fellow broke in and out of Hebrew, interpreting himself as he frantically addressed Joshua.

"We want no violence here!" he cried. "Joshua, son of Nun, take your people hence! We will have no war in our desert!"

Dumbfounded, Joshua watched as the stranger bounded across the sands toward him. He was certain that he heard him clearly, now. But his words made no sense.

"Do not fear," Joshua called, as the man reigned his camel close beside him. "We come in peace, I and all my people."

Breathless, the bedo leaned down from his high saddle, and flailed his arms. "Peace?" he cried. "We have heard of your exploits against Pharaoh! We are not fools. And neither are our neighbors!"

Joshua would have laughed, so desperate did the man appear. But he respectfully restrained himself.

"Good man," he replied, "it was not we who overcame Pharaoh, but our God. No Israelite has ever gone to war!"

For a moment, the bedo was silent, seeming to ponder this statement. But at last his lips parted in a sneer, showing a gleam of large white teeth against his black beard.

Bowing low, he nodded. "Very well," he said, "so it was your God who fought for you. Pharaoh had a god or two himself. We all do. But there shall be no violence in this desert! When the sons of Amalek come against you, turn around and go home!"

"The sons of Amalek?" Joshua marveled. "What have they to do with us?"

The bedo sat up and studied Joshua in disbelief.

"You are a commander of your people, and you do not know?" he laughed. "The Amalekites claim the very land you enter! And they are prepared to fight!"

Of course Joshua had heard of the Amalekites, one of the oldest nations on earth, and he knew that they claimed this desert as their own.

"This is a land of many peoples," Joshua argued. "It is a wilderness, and open to all."

"Ha!" the bedo scoffed. "Wouldn't I like to think so! I am chieftain of a tribe myself. But I know when I am outdone. I bow to the Amalekites, and so should you! Take your people and go back to Egypt, before the blood of Israel floods the sands!"

At this, the bedo reigned his camel about and fled back across the desert.

Swallowed by the night, he left Joshua with nothing but the drumming of his heart.

10

All night long a council fire burned in the compound where Joseph's sarcophagus rested. The tent of Moses was not large enough to accomodate all the leaders of the people whom the prophet had summoned.

In the sky above the great circle of men gathered there, the fiery pillar kept vigil, and far into the wee hours the elders talked of war.

When Joshua had returned to camp, he had gone straight to Moses with news of the bedo and his words. He had not told another soul of the stranger's fearsome warning, knowing it could spark panic among the changeable Israelites.

Sending for Aaron and Caleb, Moses sent them forth with Joshua to call a select council, and once gathered, the leaders considered what to do.

Peppering their conversation, the word "Amalekites" never failed to inspire fear. For the huge nation, which claimed for itself several kings and numerous territories from Palestine to Sinai, was the most warlike of all Semitic peoples.

Although, as Joshua had said, the wilderness into which the Israelites traveled was open territory, most tribes of the area bowed to the sons of Amalek, and across the Sinaitic Peninsula was evidence of the Amalekites' conquest in thick stone buildings set up as check stations for their occupying troops.

Sitting near Moses tonight was not only Aaron, but Amram, their father. And with Caleb and Joshua sat their own fathers and grandfathers: Nun, Elishama, Jephunneh, and Hezron. But the number of leaders was in the hundreds, men who had shown themselves over the past weeks and during their time in Egypt to be wise, reputable, and courageous. While there was, as yet, no census among the Israelites, and no clear registry of tribes, the men present this night represented a good cross section of families and clans.

As they discussed the matter at hand, it was obvious that none of them underestimated the strength of the enemy.

"They have likely sent ambassadors to all the nations hereabouts," said Hur, a leading Judahite. "We can be sure that if they come against us, we will have no allies, for they will have stirred up the whole region to hate us!"

At this, the council murmured, shaking their heads and huddling in anxious agreement. Though Hur's observation was not made to incite panic, it was a reasonable deduction. Who, after all, would side with three million renegades, whose entrance into the area was so mysterious, and about whom such fearsome reports were circulating? If Israel had "overcome" Pharaoh, as the bedo believed, they must mean to establish a land for themselves, and undoubtedly dreamed of conquest.

"As for the number of nations who might join them," Nadab added, "we would do well to think largely! Are there not many different tribes in Sinai?"

The question was directed at Moses, who had lived in the area for forty years. Thus far the prophet had said little, allowing the men to grapple with the issues. When he did not readily reply, Abihu spoke for him.

"Of course there are!" the Levite said. "Surely, Moses, when you worked here with your father-in-law, you had dealings with dozens of tribes."

Moses looked about him, surveying the worried faces in the company. "Yes," he answered at last, "there are many various people in this land. And most likely they will side with Amalek. And," he said, rising to his feet, "if we look at our options in human terms alone, we have reason to sink from fear. But we must remember that we do not fight in our own strength. If Yahweh is with us, any who come against us are *his* enemies, not ours alone!"

As Joshua listened, he remembered the night when he and Aaron had been summoned to the master's tent. When Moses had told them they must turn back toward Egypt, that Pharaoh was going to come against them, he had wondered how the untrained Israelites could ever successfully take up arms.

Breathing deeply, Joshua smiled up at his mentor. So once again the prospect of war loomed before them. Surely, once again, they would be rescued by a miracle!

Unbidden, he too stood up, taking a place beside the prophet. And presuming he had permission, he began to exhort the crowd.

"Listen to Moses," he said. "When will we ever learn? Has not Yahweh always fought our battles for us? Remember the Reed Sea? 'Stand still and see what the Lord will do,'" he quoted the prophet. "Will Yahweh forsake us this time? Surely we are not men of war!"

Rapt, the great circle of men considered Joshua's words with a hush. Never had the young man used his position as Moses's servant to speak so boldly.

Surely he was right, they thought. When they began to applaud him, Joshua bowed his head.

But soon, his moment in the sun was cut short. When Moses drew near and placed a hand on his shoulder, it was with a look of disapproval.

"May Yahweh reward you for your faith, my friend," the prophet addressed him. "But the Lord has never said we must not take up arms."

Stunned, Joshua listened, his face burning as Moses corrected him before the elders.

"Tomorrow you will go forth among the people, and choose an army," the prophet directed.

An army? The words hung in the air like battle banners.

"*I*, sir?" Joshua stammered.

"Yes," Moses replied. "You are no longer my servant, only. You are now commanding general of all my forces."

11

If ever there had been a reluctant warrior, it was Joshua.

It had been one thing to stand with Moses before Pharaoh, lending support to the man of God as he called down the power of the Almighty against Egypt. It had been one thing to, by faith, sprinkle blood upon his doorpost and await the coming of the death angel through the streets of Raamses. It had been one thing to set out across miles of barren desert, in quest of an unknown destiny. It had been one thing to stand on the banks of Lake Timsah, trusting the words of Moses that God would save them from the oncoming Egyptian troops.

It was quite another to know that within hours he must take a cold spear in his hand, hoist a heavy shield to his breast, and charge into a bloody fray.

Joshua was not a coward. A coward would never have sided with Moses in the first place. But Joshua was a reasonable man. He knew that tomorrow he must raise up an untrained force to battle against the most cunning of enemies. He knew the odds were overwhelmingly against him.

Though the Amalekites were barbarians in comparison to the fine-tuned war machine of the Egyptian forces, they were ruthlessly bold on the battlefield. Caring more for combat than for their own lives, they had made a name for themselves by recklessly rushing into conflict. By sheer bullheadedness alone, they had won countless wars, savagery making up for lack of formal discipline.

Despite all this, however, Joshua would have been less apprehensive if it had not seemed Yahweh had changed his dealings with Israel. Never before had the Lord left them to their own devices, yet this seemed to be the word Moses had given.

With dawn only a few hours away, Joshua sat in the prophet's tent, undergoing an accelerated course in military strategy. Moses had been trained in warfare in the finest military academy on earth, the school for Egyptian princes in the court of Pharaoh. Though he had never been obliged to fight in the king's army, or to lead a force in battle, he well remembered the theories learned as a young man.

"Begin by sending the council elders back to their camps," Moses directed him. "Since, as yet, there is little stratification among the people, and no demarcation according to tribe or household, instruct the elders to call forth the most capable men they can find, register them on tablets, and send them to the front, to stand before you."

Grateful for this guidance, Joshua agreed. "Yes, sir. What next?"

"These men, once gathered at the head of the company, must likewise be given orders to seek out other able men. When you have done this, come back to me, and we will talk further."

Hastening away, Joshua did as Moses suggested. And as the troops were being gathered, he took further counsel.

"Soon you must address your men," the prophet said. "Encouragement is the word of the hour. Let everything you say inspire confidence and daring."

Joshua nodded, but ran a nervous hand through his dark hair, wondering how this was to be done. He longed to tell his men that Yahweh was with them, that he would fight their battle for them as he had done in times past. But he was apparently not free to do this.

"Charge the young men to obey their elders, and the elders to obey you," Moses went on. "Appoint a small party of men to remain near the water of Horeb, to bear it out to the troops, and another to take care of the women and children. Let them know that their role is of equal value to the role of the warriors, but choose the less able-bodied for this duty. Instruct your men to shine their weapons, and to carry them with poise and valor. You have no time to drill them, but you must demand orderliness."

"Yes, sir," Joshua assented. His brow was furrowed and inwardly he trembled at the task before him. But keeping his feelings to himself, he rose to go. "Your advice is most appreciated," he said. "I shall do my best."

Though he did not look Moses in the eye, the prophet easily read his apprehension.

"Joshua," he called, as the general turned to leave, "is there something you wish to say?"

"No, sir," the young Hebrew lied. But Moses knew him well. Stammering, Joshua turned about and faced the man of God.

"Yes, sir, there is," he confessed. "I do not understand the ways of our Lord. We need him now as much as ever. Yet he has withdrawn himself."

Amazed, Moses looked at his servant wide-eyed. "How can you think this?" he marveled.

"You said so yourself," Joshua replied, his face reddening. "Just last night, before the elders."

Thinking back, Moses sorted through the events of the evening.

Suddenly realizing the source of Joshua's concern, he shook his head. "My dear friend," he sighed, "do you think that because Yahweh requires us, this time, to bear arms, he will not be with us, in our very midst?"

When Joshua only gave a perplexed shrug, Moses stood up and placed his hands upon Joshua's shoulders.

"It is true that you and all your army must take up sword and shield," Moses said, "but tomorrow, when the enemy comes against us, I will be stationed atop the hill of Horeb Rock. In my hand will be another weapon, the staff of God. So long as it is raised to heaven, no army on earth can conquer Israel!"

12

By the time dawn had arrived, seven hundred and fifty thousand strong young men awaited orders at the foot of Horeb Rock. Riding his horse halfway up the hill, Joshua overlooked the huge company. Enormous though it was, it was composed of the most disheveled, awkward-looking "soldiers" any commander had ever claimed.

There was no order to the ranks. In fact, there were no ranks. Each man was an entity to himself; no man dressed like any other, and every man, though fearful, stood at ease. They had not been trained to salute. They held what weapons they had in clumsy hands, shields dragging on the ground, spears pointing every direction.

They had come from Egypt as children at heart, raised in a slave system, stripped of a sense of power. They had not studied war, and if they were to succeed in this battle, it must be by force of will.

As Joshua surveyed his "army," he tried not to appear dismayed. But he could not help but wonder just how much force of will they had. In four hundred years they had not risen up against their oppressors. Any sense of duty or obedience they had learned was that of subservience. They did not see themselves as a force to be reckoned with.

And now, their commander must address them.

Glancing over his shoulder, he saw that Moses had taken a station on the top of the hill, and that beside him stood supportive comrades, Hur the Judahite, and Aaron. Taking a deep breath, Joshua wondered how his next words could ever command the same attention as an address from the prophet of God.

Sitting straight and tall in his saddle, he assumed the air of an experienced general, though he felt quite foolish.

"Men of Israel!" he cried. "It is by the grace and assistance of Almighty God that you have been brought out of Egypt, and have attained freedom. Be of good courage and strong heart. Rely today on that same Guiding Hand that has given us victory time and again!"

At the sound of their commander's voice, the troops grew quiet, and Joshua listened to the echo of his own words pass over the plain.

"We go out today," he cried, "against a force that would strip us of all God has given us. We must not think them capable of undoing the work of the Lord!"

Murmuring enthusiastically, the men took heed and seemed now to stand a little straighter.

"You must not imagine that the Amalekites are any more numerous than we, nor that their weapons are any finer," Joshua went on, "because we have on our side the hosts of heaven and the sword of Yahweh!"

At this, a cheer arose from the field, and the men raised their spears and swords to the sky.

"In the eyes of God, the army of Amalek is weak and small!" Joshua shouted. "They have no weapons to frighten the Almighty!"

Another cheer arose, and praises all about.

"What is war?" Joshua cried. And scarcely believing his own wisdom, he answered, "It is a fight against men, only. But you have endured trials far greater—hunger and thirst and oppression of every kind. With God's help you have conquered deserts and the great sea!"

"Yes, yes!" the men shouted.

At Joshua's command, they filed themselves behind select leaders, and began to look the part of an army. With the hems of their garments and the winding cloths of their turbans they began to shine their weapons. And within an hour they had transformed themselves into a reasonably sharp company, spears held erect and chins held high.

As they stood at attention, Joshua descended the hill a little way and passed back and forth before them. He had reason now to be proud. And though his soul still shook at the thought of the conflict ahead, he did not show it.

Turning about, he faced the men on the hilltop. "Master Moses," he cried out, "I present the army of the Israelites!"

A deafening shout ascended from the troops, and Moses smiled.

But as the eager cry filled the sky above Horeb Rock, it was met by another sound, equally deafening and terrifying.

It was the cry of the sons of Amalek, as they raced toward them across the Sinai sands.

13

More fearsome than the sound of Pharaoh's legions was the awesome thunder of one hundred thousand galloping camels. More terrifying than the well-groomed threat of Egypt's marching troops was the helter-skelter onslaught of nearly a million barbaric bedouins.

Dark of face and spewing hate, they careened across the desert toward the uninitiated Israelites. Their long headscarves trailing in the sandy wind, the riders lunged forth upon their gangly steeds, waving razor-sharp swords and broad-bladed machetes in the air. Calling on their god, Allah, foot soldiers raced behind them, swords and clubs held in sweaty hands, and scabbards empty in their wide, cloth belts.

This fighting force bore few shields, so eager were they for hand-to-hand combat. It seemed they had no fear, as they recklessly ran toward the "invaders."

Stunned by the sight of this human stampede, Joshua and his flegling fighters were momentarily paralyzed. But Moses still stood atop Horeb Rock, and when Joshua looked toward him he saw that the prophet had raised his staff above his head.

"Charge!" the commander cried. And with a mighty shout, the childlike troops dashed straight for the oncoming horde.

Slashing and yelling, the newcomers raced directly into the front lines of the Amalekites. They had few camels of their own, and had not ridden them into battle. But they daringly took on the riders, who swooped at them from their high mounts with spears and blades.

So thick was the red dust raised by the troops and

animals that it was a wonder anyone could see to move. Within moments, the Sinai sands were redder, speckled and splattered with the blood of men and camels.

Joshua, buried in the middle of the fray, saw hundreds fall to every side. But he had no notion as to who had taken the worst until a sudden rift grew between the two companies.

To his amazement, the Amalekites were retreating, chasing back across the desert.

As the dust settled, the Israelties looked at one another in bewilderment. But as they realized they had actually driven back the foe, they began to laugh and cry with astonishment.

Embracing one another, they danced up and down, clapping one another on the back and slapping hands together.

Joshua, as astounded as any of them, circled out from the troops and rode quickly toward the foot of Horeb Rock. As before, Moses stood there, Aaron and Hur beside him, his staff raised over his head. Perhaps he was just as bewildered as Joshua, for as the general stood below him, he shrugged and lowered his staff.

Counting casualties, the host of Israel found that relatively few of their men had fallen, as compared to the great many dead who littered the path of the Amalekites.

But they were not so foolish as to congratulate themselves on an early end to the war.

From the direction of Mount Sinai could again be heard the sound of a rushing army. The Amalekites had not accepted defeat but had only regrouped, this time coming forth with reinforcements, having been joined by allies of many nations round about.

To this point, the numbers of each side had not really mattered, for the first battle had seen fighting mainly along the front. Now the war would be more bloody. The chagrined Amalekites were more determined, and the fight would move deeper into the ranks.

This time, also, the Israelites would face multiple enemies spread out to north and south, as well as east.

When Joshua shouted the command to again go forth, Moses once more raised his sacred staff above his head. But the staff was no longer just a bare stick. The prophet had removed his striped mantle from his head—the one in which his mother had wrapped him when she placed him in the bulrush ark, the one beneath which he had said his first contraband Hebrew prayers in the house of Pharaoh—and he had attached it to the top of the rod.

It was a Levite shawl, and it was now the banner of Israel. Over the fray it would wave, until the war be finished.

* * *

It hardly seemed possible, but so long as that banner graced the hilltop, held aloft in Moses's hands, the army of Israel was invincible.

Whenever Moses allowed his arms a rest, the tide of battle turned, and Israelite losses soared.

It was high noon when Joshua first realized this. The battle had gone back and forth between the contenders several times, and each time the Israelites were routed, he noted that Moses had let down his hands.

This fact would have been more obvious to the prophet had he been down on the war stage beside his commander. As it was, with the dust and the inscrutable scuffle of the valley floor, the truth of the matter was not so evident to the three spectators on the hill.

There were now nearly twice as many Amalekites and their allies as there were Israelites. Things had not gone well for Israel for the last hour, although Moses kept his staff aloft most of that time.

Grabbing Caleb, who rode beside him, Joshua commanded him to go to Horeb Rock. "Tell the man of God he must not let his banner slip . . . not even slightly!" he cried.

Hastening to comply, Caleb raced away, and soon the banner was seen flying higher upon the hill, the prophet standing tall beneath it.

Throughout the afternoon, from this point on, the army of Israel made valiant strides. Though they were far outnumbered, and though the daring men of Amalek were far more capable, the Israelites forced them back toward Sinai.

Joshua's heart surged as he saw the enemy retreating. On the hill behind, Moses now sat upon a large stone, apparently placed there by his two friends. Joshua knew that his arms must be drained of blood, his muscles unable to maintain the banner on their own. To either side of him sat Aaron and Hur, supporting his numb arms, and keeping his hands aloft.

Not once, since Caleb had taken Joshua's message to him, had Moses lowered the staff. Whenever the troops wearied, the sight of the Levite banner, waving over them, gave inspiration.

At sunset, as the last of the overwhelmed Amalekites scurried toward the eastern horizon, the red sun glinting off their lowered spears, such a cry of jubilation went up from Israel, the whole world must have heard it.

PART III
The Right-Hand Man

14

At the foot of Mount Sinai, on the very ground where the enemy had retreated, Israel set up camp. There were no Amalekites left in the plain, and none had been seen since they had been routed.

This night, in the shadow of the holy mount, a great celebration was about to begin. This site had been Moses's first goal since leaving Egypt, and it had been reached over seemingly impossible odds.

Joshua's father and grandfather fussed over him as he made ready to go forth from the family tent. Moses had summoned him to stand before the people, that he might honor him tonight. The two elders helped him look his best, holding up a hand mirror and smoothing his finest tunic in the yellow lamplight.

"You have done us proud, Hoshea!" Elishama boasted, as he coaxed into place a stray lock of Joshua's wavy hair.

"Never was a father more proud than I!" Nun enthused, as he walked around his son, surveying him up and down. "To think! I raised a mighty warrior, and did not know it!"

Joshua smiled, and headed for the door. "Never did an Israelite have finer fathers," he answered, and securing his sword to his belt, he quickly hastened away.

Throughout camp, a million torches competed with a coral sunset, and with the deepening glow of the sky-pillar. Up ahead, at the base of Sinai, Moses waited for him, standing at the very site of the miraculous burning bush. Tonight there was no mysterious flaming bush, but the whole desert was flooded with orange firelight.

Apparently the entire nation of Israel awaited Joshua's appearance. As word spread that he was going forth, music and applause broke loose on every side, and barely could he make it through the pressing throng.

When he at last stood before his mentor, Moses took him by the arm and led him a little way up on the mount, so that he might be seen by the masses.

On the Sinai slope, the prophet had constructed a stone altar, and perched atop it was the sacred staff, adorned with the Levite shawl.

As the great crowd grew quiet, Moses took from inside his sleeve a small scroll. Opening it, he turned to the congregation, and announced, "The Lord has told me to write a memorial, and to recite it to Joshua."

So powerful was his voice, no one would have believed he once objected to the Lord that he needed a spokesman, that Aaron must speak for him because he was "slow of speech" and "slow of tongue."

"Thus says the Lord," he declared, "'I will utterly blot out the memory of Amalek from under heaven!'"

At this a jubilant cry went up from the people, and Moses raised his hands to quiet them.

"By his own hand, the Lord has sworn!" he shouted. "The Lord will have war against Amalek from generation to generation!"

Joshua's skin prickled as Moses looked him in the eye, and when the prophet placed hands on his head, he knelt to the ground, removing the sword from his belt and laying it at his master's feet.

"Joshua," the man of God announced, "you have proven yourself worthy of honor among your people. Always remember that the Lord is your banner."

With this, the prophet took a small vial of oil from his belt and anointed the warrior in the witness of all.

Then drawing Joshua up, he led him to the altar, where a slain goat had been placed.

Taking a torch, he held it before the commanding general.

"Do this for the people," Moses directed him.

Scarcely believing the holy man could pass this duty to him, Joshua hesitated.

"But, Master," he stammered, "I am not their minister. How can I light the fire of sacrifice?"

Moses studied him compassionately. Taking the staff from the altar, he laid it beside Joshua's sword. "With your weapon you have served the Lord, just as I serve him with my staff. You are worthy, Joshua."

Trembling, the warrior, the one who had feared to fight and who had reluctantly gone to battle, touched the torch to the altar kindling.

Instantly, a fire raged, consuming the sacrificial goat.

Overcome with holy awe, Joshua turned to the people. And raising his hands, he cried, "The Lord is my banner! The Lord, mighty in battle!"

Like a war cry it spilled over the plain, capturing the heart of Israel. And soon, the entire congregation echoed the slogan.

"The Lord is my banner!" they cried. "The Lord, mighty in battle!"

15

All that night, there was a celebration in the camp of Israel.

The mood in the vast company had been festive ever since the defeat of Amalek. But the official celebration had begun on this, their first evening at Sinai.

Indeed, it was not only a celebration of victory in war, but of their arrival at the holy mount.

The ex-slaves had learned how to be festive in Egypt. Under the oppression of bondage, any small happiness was enough to inspire revelry. It was a matter of soul-survival that the slaves learned to forget, however briefly, their hard life, and turn their minds to frivolity. Given their new liberation and the recent evidences of God's blessings, they practiced the art of merriment with greater zest than ever.

Joshua sat with Moses tonight, in the company of Israel's most respected elders. The vicinity of the prophet's tent was always headquarters of the traveling nation, and here the leaders congregated about their own fire, with their own musicians. In the shadow of Joseph's casket, beneath the spiraling light of the fiery pillar, lovely virgins danced, their long skirts and wild hair flying as they twirled and swayed.

As wine was passed, the men laughed and talked together, of freedom and victory and the days ahead.

Mostly, however, their attention was focused on an old man, bushy-bearded and dark of face, who spun an intriguing tale.

Never in his life had Joshua seen a fellow like this one. Except for the bedouin sheik who had challenged him on the desert the night before the war, he had never been close to an Arab patriarch. The Amalekites were wild desert dwellers, but not one of them had been so colorful.

Dressed in heavy, striped robes, he was bedecked with countless charms and baubles. Upon his wide sleeves there dangled little prayer boxes, and his mantle hood sported a dozen more. White teeth gleamed between a black moustache and grizzled beard, complemented by the whites of smiling eyes in an otherwise ruddy face.

When he laughed it was at Moses's expense. For the tales he told were of the young, runaway prince who had become his son-in-law.

Yes, this was Jethro Reuel, priest of the tribe of Midian, and father of Moses's Midianite wife, Zipporah. Moses did not seem to mind his good-natured jabs. The delight they had in one another's presence had been evident from the moment Jethro appeared on the eastern horizon.

Word of his approach had followed on the heels of the ceremony at the site of the burning bush. One of Jethro's servants had been sent ahead, and had come to Moses at the mount, telling him, "Jethro Reuel, priest of Midian, your father-in-law, has heard of all that God has done for you and for Israel, how the Lord has brought Israel out of Egypt. He says to tell you 'I, your father-in-law Jethro, am coming to you with your wife and her two sons.'"

Leaving the holy mount, Moses had wasted no time in rushing out to meet the long-lost family. It had been months since he had left his wife and sons in the desert, returning them to the tribal camp in Midian, and going off to Egypt. Taking Joshua with him, he had ridden quickly into the eastern night, and when he had seen the little company advancing, he had leapt from his camel, bowing and running, bowing and running, until he embraced them all.

Feeling a little out of place as he witnessed this intimate reunion, Joshua had nonetheless observed it with pleasure. He had heard of Zipporah, and he knew Moses had a family on this side of the world, but seeing them together brought the prophet's humanity into sharper focus.

As did the stories Jethro told tonight around the campfire.

"He barely knew a donkey from a mule, when he came to us," the old fellow chuckled, clapping Moses on the back. "Oh, it is good to be with you again, my son!"

For the tenth time since Jethro's surprise arrival at sunset, the two men embraced and tears filled their eyes.

"And you have joined us on our most happy night since leaving Egypt, my father!" Moses enthused. "My life has surely never been fuller!"

As he said this, his gaze traveled past the fire to the radiant face of a woman, the only woman allowed inside this otherwise male gathering.

"Sit with me, wife," he called, extending his arms and beckoning her forth.

Who dared to question this gesture? Was not Moses governor of Israel? If he wished for Zipporah to sit with him, she had every right to do so.

Joshua watched with a lump in his throat as Moses rose to receive her. The look of unfaded yearning upon the master's face tugged at the young Hebrew's heart.

What must it have been like, he wondered, for the mighty prince of Egypt to fall in love with an Arabian shepherdess? Such a romance they must have had—the ruddy, wild girl, and the refined and regal runaway!

In all the fables of every nation, there were such stories. Unlikely lovers—princesses and tinkers, noblemen and beggarwomen—always made for romantic fare.

But the two whose fingers entertwined this night were not the domain of fairytales. They were real and breathing, and as an aging Zipporah cuddled close to a graying Moses, the lingering glances they exchanged pricked Joshua's lonely soul.

Wistfully, he listened as Jethro told of the couple's first encounter. While Moses and Zipporah were real enough, the tale of their meeting was more beautiful than any fanciful lovestory Joshua had ever heard.

"My daughter and her six sisters were tending their flock beside a well in Midian," Jethro recounted, "when they were set upon by Ishmaelites, who meant to run their animals away from the water, and do who-knows-what evil to the girls."

Zipporah nodded, remembering the incident clearly.

"Suddenly, atop a nearby cliff, a strange-looking fellow popped up, hailing the Ishmaelites, and calling over his shoulder, as if to summon a mighty army against them!"

Jethro looked at Moses, who shrugged and laughed a little.

"How were the wildmen to know there was not a soul with the phantom Egyptian!" Jethro laughed. "And how was Moses to know that from that day forth he would be responsible for the eldest girl he rescued!"

Zipporah leaned into the crook of Moses's shoulder, a broad smile stretching her lips.

"Ah, but you have not told the entire truth," Moses jibed, recalling the slippery manner in which Jethro had "bestowed" his bride upon him. "You have not told that it was trickery, pure and simple, that saddled me with this woman!"

Zipporah pulled away, pretending to be offended. But though the audience was not privy to the details of that long-ago transaction, the twinkle in the woman's eye let them know there had never been a happier marriage.

"If you have been saddled," Jethro countered, "it has been willingly. Never did I see a man take the bit in his mouth so eagerly!"

Delighted by this exchange, the listeners applauded.

On and on the stories went, as Jethro and Moses reminisced, and as Moses's sons, Gershom and Eliezer, and

Jethro's son, Hobab, added their own memories to the chronicle.

But as a gigantic moon rose on the horizon, casting the gathering in silvery halo, the mood around the campfire mellowed.

It was hard to be frivolous beneath such a moon. Instinctively, their spirits were stirred, drawn toward higher things.

As the rest of the Israelites celebrated through the night, the elders and leaders of the camp recounted for Jethro the many miracles with which Yahweh had proven himself their protector.

Chapter by chapter, Moses told the glorious story of what God had done to Pharaoh, of the hardships that had befallen Israel on their journey, and how the Lord had delivered them time and again.

The men described for Jethro the parting of the Reed Sea, the gift of the quail and manna, and the miracle of the water at Horeb. As they reported the details of their most recent victory, the defeat of Amalek, Jethro bowed his head and closed his eyes.

"It is too much!" he groaned. "My heart can barely contain such joy!"

Suddenly, the old man stood up, raising his hands and drawing the crowd to its feet.

"Blessed be the Lord who delivered you from the hand of the Egyptians and from the hand of Pharaoh!" he cried. "Now I know that Yahweh is greater than all the gods!"

At this, he turned to Aaron, who sat beside Moses.

"I understand that you have ministered to your brother since he left my camp. I am a priest," he said, drawing Aaron close, "but you are more worthy than I, for you have *seen* the hand of Yahweh, and I have only believed in him. You *know* him, and I am only learning. Come with me."

To the amazement of all, Jethro led Aaron toward the site of the altar, where only hours earlier Moses and Joshua had sacrificed to the Lord.

Summoning all the elders before him, he requested that another sacrifice be made, this time by the hand of Aaron, invoking the guidance of Yahweh on them all.

As flames parted the dark above the altar, Jethro embraced Moses his son-in-law again.

"I was once your teacher," he said, remembering the naive fugitive who had first entered Midian. "Now you shall teach me. Though you are hated by Ishmaelites and Amalekites, though you will endure the reproach of many nations, my people and yours shall be one together, sons and daughters of Abraham!"

16

Joshua crept forth from his tent, rubbing his eyes in the morning light. The celebration of the night before had lasted until near-dawn, so that by the time he had slipped to bed, only a few hours of sleep were his.

Beneath one arm he carried a bundle of scrolls, a record of disputes between the people, which had been brought to Moses since the journey from Egypt had begun.

At various intervals along the trip, Moses had set aside time to hear such matters. In a company as huge as Israel, there were many contentions. Tempers were short among the weary travelers, and with few distinct boundaries and fewer clear rules, arguments and rivalries escalated from hour to hour. The days of the hearings were always arduous, as Moses sat in his camp and the contending parties came before him, hundreds of them at a time.

Joshua was not looking forward to the ordeal. He was Moses's attendant, and it was up to him to keep order as the people waited in the hot sun for their turn at court.

Though the master sat as judge from morning until night, he had never once cleared the docket of disputes. Some of the scrolls that Joshua carried with him today went back to their stay at Timsah.

What would make matters worse this day was the fact that many of the people who would come before Moses would be suffering the effects of the previous night's revelry. As Joshua arrived at Moses's tent, nearly two hundred disheveled, bleary-eyed folk awaited trial.

The master himself was not in the best of spirits. As Joshua called to him, entering his striped shelter, he found the man of God just pulling on his sandals, his brow furrowed.

"What is the first subject I must deal with?" he asked, hardly glancing up at his servant.

"One we have discussed before, master. The matter of the young girl who cried 'rape.'"

Moses shook his head. "Did we not settle that?" he groaned. "That was weeks ago."

"It was, sir," Joshua sighed, "but her father is not satisfied. He wants to see the man marry her."

Moses shrugged. "Poor girl. Caught in the middle. I am sure her attacker is the last man on earth she wishes to spend her life with. But who will have her, now?"

At this, he stood and threw back the tent flap, squinting against the desert sun.

He did not stop to see how many stood outside, awaiting his emergence. Walking straight for the chair of judgment, a highbacked throne brought from the palace of Egypt and placed atop a mound of crates, he sat down and took the first scroll from Joshua's hands.

"What else?" he muttered softly, so that the crowd would not hear.

"I am sure the girl's father will have more witnesses. You will be involved with her trial until noon."

"And then?" Moses snapped, already weary.

"Well, sir, there is an accusation of thievery against a Kohathite, by his younger brother. The man claims that the elder took more than his share of the birthright when his father died during this journey. The elder claims the possessions were never his father's in the first place, as he himself took them for spoil from his own Egyptian master."

"Witnesses?" Moses asked.

"On both sides," Joshua replied.

The prophet now looked up, quickly surveying the host of petitioners and defendants who anxiously waited for a moment of his time.

"I am ready," he said.

Joshua felt the weight of his master's responsibility as he faced the crowd and called forth the first party. It was good that Israel had finally come to rest for a time at Sinai. The roster of hearings could well take several weeks.

* * *

It was nearing sunset. Moses had heard four trials this day, and had reached decisions on them all, a feat which amazed his servant, Joshua. Yet still, there were one hundred and fifty Israelites, representing over thirty unheard cases.

As he sent these people back to their camps, he could feel Moses's exhaustion as if it were his own.

He had just rolled up the last scroll and was about to accompany his master to the headquarters tent, when a voice from the twilight hailed them.

"Son, may I have a word with you?"

It was Jethro, and Moses greeted him with a vague smile.

"Joshua will prepare us a cup of wine, Father," Moses replied. "Do come."

As the three of them sat in the smoky lamplight of the prophet's tent, Jethro intently studied his son-in-law's face. In his always-direct manner, he came to the point of his visit.

"What is this thing that you are doing for the people?" he asked. "Why do you alone sit as judge, and all the people stand around you from morning until night?"

Taken aback, Moses sputtered, "Well, because, Father, the people come to me to inquire of God!"

Jethro looked at the floor, and Joshua wondered what he was thinking.

"When they have a dispute," Moses went on, "they come to me, and I judge between one man and another, and make known to them the statutes of God and his laws."

"These laws," Jethro paused, "they are made known to you of the Lord?"

"They are," Moses replied. "At least, I trust that they are."

Jethro leaned back, and gazed at the goatshair ceiling. "I remember when you used to come to me, asking how we may know the right from the wrong. You wanted to know how a nation and a people may be righteous."

Moses, too, remembered those long-ago conversations.

"I wanted to know about the 'covenant' of which your people so often spoke," he acknowledged. "'Be perfect, as I am perfect,' was God's demand, so you told me."

"You were not very satisfied with that, were you?" Jethro recalled.

"I did not see how such a command was specific enough," Moses admitted.

"So...now the Lord tells you, and you alone, every day, just what is right in every case?"

Moses squirmed, obviously uncomfortable with the intimation.

"It seems so," he answered. Then he defensively pulled forth the thick scroll he had once shown Joshua, on which were scrawled dozens of edicts. "As the Lord gives me his judgments, I write them down. These are the laws of Israel."

Looking at the collection, written in bits and pieces along the journey, Jethro seemed doubtful. "Very well," he said. "But the thing you are doing is not good."

Joshua felt for his master. What did Jethro know of the pressures he endured day after day? But the young Hebrew did not interfere.

Sighing, the Midianite summoned his most diplomatic skills. "I am only concerned that you require too much of yourself," he explained. "I, also, am master of a nation," Jethro reminded his son-in-law. "Were I to try to administer justice as one man, I would go mad!"

This seemed to take Moses up short. "Yes," he acknowledged. "I know you handle things differently."

"Well, then, take my advice," Jethro said. "You will surely wear out, both you and the people who are with you, for the load is too heavy for you. You cannot do it alone."

Leaning close to the lamp, so that his aged features were illumined clearly, Jethro insisted, "Now listen to me. I shall give you counsel, and God be with you. You will still be the people's representative before God, and you will bring the disputes to God. But teach them the statutes and the laws, as the Lord gives them to you. And make known to them the way in which they are to walk, and the work they are to do, once and for all. Furthermore, select out of all the people able men who fear God, men of truth, those who hate dishonest gain, and place these over them, as leaders of thousands, of hundreds, of fifties and of tens. Let them judge the people at all times. And let them bring every major dispute to you, but every minor dispute they themselves will judge. So it will be easier for you, and they will bear the burden with you. If you do this thing, and God so commands you, then you will be able to endure, and all your people will complete their journey in peace."

Astounded, the two Israelites took in the wisdom of the Midianite. As though a huge weight had been lifted, they looked at one another with brighter eyes.

"Last night you said I was to be your teacher," Moses sighed, laying a hand on Jethro's knee. "But once again, you prove yourself the wiser man."

"By experience, only," Jethro said with a smile. "God speaks to all people in all places."

Hugging Moses to him, he added, "But surely the Lord

has great truths to show you, greater than anything I have ever taught. When he reveals to you the full meaning of the covenant, share it with the world."

17

After Jethro left the tent, Moses asked that Joshua stay for a while. As it turned out, the young servant never went back to his own camp that night, but sat up talking with the prophet till dawn.

Though he had come to know Moses well during the journey, that night's conversation exposed to him parts of the master's soul which had before been hidden. As never before, he came to understand what a toll leadership could take, and as never before he came to appreciate the heart of God's chosen one.

For some time, they discussed who might best fulfill Jethro's description of the judges to be set over Israel. Moses best knew the elders of the nation; Joshua the younger, rising leaders. The names of Hur, Amminadab, Zuar, Helon, Shedeur, and others came easily to mind, for these were the most reputable and respected patriarchs of various tribes. And then Caleb, Nahshon, Nethanel, and Eliab, to name a few, seemed likely candidates to put beneath them, training to take their places when necessary. It seemed reasonable that the first should be placed over the "thousands and hundreds," as Jethro suggested, and the younger over the "fifties and tens."

Of course, Moses would confer with Aaron on these matters, but for now, he seemed content to consult Joshua alone.

Though the choice of governors was crucial, Moses often sidetracked to a discussion of "covenant," that mysterious concept which had apparently been a theme of frequent debate between himself and Jethro in years past.

It was when he spoke of covenant that Moses revealed his most personal agony.

His face pensive, he seemed to hope the ex-slave whom he called his right-hand man would be able to illumine the subject.

"I used to torment my poor father-in-law," he confessed, "with my need to know more of God's demands. But, as you have seen, Jethro, for all his savvy, is a rather simple man. For him, the way of God is the way of the desert. He does not dwell deeply on the ways of 'righteousness,' for right and wrong are a matter of expedience and survival. To be perfect, in Jethro's unwritten code, is to be both strong and kind. When problems of justice or issues of cleanliness are brought before him, he follows an elementary code: Do unto others as you would have them do unto you."

As Moses spoke, the young Hebrew sensed that he was still debating with the old priest, at least in his mind.

Joshua shrugged, and prodded the tent fire with the sword he was now accustomed to keeping with him.

"In Jethro's defense, sir," he offered, "his nation is very old, and its ways well established. He is not faced with the complexities of our new society, with the variety of people, and with the confusion that comes with their new freedom. If he were, he would understand the necessity of a fully defined code."

Standing, Moses paced the small chamber, his fists clenched. "I, of all people, should have such a code at my fingertips!" he complained. "What laws are more intricate and sophisticated than those of the Egyptians? I would have been Pharaoh! Yet I cannot compose a set of regulations for this most childlike of people!"

Joshua, not knowing what to say, gazed into the fire.

"What good will it do to assign ten thousand governors, if they have no laws to govern by?" the prophet went on. "I have searched my memory for help from Hammurabi, the Babylonian lawgiver. I have pondered the laws of my Egyptian mother. All of these help. But this is not Egypt or Babylon. These people have known only the law of whip and chain, and cannot govern themselves. Every morning I am faced with unique problems, demanding a wisdom which is beyond me."

By now, Moses had gone to the tent door, and stood looking out at the moonlit sky. Over all there was the every-night glow of the spiraling pillar. But the master's face was dark with gloom.

Turning about, he inquired of Joshua, "What am I to do? Oh, Joshua, how I would love to say, 'Go to, Israel! Judge yourselves by this or that code!' But God demands perfection, and there is no perfect code."

18

Joshua's heart was heavy. He had known fear on this journey, and joy. But he had not known heaviness since he laid aside his slavery and joined the exodus.

The master had been gone for days, and he missed him. Moses had excused himself from his duties, leaving Israel in Joshua's charge, and he had disappeared into the folds of the mountain.

He wanted to be alone, he said. If he was to establish the laws of Israel, he must have guidance. God had spoken to him on Sinai before, and he would not leave the mountain until he spoke with him again.

That had been three days ago, and no one had seen or heard from the prophet. Though Joshua was kept very busy as commander of three million people, desperate thoughts sometimes raced across his mind, fears for the master's safety, and fears that he might be Israel's overseer indefinitely.

The young administrator had called a gathering for this afternoon of all the elders and leaders whom Moses had approved, the chosen judges of the new order. For the first time they were meeting together, and they all expected that Joshua had some important word for them.

Indeed, Joshua had expected to have more to offer. When he had announced the meeting yesterday, he had hoped that Moses himself would be here, to take charge and pass to his men the Lord's commandments.

Instead, he was left alone to face the most prominent Israelites in the nation.

As he looked over the crowd, congregated in the shadow of Joseph's coffin, he felt a lump rise to his throat. There must have been hundreds looking to him who were far more worthy to carry such responsibility, and who would have done the role greater justice.

Would he ever have the confidence of a Moses or an Aaron? Once again, he found himself wondering how he, of all people, had attained such a position.

Raising his hands, he called for quiet in the milling audience. Though many of the leaders were older than he, they respected him as a military hero, and as Moses's servant. Quieting, they sat down upon the ground, their mood eager.

"Three days ago, our governor, Moses, went into the mountain," he announced. "We have all been waiting for his return. As yet, he has not chosen to come down."

Obviously disappointed, the men turned to one another, murmuring among themselves.

Quickly, Joshua covered. "This is not necessarily a bad sign, gentlemen. Surely, the Lord has met with our master, and the time is well spent. The longer he is away, the more he will have to tell us!"

Perhaps Joshua's tone was not convincing, for the men only shook their heads and muttered more loudly.

"Didn't he say when he would return?" someone challenged. "Did he leave you with no instructions?"

Joshua thought he heard laughter at the back of the crowd. But he lifted his chin.

"It is enough for you to know that I *am* in charge!" he retorted. "Until we hear otherwise, we shall conduct ourselves as Moses would wish."

This silenced the challenger, but the men grew more restless.

"We understand that we have been chosen to help Moses govern Israel," another called out. "We need to learn just how to do that!"

Joshua nodded. "And so you shall," he replied. "You have been chosen for your wisdom and endurance. Let patience accompany these qualities."

The crowd sensed that the general was buying time.

"Would you have us go back to our camps with no instructions?" someone else inquired. "How can we be effective? We will be laughed to scorn!"

"Hear! Hear!" others agreed.

"We know you are a mighty warrior, Joshua," one of the younger men shouted, "but how do we know that Moses left you to rule over us?"

"Yes," another cried, "perhaps Moses is not returning, and you have taken the lead presumptuously!"

Joshua's heart stuttered. How could they make such accusations? Daily he was gaining a greater appreciation for the endurance Moses displayed in the face of the headstrong and hot-blooded Israelites.

Again, he raised his hands, demanding silence. But many of the men were standing, turning to leave.

"Call us when Moses returns," they hooted.

Humiliated, Joshua watched them disperse. And with stooped shoulders, he turned toward the master's empty tent.

But suddenly, the crowd was called to a halt by a voice, loud and commanding, ringing from the mount.

"'You have seen what I did to the Egyptians,'" it cried, "'how I bore you on eagles' wings, and brought you to Myself!'"

There was no mistaking the voice of Moses, and everyone knew he spoke for the Lord. Hurrying back toward the foot of Sinai, the men huddled together and watched their prophet descend the mountainside.

"'Now then, if you will obey my voice and keep my covenant, you will be my own possession among all nations, for all the earth is mine!'"

Trembling, Joshua listened with the others, to the awesome pronouncement.

"'And you shall be to me a kingdom of priests and a holy nation,'" Moses concluded. "These are the words of the Lord!"

Joshua was forgotten in the tide of wonder that overswept the audience. Joshua himself forgot his shame as he watched his beloved mentor striding down the jagged slope.

"All that the Lord has spoken we will do!" the men cried out. "Tell us, Moses, the words of God!"

Passing his hands over the crowd, Moses stilled them, and one by one, then as a body, they fell to their knees.

"Consecrate yourselves!" he commanded. "Wash your garments, and make ready. For in three days, the Lord himself will come to you. In three days, the Lord himself will speak to you. At the sound of a trumpet blast, he will descend!"

19

With blistered hands, Joshua gripped the tongue of a wagon and pulled it into line behind a hundred others, helping Caleb and a dozen young men construct a barrier along the foot of Sinai Mount. All night they had worked, fulfilling Moses's command that a barricade of carts and bales must be made between the people and the site where Yahweh had promised to appear.

Word spread quickly of Moses's encounter with the Lord, and of the revelation soon to come. Like a tide, the mass of Israelites spilled toward the mountain, pressing in about the barricade, so that Joshua was afraid it would not hold.

"Back!" he cried, gesturing to the people. "The prophet has told us that we must not go up on the mountain or touch the border of it! Whoever touches the mountain shall surely be put to death!"

Crushing in upon the makeshift boundary, the Israelites waited for dawn, sensing that sunrise would herald the Lord's approach. When Moses emerged from the headquarters tent, just as the sun broke over the horizon, a hush of awe spread through the crowd.

Stepping back, Joshua let the prophet pass, and quickly closed the boundary again. He was almost afraid to say a word, but so insistent were a thousand would-be trespassers that he cried aloud, "You must not break through! He who looks upon God Almighty shall surely die!"

His heart drumming, he then turned about, watching his master ascend the dewy slope.

Suddenly, as the prophet trekked high enough that all the people could clearly see him, the earth quaked. It was dawn, the sun was shining, but in an instant a thick blackness arose from the mountaintop, cloaking the sky above the highest pinnacle, and blotting out the light just breaking across the easterly summit.

From the midst of that black cloud there came a rumbling, as of thunder—a thunder sympathetic with the rumbling of the earth. And out of the shroud's interior there flashed lightning, jagged bolts of searing white.

Clutching a wagon rail, Joshua tried to stay erect on his wobbly legs. But when another sound, the blast of an unearthly trumpet, shook the mountain, he could no longer stand. Slumping behind a hay bale, he closed his eyes and tried to control his chattering teeth.

It seemed the trumpet took on the semblance of a voice, dreadful, indecipherable. Finding courage to peer through the slits of his eyes, Joshua saw that the cloud was descending the mountainside, and as the trumpet voice grew louder and louder, he stopped his ears, fearing he would go mad.

Again, a quake shook the earth, this time rattling through the mount itself. Smoke and fire, as if from a colossal furnace, belched into the air above Sinai, so that Joshua thought the mount would be consumed. In horror he watched as Moses ventured into the heart of the holocaust, and was swallowed by the living cloud.

It seemed the prophet was gone an eternity. Actually, he descended once or twice, warning the people to stand back, for the Lord would surely break through upon them if they disobeyed. But all this was like a dream to Joshua, who waited in the darkness, alone and fearful, waited for the quaking and the nightmarish voice to end.

As horror and wonder stretched into hours, Joshua felt as though his soul was not his own. It seemed to scale the mountain heights, wandering through the loud phantasm like a ghost. And it seemed an unclean ghost, sorely in need of redemption.

Joshua had dwelt often in his life on God and on things holy. He had done his best, according to the light he had, to lead a holy life. But today he felt unclean. In the presence, or beneath the presence, of an almighty God, he sensed the raw weakness of all his efforts.

Sinking further down behind the hay bale, he forgot his whereabouts, lost as he was in the supernal horror of heavenly blackness.

Sometime that day Moses came again to the people. On every side, and stretching back as far as the eye could see, men and women lay prostrate upon the ground, all fearing, like Joshua, to look upon the mount, upon the lightning and the dreadful cloud. Everywhere men and women shut their ears, terrified of the howling trumpet, the sealike voice.

"Fear not!" the prophet cried. "God is testing you, so that the fear of him may remain with you, and you may not sin!"

Sin! Such a confounding word. Joshua had never felt sinful in his life, not until today. Today he hid his face in shame, despising the feel of his own unclean hands upon his face.

But somehow, he managed to stand again. Not because he was haughty, but because he longed to be whole.

"Moses!" he replied, shouting toward the mount. "We would be holy, just as God is holy. But we do not know how! We cannot understand his ways!"

Through the smoke and dusty ash, Moses's eyes met the eyes of his beloved servant. The prophet knew he spoke for the entire nation, and listened respectfully.

"Tell us the ways of God!" Joshua pleaded. "Speak to us yourself, and we will listen!" Tears poured down Joshua's face and into his dark beard. Like a child he wept, his arms thrown open wide. "Please!" he cried. "Tell the Lord to keep silent, lest we die!"

20

Two weeks later, Joshua sat in a niche of the mountainside, high, high above the camp of Israel.

The warning of Moses, declared over and over, during the great revelation, still haunted him: "Beware that you do not go up on the mountain or touch the border of it. Whoever touches the mountain shall surely be put to death!"

Yet, here he sat, having been led by his master into the very sanctuary of Yahweh.

So much had happened since the great day when the mountain had shaken that Joshua would never recall it perfectly. He knew that Moses had descended to the people, recounting for them all the laws that God had given them, a multitude of ordinances, some general, and many more specific, regarding the behavior expected of them as a holy nation. But the commandments had been so foreign, and so numerous, Joshua wondered if they could be kept.

Only the first ten had pierced his heart, and had riveted the attention of all the listeners, for they cut through all confusion. On these Joshua had dwelt these two weeks, hoping to inscribe them on his memory:

You shall have no other gods besides Me...

You shall not make for yourself any graven image...

You shall not take the name of the Lord your God in vain...

Remember the sabbath day, to keep it holy...

Honor your father and your mother...

You shall not murder...

You shall not commit adultery...

You shall not steal...

You shall not bear false witness...

You shall not covet...

Again and again he had pondered these words, finding them more than enough to live up to.

More potent, however, than thoughts of God's law, was the memory of the sight of him.

Yes, Joshua had seen God!

He, along with Aaron and seventy elders, had been summoned by Moses to the mountainside the day after the laws were given. That morning, at the site of the burning bush, Moses had constructed yet another altar, this one surrounded by twelve pillars, one for each of the twelve tribes of Israel. Young men had been chosen to offer burnt offerings upon those pillars, and Moses took half of the blood and put it in basins, and the other half of the blood he sprinkled on the altar. When he had once more read all the laws to the people, they cried out, "All that the Lord has spoken we will do, and we will be obedient!"

Sprinkling the blood of the basins over the audience, Moses had announced, "Behold, the blood of the covenant, which the Lord has made with you in accordance with all these words!"

Then, taking Aaron and Joshua by the hands, and followed by the seventy elders, Moses had led them higher up on the slopes of Sinai.

This very moment, Joshua could remember the feel of the master's hand in his. Terrified of letting go of it, he had held on tight.

Leading them into the very midst of the smoky darkness, Moses told them to shield their eyes. And when they were completely enveloped, he bade them sit down upon the ground.

Suddenly, the air about them shimmered with stillness, and through their closed eyes they sensed that light surrounded them.

One by one, they took courage to look up, and to their astonishment they found that a brightness divided the dark in a halo.

Though no one on the plain below could have known it, in the center of the swirling roar of smoke and cloud that blanketed the Sinai summit there existed a chamber of perfect calm, flooded with an aura indefinable in human terms.

As their eyes adjusted to this brightness, a figure, tall and glimmering, became distinct before them. At his feet was what looked like a pavement of sapphire, clear as the sky itself, and from his face radiated beams, as pure as sunlight.

Falling down, Joshua lay prostrate, just as did Aaron and all the elders. From deep within him Joshua felt a quaking, a tremor moving from his innermost soul to the tips of his fingers and soles of his feet.

Surely he would not survive. Surely he would never stand again or breathe again.

Today, as he sat in a lonely niche of that same mountain, not far from the very site where he had seen the Lord, he could scarcely remember more. He knew that somehow he and the elders had been encouraged to rise up, that food and drink had mysteriously appeared before them, and that they had partaken of a celebration meal in Yahweh's presence.

But this he could only vaguely recall.

The laws of the Lord and the Lord himself were his sole concerns. On these laws he had dwelt day and night since that hour.

But he was now alone, and loneliness also consumed him.

When the meal had ended, the Lord had vanished, taking the light with him, and night had covered the mountain.

Sending the elders and nobles back toward camp, Moses had singled out Joshua, and told him to accompany him further up the mount.

"We will return," Moses told the others. "Wait for us and take charge of Israel. If any disputes are brought before you, on which you need advice, bring your questions to Aaron and Hur."

He did not explain to Joshua why he must stay with him. But together they had hiked nearly to the peak of the highest pinnacle of Sinai.

Slipping and sliding on the red sandstone, they arrived at a flat spot near the top, their hands and shins scraped and bleeding.

"I will leave you here," said Moses. "You may not enter the holy of holies. Make camp here, and wait for me."

Camp? Joshua had no provisions for a camp, no tent, no firewood. But without further word, Moses disappeared up the highest slope, into a misty veil.

Night was coming on. It was much colder here than in the desert, and a shrill wind stung Joshua's eyes with red grit.

Through a glimmer of biting tears, he spied a fissure-like cave notched into the mountainside. Quickly he scrambled toward it. At the mouth, a clump of brittle sage, the only vegetation on the lifeless slope, offered fuel, and rummaging in his pouch, he drew forth the flint with which he had sparked a hundred campfires during the journey from Egypt.

If he built a fire at the cave's entrance, he might be safe from prowling beasts. Deftly he did so, and soon he was bundled in his mantle, deep within the rift, drowsily watching, through the thick cloud, the leaping flames and the swirling fiery pillar that lit the valley below.

Thoughts of food would wait until morning, when his growling stomach would awake him.

* * *

Where was Moses, he wondered, as sunlight penetrated the cave. How had he fared through the lonely night? Or *was* he alone? Perhaps he was, once again, in the company of Yahweh, and only Joshua must spend the bleak hours in solitude.

Solitude. Moses had often spoken highly of the condition, saying that his greatest spiritual lessons had been learned during his forty years in the wilderness.

Joshua shivered at the thought. Were he to spend a week here, he believed, he would go mad.

That had been two weeks ago. In that time, he had learned to track down his food, to stab lizards (or anything that moved) with his sword, to roast them over his daily-gathered brush fire, and to swallow the most noxious fare with a less-than-queasy stomach.

In these two weeks, he had seen Moses three times. Each time the prophet had come from the summit famished and exhausted. Though his face was radiant, having confronted the face of God, he did not speak of his hours in his presence, and was drained of strength.

Eagerly, Joshua would prepare for him a meal, stoke the campfire that he might be warm, and remove his sandals. But all too soon, the master would rise again to go. And each time he vanished up the mountain, Joshua was more miserable.

Today it seemed even the ten laws which had thrilled his soul were difficult to recite. He wondered if he would be able to obey them if they were lost to mind all together.

But then, if Moses never came to him again, if he had

disappeared forever into the mountain heights, what purpose did the laws serve?

What purpose did Israel serve?

Gathering his robes close to his legs, Joshua drew his feet under him and tried not to fear. Like a loyal dog, he listened for the sound of his master's footstep on the slope outside.

To Joshua, Moses was Israel, Moses was the law. Without him, there seemed no purpose to anything.

21

Forty days and nights had passed. Joshua lay at the mouth of his cave, his hollow eyes closed and ready for death.

He was healthy enough. He was worn, but strong. It was not physical depletion which had beaten him down, but loneliness and doubt. It was not the elements or the cruel mountain that had defeated him, but emotional exhaustion.

Joshua had been a mighty warrior before the Lord, but he was not well trained in prayer. Forty years in the wilderness may have lifted Moses to spiritual greatness, but forty days had brought Joshua to despair.

With only sporadic visits from Moses, and with his sole duty that of survival, Joshua sorely wished he had remained a slave in Egypt.

This morning a light frost covered the ground where he lay. Fitting, he thought, with what strength he had for thinking. Frost and death were good companions, and if he never had a grave, snow would be a fitting shroud.

Half-consciously he moved his fingers through the frost, and lifting its moisture to his lips, he left a residue of dirt upon his mouth. To his dreaming mind, the frost was manna, and the red earth was meat.

Across the years his drowsy thoughts meandered, to times in his Egyptian master's stable. Reliving those years in his confused state, he thought he groomed one of the glorious horses, and that, as chief valet, he rode him through the streets of Raamses.

On all sides, people cheered him, for was he not a military hero? When the streets of the king's capital became the desert highway, and he rode in the ranks of Pharaoh's army, tall and proud, he suddenly awoke.

His heart was pounding to the sound of Egyptian drums ringing through his dream, and as he realized how perverse was this fantasy, his face grew hot with shame.

Struggling to a sitting position, he ran a hand across his brow. It seemed a fever raged within him.

"Forgive me, God!" he cried out. "I am an Israelite! A son of Abraham! And I love you!"

A brilliant winter sun seared the cold sky. There was surely no winter like winter in the desert, at once chilling to the bone, yet demanding a lively heart.

Joshua stood up, still reeling from the shame of his dream and hoping Yahweh could forgive such trespass, when he was hailed by the voice of Moses.

Wheeling about, he saw the master descending the mountain, this time not with an exhausted stride, but with determined purpose. In his arms he carried something. Joshua could not make out what it was, but joyously ran to greet him.

Yes, Joshua ran! The man who had lain half-dead moments before was suddenly infused with zeal.

"Master!" he cried, leaping up the slope, dodging crags and shale like a mountain goat. "Is it over? Are we going home?"

Moses would have embraced his beloved servant, but would not release the burden he bore in his arms.

"What are these?" Joshua marveled, seeing that the objects were two smooth stone tablets, etched with perfect characters. Sensing that they were very holy, he feared to touch them, and as he gazed upon them, his soul trembled.

"My friend," Moses replied, "they are the words of the Lord, engraved by his very own hand. Without them, we are prone to evil. But with them, we may learn to keep the covenant by which we are true sons of Abraham."

PART IV
The Faithful Friend

22

It was with a light heart and a nimble foot that Joshua descended the mount with his master, Moses. Night was settling across the wintry desert, but he was not any longer afraid.

As he trekked down the Sinai slope, he often glanced at the miraculous stone tablets cradled in the prophet's arms. Such strength they gave him, just to gaze upon them!

For engraved there were the most awesome words ever recorded, the ten commandments that would forever constitue the covenant between the Lord Almighty and his people, Israel.

How long Master Moses had sought after the simple thoughts contained there! During his forty years with Jethro he had yearned to know God's requirements, and now that they were established, how compact they were!

Nor were they written on parchment only, or transferred by word of mouth. They were registered in rock, a permanent record for the nation to embrace.

So long as Israel had these two tablets, it had the mind of God.

So it was that Joshua was lighthearted, able-footed as he headed with the prophet back toward camp, eager to witness the celebration certain to commence when the tablets were displayed before the people.

They were only halfway down the mountain, however, when a frightening noise ascended from the valley floor. Loud shouts and the rhythm of drums hammered up the slope, filling Joshua with apprehension.

Automatically, his hand went to the hilt of his sword, secured in his belt.

"Master," he gasped, "there is a sound of war in the camp!"

Moses had already stopped, and stood still in the path, his head cocked as he listened to the reverberations.

Suddenly, his face was clouded, and Joshua wondered if that was anger flashing in his eyes.

But before he could inquire, the prophet was heading downhill again. "That is not the sound of war!" he shouted over his shoulder. "It is not the cry of triumph or defeat, but the sound of singing I hear!"

Singing? Joshua followed after him, racing behind the elder who moved at a surprising pace. What kind of singing was it? he wondered. As he drew closer, its gyrating beat pulsed through him like the throb of unclean thoughts.

And to his dismay, the scene he came upon, when they reached the foot of the mountain, was far worse than the music suggested.

Reminiscent of the free-for-all festival of Bast, which annually raged through the streets of Egypt, the licentiousness of the people was beyond recounting. Apparently having given up hope that the prophet would return, they had also given up all decency, abandoning themselves to revelry of orgiastic proportions.

In the leaping light of bonfires, aflame throughout the camp, could be seen the silhouettes of lewd dancers, and at the head of camp, in the very place where the sacred bush had burned, a golden image reflected the glowing fires.

Pausing behind his master, Joshua stood with him, gazing in horror at the excesses of his people.

Glaring at the image of a golden calf, which profaned the holy site, Moses clutched the tablets to his breast.

"The Lord told me the people had corrupted themselves!" he groaned. "Oh, I did not want to believe it!"

Then he was off again, striding downhill with great

fury. Joshua ran to keep up with him, feeling the slap of master's robes against his own shins.

From Moses's dark brow sweat streamed, and if a face of retribution could kill, the entire nation would have been leveled.

Casting his arms wide, Moses straddled the mount above the camp, and holding aloft one tablet in each strong hand, he shouted over the din, "How quickly you have turned to sin!"

Over and over he repeated the words, until the music and the dancing ceased, and the cry of the camp was silenced. All eyes traveled to the mountain, and the besotted gaze of the people met the angry countenance of God's man.

Gesturing to the golden calf, Moses cried, "Is this your god, O Israel, who brought you up from the land of bondage?"

Chagrined, the revelers covered their nakedness and slumped to the ground, shielding their shameful faces.

Unable to contain his fury, Moses raised the sacred tablets, the stones carved by the hand of God himself, and threw them to the ground. Into a thousand pieces they shattered, and though the people did not know what they were, they gasped with terror.

His hands now free, Moses approached the profaning idol, and toppling it from its pedestal, sent it likewise crashing to the desert floor.

"You deserve no greater god than a golden calf!" he howled. "May the Lord reject you!"

Whipping his robes about him, he turned, trudging into the black of the Sinai heights.

Stunned, Joshua fell to his knees. Before him, in the sand, the remains of the tablets lay scattered about the fallen baal.

Through a haze of tears, he rummaged through the dirt, trying to retrieve the covenant.

But it was no use. The site of the burning bush and the words of the Lord had been profaned. Israel was still enslaved and should have stayed in Egypt.

23

The next day there was another cry in the camp. This time it was not the cry of riotous celebration, but of mourning.

Joshua sat outside his master's tent, far out on the desert. Incensed by the sin of the people, Moses had removed his headquarters a great distance from the population, and the young servant stood vigil as the prophet prayed inside.

There was much to pray about, much to grieve. After destroying the tablets and the golden calf, Moses had summoned the sons of the tribe of Levi, the only group which had largely abstained from the follies of the apostate crowd. Commanding them to strap their swords to their thighs, he had sent them throughout the congregation with orders to kill those most responsible for the sinful excesses. In that night, over three thousand men had fallen. Regardless of their status, even if they were friends, brothers, or sons of the avengers, they were cut down. And by morning the sands of the Sinai valley were crimson with blood.

"Take off your ornaments, take off your party clothes!" Moses had cried to the horrified onlookers. "Let the widows, the orphans, and all the bereaved weep for their own sin, in sackcloth and ashes! Weep for yourselves, and not for the fallen ones only. For the Lord says whoever has sinned against him, he will blot out of his book!"

As the dawn sun touched the blood-soaked earth, a putrid steam arose from the ground, and the people sat in the doors of their tents weeping and wailing.

"Listen to the words of the Lord!" Moses challenged. "From this day forth he leaves us to ourselves! Though he will send his angel before us, he himself will stand afar off. For you are an obstinate people, and should he stay in your midst for one moment, he would destroy you!"

At this, Moses had turned from the great company, and had trekked out into the desert, to the site where Joshua had moved his tent. The pillar of cloud, the symbol of the Lord's presence, had followed him, standing a good way off from camp, hovering over the prophet's sanctuary. All day long, Moses had been inside, weeping and wailing himself, for the iniquities of Israel.

And all day long, Joshua had sat outside the tent, guarding it. He had not gone inside, for he could hear more than one voice through the tent flap. Yahweh was visiting with Moses, and Joshua dare not look in.

Sometimes the conversation emanating from the interior sounded like an argument, not violent or loud, but a bargaining session, full of pleas and objections, requests and concessions. Now and then, Joshua caught a phrase or two, though he tried not to eavesdrop.

"Forgive them," he once heard. And to his horror, he had clearly picked up the Lord's response. "Whoever has sinned against me, I will blot out of my book!"

Yes, Moses had told the people this was true. But to hear it direct from the Almighty caused a tremor to pass through Joshua's soul.

"If you do not go with us, do not lead us any further!" Moses had wept.

On through the day the dialogue had continued, until Joshua wondered that the master did not faint dead away.

And the cloud remained at the entrance to the tent, hovering over the desert floor, until the sun began to set and the pillar took on its reddish glow.

Perhaps Joshua fell asleep. He only knew that when Moses at last emerged from the tent, he was unprepared for him, and jolted by the sound of his voice.

"Stand up!" Moses commanded. "Come with me!"

Rubbing his eyes, Joshua obeyed, trudging out with his master across the desert.

Glancing over his shoulder, he saw that the fiery pillar no longer stood over the tent's entrance, but had risen again to the sky and taken its customary place above the camp.

Did this mean that the pleas of Moses had prevailed? Would the Lord once more dwell in the midst of the people?

Anticipating his question, the prophet pointed across the sands. "Ahead is the Rock of Horeb," he said. "We must cut out two new stone tablets. The Lord is going to restore the covenant."

24

Joshua sat at the top of a great dune, overlooking the westerly desert. In the distance, three days' journey from the setting sun, could be seen the craggy summits of Mount Sinai, where the law and the covenant had been given and restored.

So much had happened on the journey from Egypt and during a full year at the sacred mountain that the children of Israel might always have considered Sinai their home, had the great pillar of cloud not lifted and begun to lead them to the east. They were not intended to live forever in the sifting sands of the Arabian Peninsula. A land had been promised to them centuries ago, to their fathers Abraham and Jacob. A destiny greater than Sinai beckoned to them.

This evening, Joshua, Moses, and Aaron waited on the crest of the great sand hill, looking back across the wilderness as the three million whom they had led out from the holy mount spilled toward them in waves.

The sight of this huge company, when viewed from any distance, had always been awesome. But never more than now.

When the fugitive slaves had left Egypt, they had been a disorderly mob, with no sense of rank or file. At Sinai, a degree of division and hierarchy had been established, with the assignment of judges over thousands, hundreds, fifties, and tens. And by then, the people had largely arranged themselves according to what they knew of their ancestries, into tribal companies.

Before setting out from Sinai, however, Moses had assigned more specific order, and along with teaching them the laws and ordinances of Yahweh, he had instructed them to build a tabernacle for the Lord, a traveling sanctuary to be the fulcrum point from which all justice would be dispensed, and to which all reverence and homage would be made.

No longer would the humble tent of Moses be the only council chamber of Israel. A glorious meeting place would go before the people, the house of God himself, upon which the presence of the Lord would continually dwell.

Little by little, the nation of Israel was becoming a formal entity. Though it was on the move, with no fixed resting place, it had its seat of government and its own intricate legal system. It had its governors, its priests, its rituals, and its army. It was becoming a formidable force, and the lands across which it traveled quaked at its coming.

This evening, as Joshua watched the Israelite tide spill across the desert, he marveled that this was the same throng that had only months before fled for their lives from the Nile Valley.

They tramped across the sands in cadence with the rhythm of drums and flutes and singing. Had one been blind, upon whom they had come, the sound alone of their marching and their music would have inspired great fear. But the appearance of the vast congregation was enough to make the heart stop.

Divided into seven neat companies, they were headed by the camp of Judah, with the tribal armies of Issachar and Zebulun. Behind these came the Levite tribes of Gershon and Merari, bearing the dismantled tabernacle, and followed by the camp of Reuben, with the tribal armies of Simeon and Gad.

The Levite tribe of Kohath was next, bearing the most holy elements of the sanctuary, the very house of God himself, and behind them came the orderly ranks of Ephraim, with Manasseh and Benjamin; then the camp of Dan, with Asher and Naphtali.

Bringing up the rear of the mammoth march was a mixed multitude, the multicolored, multilingual horde of people who had sympathized with the Israelites during their struggles in Egypt, many of them Egyptian themselves, or members of countless Semitic and African nations who had likewise endured oppression under Pharaoh's cruel hand.

At the head of each great camp was a banner, the green standard of Judah leading them all, and graced by the design of a noble, golden lion. The banner of Reuben was scarlet, its motif a human head. And last to come into view was the eagle-crested flag of Dan, its red and white emblem flashing in the sunset.

Before the banner of Dan, however, was one other, and upon this regal standard Joshua's eyes lingered longest. For it was the golden flag of Ephraim, and though Joshua was privileged, as Moses's servant, to travel at the head of the company, his heart was with his family and with the host that carried Joseph's coffin.

Strange, he thought, as he sat upon the dune, absorbed in the wonder of the oncoming throng. Strange that he was equally proud to be an Ephraimite as an Israelite.

"Sir," he sighed, leaning close to Moses, "did you ever think so many different people could march together in harmony?"

Moses scanned the ranks who pressed toward them. At the very head of the march, coming even before the camp of Judah, was a small cluster of men, bearing poles upon their shoulders. Atop the poles was a gleaming gold box, overwatched by the likeness of two golden angels, their wings stretched across it. It was the ark of the covenant, containing the tablets of the ten commandments, and it always led the way before the nation.

Pointing toward the hallowed box, Moses replied, "So long as the covenant is our guide, we will work together, and our enemies will be scattered before us."

25

It was true that as they marched in their orderly files, each family and tribe in its place, each banner held proudly aloft, the nation of Israel appeared to be harmonious. But their unity was a tenuous thing, easily weakened by the least adversity.

On the seventh day out from Sinai, Moses stood with Joshua at the head of the camp, preparing to say the evening prayer for safety over his people. As his servant lifted the sacred mantle over the prophet's head, Moses raised his hands toward the pillar of light. "Return, O Lord, to the many thousands of Israel!" he cried. And the pillar, which had come to rest over the congregation, descended, marking the end of the day's journey.

But though the pillar rested, the people were anything but serene. Throughout this past week of travel, as had so often happened in the past, they were complaining.

As Moses and Joshua walked back through camp, women were fretting over their cooking. They had grown very weary of manna. They were tired of gathering it, grinding it, beating it into batter, boiling it in pots, and pounding it into cakes. Men sat in their doorways griping that they had no meat and recounting fondly the variety of fish and fowl they ate in Egypt; the succulent cucumbers and melons; the zesty leeks, onions, and garlic.

"Who will give us meat?" they cried out as Moses and his servant passed by. "What became of the quail the Lord provided before Sinai? Will he never do so again?"

Joshua walked close to his master, shaking his head as Moses sighed, "Do you believe it? After all the Lord has done for them, they still complain!"

Moving faster, Moses angled out from camp, toward his own tent. Joshua could see that he was anxious to be free of the protesters.

"Well, sir," he tried to console him, "they *do* grow weary of the same fare day after day. I suppose even a miracle can become bland when it is revisited too often."

When Moses turned on him with a storm in his eyes, Joshua looked at the ground. "I...I only meant..."

But the man of God was right to be angry. And Joshua was chagrined as Moses lifted a tormented face to heaven and began to remonstrate.

"O Lord!" he groaned. "Why are you so hard on me? What did I ever do to deserve these people? Did I conceive them? Did I give them birth, so that I must carry them like babies?"

They had come to the tent now. All the way out from camp, Moses had ranted. "Where am I to get meat for so many? 'Give us meat! Give us meat!'" he mimicked them.

Dejected and frustrated, the prophet did not even bid Joshua good night as he threw back the flap of his tent and disappeared inside. Joshua's ears burned as he rolled out his own pallet and made ready for bed outside the door.

He knew the burden of his master was great. But he feared Moses took too seriously the cries of the disgruntled masses. And his own heart sped fearfully as he heard the despair in the prophet's voice, still raving within the shelter.

"I cannot bear it!" the master cried. "These people are too much for me! If you are going to deal thus with me, please kill me at once! If you love me, kill me! Do not let me suffer any longer!"

* * *

All night the prophet struggled with the Lord. Joshua slept fitfully, awaking often to the sounds of anxious and angry conversation issuing from the shelter, and trying not to eavesdrop.

At dawn, the man of God emerged, a look of retribution etched upon his face.

Joshua hung back, following at a distance as Moses strode across the sands toward camp.

Every other morning since leaving Sinai, the prophet had gone to the head of the nation and had called upon Yahweh to lead them forth. "Rise up, O Lord!" he would cry, lifting his arms to the pillar of cloud. "Let your enemies be scattered, and let those who hate You flee before You!"

At this, the cloud would lift and move northeast across the desert, guiding the people toward the promised land.

But today, no such prayer would be said, no such guidance would occur. Instead, the prophet trudged to the top of a high dune and shouted to the people, "Consecrate yourselves! For tomorrow you shall eat meat! You have wept in the ears of the Lord, saying, 'Oh that someone would give us meat to eat! We were well-off in Egypt!' Therefore the Lord will give you meat and you shall eat!"

The millions who heard this proclamation might have cheered heartily had it not been for the vengeance in their leader's voice and his angry gestures. Bewildered, they listened breathlessly as he declared the Lord's intent.

"You shall eat, not one day, nor two days, nor five days; neither ten days, nor twenty days! But a whole *month*, until it comes out of your nostrils and becomes loathsome to you! For you have rejected the Lord who is among you and have cried before Him, saying, 'Why did we ever come out of Egypt?'"

Aghast, the people heard their fate, and not daring to dispute, they bowed to the ground, weeping this time for shame.

Joshua's throat was tight at the witness of the repentant horde. How many times had he seen them driven to their knees? Would they never grow beyond their faltering faith?

Observing his master, who stood upon the windswept hill with his eyes closed and his head back, Joshua was grateful for his example. He, the prophet's servant, was also weak of faith, and he knew he would have been among the dissenters had he not been afforded months of intimate companionship with the man of God.

At that moment, as the three million crouched upon the ground, pleading for forgiveness, and as Moses stood strong and tall before them, Joshua loved him more than he ever had. At that moment, also, he realized what a dreadful void would be left in his heart and in his soul should the master ever leave him.

Though the prophet was a pillar of strength this morning, his words of the night before still haunted his servant: "O Lord, please kill me at once! If you love me, kill me! Do not let me suffer any longer!"

Joshua knew very well his master's humanity. Moses had experienced the hand of God and had received many evidences of Yahweh's saving grace. But over and over he had also been tested by his temperamental and fickle followers, his always-demanding and rarely grateful children. Joshua had been privy to his moments of despair, his hours of heartbreak.

Surely Yahweh did not intend for Moses to bear such burdens, but if the Lord did not act soon to relieve him, he might not survive the journey to Palestine.

Longing to reach out to him, Joshua crept up the hillside and drew alongside the man of God. Stretching forth his arms, he was about to embrace him when Moses turned away. Unaware of his servant's presence, he blinked back tears and descended the dune, plodding in dejected solitude across the sandy waste.

26

Once again alone, Joshua waited that morning beside the tent of meeting, wondering when his master would return. The camp of Israel was busy making preparation for the ominous visitation which Moses had promised, washing and consecrating themselves as he had commanded. Joshua had completed his own oblations and tried to devote himself to prayer.

Pondering the events of the night before and the sad words that Moses had spoken, Joshua did manage to pray for his master's welfare.

But though he longed to see the prophet's burdens lightened, he was unprepared for the way in which that longing would be answered.

At high noon, a movement along the edge of camp caught his attention. A large company of men was gathering there, and another figure was leading them toward the meeting tent.

Standing, Joshua shaded his eyes against the sun and watched them approach. It was Moses at the lead, and as the group came closer the servant recognized them as members of the seventy whom Moses had taken up Mount Sinai to see the Lord.

In fact, as they gathered outside the shelter, Joshua realized that all but two of that select group were present.

"Circle the tent," Moses instructed them. Quickly they did so, and the man of God motioned to Joshua to stand back, well away from the house of meeting.

When Moses raised his hands, the pillar of cloud descended above the tent's entrance. As had happened on Sinai, a voice like thunder, but this time gentle, issued from the cloud, and something like a mantle of fire was lifted from the prophet's shoulders. Moving quickly over the elders, who waited with their heads bowed, the fiery cloak settled on one after another, until the entire meeting house was set aglow round about, and every face was upturned to the sky, radiating divine light.

As the spirit settled on them, each man in turn began to speak out with authority. Some repeated the commandments that God had given Israel, some raised their voices in songs of praise, and others entoned the warnings against ungodliness which Moses had so often given.

Amazed, Joshua huddled behind a clump of sage and watched the supernatural ordination of 68 new prophets.

But, while he could have been delighted at this intervention on behalf of his master, he was not. When governors had been raised up to help Moses bear the burden of judging and overseeing the people, Joshua had been grateful. But to think that his master's gift of prophecy should now be shared among these men sparked a protective jealousy he did not know he possessed.

This was obviously the work of the Lord. What right did he have to question it? Certainly he would not do so in the presence of the men themselves.

Still, he bowed his head and stared at the ground, tracing his toe aimlessly back and forth through the sand. And as the prophets continued to preach and sing, his brow furrowed.

Barely did he understand his own emotions. He surely did not admit to himself that he was envious. But when opportunity presented itself, he was surprised by his own response.

His fretful ruminations were interrupted when a voice hailed the master. Running out from camp was a young fellow, one of the nobles who served with Aaron in the service of the altar. Although he was respectful of the events transpiring about the tent, he bowed furtively and spoke in urgent tones.

"Sir," he called, catching his breath, "strange things are happening in the congregation!"

Gradually the elders ceased their expounding and their singing, listening as the young man exclaimed, "I thought you should know, sir, that there are two men prophesying in the camp! They say they are among the seventy you called, but they did not come out with you to the tent, and they are wandering through the camp, preaching!"

Now this was all Joshua needed to give courage to his jealousy.

"Preaching? In the camp?" he snarled, as though it mattered greatly where such activities were carried on. "Who are they?"

The young noble, surprised at Joshua's interruption, replied, "Eldad and Medad, sir. Are they among the seventy?"

Indeed they were. But Joshua, already incensed, did not care whether they were or not.

Turning to the man of God, he heaved an exasperated sigh. "Moses, my lord," he pleaded, "restrain them!"

Taken aback, Moses surveyed his servant's distraught face. Quickly interpreting Joshua's reaction, he shook his head.

Placing an arm about his shoulders, Moses looked deep into Joshua's eyes.

"My friend," he replied, "are you jealous for my sake?"

When Joshua only looked away, his face coloring, the man of God declared, "Would that all the Lord's people were prophets, and that the Lord would put his spirit upon them!"

27

The visitation of the Lord, against which Moses had forewarned the people, was meant to be a punishment. But by their reaction to it, it seemed instead a blessing.

Initially, as it appeared on the eastern horizon, heralded by a strong wind and a dark, ominous cloud, it sparked fear. But when that cloud swooped over Israel in a flurry of wings and squawks, a shuddering cheer arose from the great congregation.

Moses had told them they would have meat. The Lord was giving them quail, just as he had done before Sinai. And as the birds toppled to the sands, tottering among them, the people went wild with greed.

Joshua stood with his father and grandfather, and with his friend Caleb, in the midst of the ravenous mob. Astonished, they watched as the manic, meat-hungry crowd gathered up the birds, wringing their necks and stuffing them into bags and baskets.

"Don't they hear the prophets?" Caleb marveled, noting that the seventy wandered everywhere through the throng, preaching destruction and warning of retribution.

On every side the people grappled over the live food, cursing and tearing it from one another's clutches. Nun and Elishama huddled together, fearing that riot would soon break out.

"They did not listen to Moses," Joshua answered. "Why should they listen to anyone else?"

Shaking his head, he led his three companions outside the camp. The sky was so darkened by the living cloud, which continued to come in from the east, that it might have been nighttime.

"Hurry!" Joshua cried. "We will be safer at the tent of meeting."

Though it was midday, people were building fires in the camp, not only for light, but for cooking. By the time Joshua and his little company reached the tent, the aroma of roasted fowl already filled the air.

He and his family had longed for the taste of meat, just like every Israelite. They too had had their fill of manna and its bland variations. But as the smell of quail, fried, broiled, and boiled, wafted toward them, they covered their noses.

Joshua held his stomach as the sounds of fighting and frantic feasting filled the desert.

He would not have eaten of the windfall were it set on a golden plate before him. And he doubted that Yahweh would long abide Israel's gluttony.

*　*　*

All that day, all night, and all the next day the people gathered and ate fallen quail. But on the third day a nauseating stench replaced the aroma of cookfires and banquets.

Joshua and his party feared to go forth to see the source of the foul odor, for they knew it was the reek of death.

They might have thought it was only the stench of rotting birds. Certainly this was part of it, for the windfall of quail was so vast it spread as far as the eye could see, a day's journey in every direction, so that the quail lay writhing in their death throes to a depth of three feet upon the ground.

Of course, the tent of meeting was within the radius of their fall. All night long and all day, Joshua and his companions had huddled inside the shelter, listening to the small, feathered bodies hit the goatshair walls and tumble to the earth about.

A nightmare it was, and the odor was disgusting. But they also knew it was not only rotting birdflesh that drew flies and choked the air with rancid steam.

People were also dying, hundreds, thousands of them.

Yes, the Lord's patience did have an end, and by the second day greedy feasters throughout the camp had taken sick. A plague tore through the huge company, and the sound of merriment gave way to weeping and mourning.

On the third night, Joshua and his three comrades emerged from their shelter. No plague had reached them there, and they hoped it was safe to venture forth.

But just as they took a few wary steps into the darkness, they decided to retreat. The moonlit scene before them, mounds of dead flesh both poultry and human, was too grotesque, and the womb of their tent was a comforting haven.

They would wait for Moses. And when the nation moved on again, they would name this place Kibroth-hattaavah, "the graves of greediness."

For here they would bury yet another rabble element. And again Israel would be purged.

28

The oasis of Hazeroth was a welcome respite from the tragedy of Kibroth-hattaavah. This pleasant dot of green in the monotonous Sinai landscape had been a stopping place for countless generations of caravanners and bedouin tribes. Many had left permanent marks here, erecting small sandstone huts and low corrals, so that the place-name meant "villages."

That a company so vast as Israel could be impressed by a tiny parcel of vegetation testified to the bleakness of their desert sojourn. They were weary. They missed not only the food of Egypt, but its temperate climate and lush riverbanks.

They had learned, for now, not to grumble over their condition. But Moses would at least allow them a time of refreshing, permitting them to stay here for several days.

Not only was Hazeroth a beautiful oasis, but it received breezes from the Gulf of Aqaba, almost twenty miles east. Indulging himself, as well as his people, Moses set up the tent of meeting, which was his dwelling place, on the east side of camp, where he could best enjoy the cool air that spilled across the dunes at sunset.

Not only did he move his shelter there, but for the first time since leaving Sinai, he brought his family out from the camp to reside with him.

Joshua might have felt awkward with this arrangement, especially considering that the family Moses invited was an extended one, including not only his wife and sons, but his sister Miriam, brother Aaron, mother Jochebed, father Amram, and his wife's brother, Hobab, who had stayed with them when Jethro departed. Rather than feeling awkward, however, Joshua was glad for the company. Though he would never have told Moses, his role as solitary servant to so private a man was often very lonely.

What neither he nor Moses anticipated was the incendiary atmosphere that would be created by bringing so diverse a group together.

Moses's kin had never lived with Zipporah and her relations. The fact that Moses had married a Midianite and had managed to coexist with her family for forty years was no guarantee that his Hebrew family would mesh well with them.

Indeed, it had only been Moses's quiet and humble personality that helped him endure the high-spirited Arabs. A more volatile temperament would have clashed endlessly with the feisty Zipporah and her hot-blooded brother.

As it was, the mixed group experienced difficulties from the beginning.

Joshua sat this afternoon in the shade of the tent, chatting with Moses's sons, Gershom and Eliezer. He tried not to glance too often toward the abode of Zipporah, the striped wedding tent that had for all her married life been her conjugal home. She had pitched it close to the tent of meeting, too close, according to Miriam, and just now the two women were outside it, engaged in a boisterous exchange regarding its location.

Joshua had heard the women argue before, always differing over one trifle or another. He had managed to steer clear of involvement, and was determined to do so again. Pretending not to notice their conversation, he focused on the two young men at his side.

But with each passing minute, the argument grew louder, until Miriam, in a huff, wheeled about and stormed toward her own tent.

"Selfish!" she was shouting, her wrinkled face livid. "I never met a more selfish woman than you, Zipporah!

How my gentle brother could have chosen you, I will never know!"

Zipporah, not to be outdone, waved her small fist in the air. "Perhaps he learned patience from dealing with you!" she cried. And with this she flung back her tent door and slapped it shut behind her.

Gershom and Eliezer looked at the ground, their faces red. Doubtless such embarrassment was not new to them, and they had learned not to interfere.

Not so with Aaron, Jochebed, and Amram. Naturally siding with Miriam, they huddled close about her, listening to her grievance. "It just isn't proper!" the spunky woman complained. "To erect a love-house in the shadow of the tabernacle is indecent. I tell you, it is not right!"

Aaron nodded and Jochebed flashed angry eyes at the colorful shelter. But though Amram agreed in principle with Miriam, he tried to calm her.

"Now, daughter," he said, "we must not be hard on her. She is new to our society, you know."

But when Zipporah stuck her head out her door and made another catty remark, even Amram clenched his fists.

"How can it be improper for the shadow of God's house to grace my marriage house?" she spat. "But then you have never been married, Miriam. You wouldn't know about such things!"

When Miriam lunged forward, ready to engage her sister-in-law, Aaron and Amram restrained her. Flailing her arms, the outraged woman yelled, "Will you teach us the ways of the Lord?"

And Aaron, unable to hold his tongue, added, "You would do well to listen to us. We know a few things about God! Has the Lord spoken only through Moses? Has he not spoken through us as well?"

To this point, Moses had been oblivious to the dispute. He had been in camp all morning, and had only just returned home. When he walked in on the contest, he was befuddled.

Running to him, Joshua beseeched him. "They are fighting again, Master. Is there nothing you can do?"

Moses had heard enough to be deeply troubled. But it was not the issue of the tent and its location that aggravated him.

"It seems my own family doubts my calling," he observed. And going directly to his brother, he demanded, "You and Miriam come with me!"

Surprised by his sudden appearance, the two drew back. But taking them firmly by the arms, Moses led them to the very door of the meeting tent.

Suddenly, from the midst of the tent, a quaking could be felt. And the cloudy pillar, which hovered over it, descended and stood before the door.

"Aaron! Miriam!" came a trumpeting voice. "Hear now my words!"

Trembling, the two squabblers shielded their gaze.

"If there is a prophet among you, I the Lord will make myself known to him in a vision," the voice pronounced. "I will speak to him in a dream!"

Aaron and Miriam took in the words fearfully and looked sheepishly at one another. Neither of them had ever had such a dream or vision, and they stood corrected before the Lord.

"It is not that way with my servant Moses," the voice went on. "He is faithful in all my household. With him I speak mouth to mouth, openly, and not in dark sayings. And he beholds my very form!"

At this, Moses also bowed his head, humbled by such distinction.

And now the pillar moved from side to side, as if surveying the prophet's shamefaced siblings.

"Why were you not afraid to speak against my servant Moses?" the voice demanded.

Still emanating anger, the cloud ascended, departing from them. But when Aaron turned to Miriam, ready to lead her away, he suddenly gasped. Creeping forward, the rest of the family looked upon her, and fell back horrified. For she was white as death, her skin suddenly leprous.

Falling to his knees, Aaron clutched Moses about the legs and wept, "Oh, my lord, I beg you, do not charge this sin to us! We have acted foolishly. Do not let her be like one who is dead, whose flesh is half eaten away!"

Leaning his head back, Moses too wept, stretching his hands heavenward and praying, "O God, heal her!"

For a long, tense moment, the family waited for a reply. And when Moses opened his eyes, he heaved a sigh.

Turning to Joshua, he instructed, "Take her. Lead her by the hand into the desert. There she must stay for seven days, until this curse be lifted. These are the words of the Lord!"

Swallowing hard, Joshua stepped toward the snow-white Miriam, toward the one whose skin had been ruddy and dark from birth, just like his master's. Fearing to touch her, he nonetheless obeyed.

And as he led her forth, Joshua saw Moses draw Zipporah to his bosom. Like a bird she nestled into his embrace. Though he sadly watched his sister depart, and though the family would no longer reside so close to the holy tent, he clearly drew great comfort from his wife's caress.

PART V
The Leading Spy

29

Joshua sat on a rim overlooking the Gulf of Aqaba, the northeastern arm of the great Red Sea. Framed by white sands, its pure, azure waters stretched to the southern horizon as far as the eye could see.

It seemed forever since the people of Israel had been near a great body of water. The last time had been when they crossed the Reed Sea, or Lake Timsah, under the miraculous intervention of the Lord. So long had they been hemmed in by desert and endless miles of sand that the proximity of water was refreshment indeed.

So was the proximity of civilization.

At this northern tip of the gulf lay the small town of Ezion-Geber. Beginning as an Egyptian outpost, it had become a full-fledged settlement, having permanent residents. While the Israelites might have been uneasy with the fact that it represented Egypt's farthest imperial reach, they were not. What could Egypt do against millions of them, so far from the Nile Valley? Instead, the sight of buildings and commerce, however modest, was consolation that they had at last come through the Sinai.

Of course, if they were to reach Canaan, they must go through more wilderness. But none would be so bleak as the desert which had been the scene of their journey thus far.

As Joshua sat on the rim of the gulf, he was stirred with anticipation. But that anticipation was mingled with another emotion, his all-too-familiar soul mate, loneliness.

Glancing north, he knew that Canaan lay more than one hundred miles ahead. He also knew that great things would be required of him as the immigrant nation of Israel attempted to take their place within its borders.

Not that Israel was truly immigrant. By the promise given to their forefather, Abraham, the land was rightfully theirs. Though they had been away for 400 years, they still believed in the covenant. And though to the current inhabitants they would be invaders, they considered themselves returning heirs, ready to lay claim to their inheritance.

Joshua drew his cloak tight to his chest. He knew that the birthright would not easily be won. He would have been a fool to think war was not inevitable.

And he was the commanding general of Israel.

Closing his eyes, he clenched his teeth. He still had trouble thinking of himself as a warrior. What he would have given for a comforting word, for a touch of human reassurance!

Despite the agitation that Moses's family often caused, Joshua envied him the tender joys of wife and sons. And not for the first time in his life, he regretted that he had never married.

But, he told himself, lifting his chin and striking a dauntless pose, it was probably for the best. A man in his position, a man who would soon risk his life, was better off without attachments.

"Good day, Joshua!" a voice hailed him.

Jolting from his ruminations, the young Hebrew glanced down the incline leading to camp. Walking toward him was Moses, his step eager.

"Such a noble look you have today," the master greeted him, "as though you could take on the world!"

Joshua's face colored. "I ... I was just thinking ..."

But he did not wish to divulge his thoughts.

"You were thinking of Canaan, and the days ahead?" Moses guessed.

Joshua gazed north again. "Partly, sir."

"That is good!" Moses said, clapping him on the back. Sitting with him, he drew forth a parchment and unrolled it on the sand.

Upon it were not the usual hieroglyphs and words of law that Joshua was accustomed to seeing. Instead, it was a map, carefully drawn.

"Here!" Moses enthused, pointing to the topmost section. "Here, my boy, is Canaan!"

"Yes, sir," Joshua replied.

"And here," Moses went on, moving his finger southward, "is Ezion-Geber."

Joshua studied the pinpoint on the map, and then the real-life village on the desert floor.

"There are many miles between us and the promised land," he noted. "How many days will it take to get there?"

Moses shrugged. "I do not think that is the question to concern ouselves with. Not yet, anyway."

Keeping the chart before him, he explained, "Hobab drew this map for us. He has traveled much for my father-in-law, and knows every inch of the terrain between here and Canaan, as well as Canaan itself. He will be an excellent aide as we approach the land. But we must not be hasty."

Joshua listened attentively as Moses laid out the plan for the next few weeks.

"We will not invade immediately," Moses began. "The people have come to me, suggesting that first we spy out the land, to see what our challenge is. After all, we have fought only once, and that was against desert dwellers. Canaanites are city dwellers, and their region is very different from the Sinai."

Joshua nodded. "Very wise, sir. Besides, the Canaanites have likely heard of our intentions by now. Surely the whole world has heard! They will be ready for us."

Even as he said this, an unwelcome twinge worked

across his shoulders. He hoped Moses did not read his fear.

"I am glad you agree," the prophet went on. "So our next task is to choose men to send forth as spies. We must choose one for each of the twelve tribes, each man a leader."

Again, Joshua nodded. But as his quick mind composed a list of likely candidates, he was unprepared for Moses's next words.

"Of course, you will represent the tribe of Ephraim."

Taken aback, the young general looked at his master in amazement.

"I, sir?" he marveled.

"Who would be better?" Moses insisted. "For their commander to accompany them would give the young men courage. Besides," he admitted, "I will rest easier if you are in charge."

Flattered, Joshua tried not to smile too broadly. And he attended closely to his master's instructions.

"Head directly north and then west," he said, tracing the route. "Avoid the King's Highway, which runs northeast. There are too many settlements there, and relations with the Edomites are uncertain. Start in the Negev," he directed, pointing on the map to the southern edge of Canaan. "Then go up into the hill country and see what the land is like, whether the people are strong or weak, whether they are few or many. And how is the land in which they live, rough or smooth? What are the cities like? Are they open camps or fortifications? And is the land rich or poor? Are there trees and orchards, vineyards and farms? It is now early spring. Try to bring back some of the produce."

Joshua took all of this in, committing the map and its place-names to memory.

"I shall do my best," he promised.

Pleased, Moses rolled up the map and handed it to his servant. "I know you will," he said.

Then with a sigh, the prophet looked over the little village below. "How well I remember this place!" he said. "When I was running from Egypt, I stopped here. This time, it is a starting point, but back then, it was like the end of the world. The end of Egypt and her reach, for sure."

His mind drifting back, Moses reminisced. "I was very frightened then, just as you are now. I knew not what lay ahead. And I was very lonely."

At this, he stopped and gazed deep into his friend's eyes. Joshua had hoped he had not detected his fear, his loneliness. But as he proceeded, the young man was grateful for his insight.

"I had no idea what I would find in Midian," he continued. "I did not know that I would dwell there so long, or that my life would be so happy. May your life be full when we reach Canaan," he smiled. "May you find life and love, as I did."

30

A cooling breeze blew across the shepherd hills of southern Canaan, caressing the faces and bare torsos of twelve young men. Sprawled beneath the open blue sky, they laughed and talked together, enjoying one of the rare hours of rest they had permitted themselves since leaving the Israelite camp in the wilderness of Paran.

They had headed out on their investigative expedition three days ago, making short work of the forty miles between the Negev and the Hebrew encampment at Kadesh-barnea.

Just this morning they had entered the shepherd district, and had donned the disguise they would wear throughout their sojourn, the long headscarf and cloak typical of Canaanite herdsmen. They hoped to avoid scrutiny by passing themselves off as just another group of transient shepherds. If they could avoid speaking much with the locals, they would do well, for their Egyptian tongue and Hebrew dialect, the only languages they knew, would surely give them away.

But though they rested, they were on the alert. A group of real herdsmen might come upon them at any time, for the hills were full of them. And finding them without a flock, they would surely be suspicious.

A few miles away, according to Hobab's map, a highway would lead them to the town of Hebron. Once on that road, they would be able to move more freely, for passersby would assume their flock was in the hands of comrades in the hills.

Keeping their eyes and ears atuned to danger, they were nonetheless grateful for the hour's reprieve.

Not since leaving the Nile Valley had their eyes been blessed with green hills, or their ears with the music of songbirds. The rounded terraces of southern Canaan were full of color and melody, trees blooming with spring flowers and narrow wadis alive with the sound of running water.

Joshua lay upon his back, his cloak open to the breeze. For a brief moment he closed his eyes, soothed by the rush of wind in tall grass.

He had just come from the brook that ran alongside the hill. Having washed his face and neck, he had splashed the cooling water all over his head, and now enjoyed the feel of sunlit air upon his wet hair and beard.

Sad, lonely thoughts had kept their distance since he had set out on this adventure. Eagerly he contemplated the next weeks, wondering what lay in store.

When a shadow moved across his face, he opened his eyes and found that Caleb had joined him. Stretching himself full-length beside Joshua, Caleb shook his own wet locks in the warm air.

"The brook feels wonderful!" Caleb exclaimed. "Much better than those stagnant oases in the Sinai."

"Are you just now done with your swim?" Joshua laughed. Gesturing toward the others, he said, "They have all dried off long ago."

"I could stay at the brook all day!" Caleb replied. "But I suppose we should make Hebron by nightfall."

"Yes," Joshua said, sitting up. "We will move out soon."

Gazing over the green folds leading toward the highway, Caleb marveled. "Perhaps I never really thought we would see Canaan. I can scarcely believe we are here!"

Joshua ran his hand through the lush grass at his side, disturbing a fat bee, who bumbled drowsily away. From someplace in the hills the sound of bleeting sheep reached his ears, and the clanking of heavy bells about the necks of milkgoats echoed up the ravines.

Reminded of a refrain from a slave song often heard among the Hebrew chaingangs in Egypt, he whispered, "Milk and honey..."

Caleb looked at him in surprise, a smile lighting his face.

"A land flowing with milk and honey!" he cried. "Oh, Joshua, I remember the song well!"

Suddenly, they were singing, rocking back and forth upon the hill, their arms wrapped about one another:

> Milk and honey,
> We shall have milk and honey.
> In the land of Father Jacob,
> In the Valley of Jehovah,
> We shall rest ourselves!

Barely were they aware that the others had now joined them, until ten more husky voices rang out across the hills, and each heart was lifted in song.

Yes, they had come at last to Canaan! Somehow, the trek through the arid Negev had not impressed them with this fact. But today, as they reveled in the joy of pleasant surroundings, in the tune of birds and bees, it occurred to them that they were the first Israelites in four hundred years to set foot upon the holy soil promised to their ancestors.

The more their souls swelled with song, the more the reality of their privileged position settled in on them, until tears filled their eyes and spilled down their ruddy cheeks.

Weeping for joy, they embraced one another, dancing up and down the hill like children.

But suddenly Shammua, representative of the Reubenite tribe, stopped short, his glistening eyes caught by a movement along a distant ridge.

"Brothers!" he gasped. "Look, over there!"

Quieting, the men followed his pointed finger to the top of the ridge, where a handful of people could be seen traversing it.

There were half-a-dozen of them, men dressed not like shepherds, but like cave-dwellers, in short skin skirts and highlaced sandals. Upon their torsos they wore nothing at all, but two of them bore upon their shoulders a long pole from which was suspended the carcass of some large animal.

Because there was so great a distance between the hill and the ridge, the Hebrews might not have realized just how gigantic these fellows were. It was the animal they carried, and the size of the men in comparison, that told Joshua and his followers that the hunters were huge.

Even if the quarry was a stag of unusual proportions, the men bearing him were over seven feet tall. And if the deer was of normal size, they were even taller!

Clustering behind some bushes, Joshua and his followers lay low, watching the hunting party descend the far slope, apparently headed for a camp in the wadi below.

"So . . . it is true!" whispered Shaphat, the Simeonite.

"What is true?" asked the Benjamite, Palti.

"The legend that Canaan is full of giants!" answered Ammiel, the Danite.

Joshua was familiar with that rumor, but quickly challenged it.

"Now, men," he warned, "we have seen many Canaanites along the way. None of them were giants!"

"We must not stir ourselves up with silly stories," added Caleb.

Looking at him wide-eyed, Geuel, the Gadite, argued, "Silly? Do you call what we have just seen 'silly'?"

"Right!" exclaimed the others.

Soon they were trading tales, of ogres and colossal bogeymen, of cannabalistic Canaanites who would as soon eat them as talk to them.

All but Joshua and Caleb. To no avail, they tried to reason with the rumormongers, until Joshua, in anger, commanded, "Put on your coats and your cloaks! We go to Hebron today! If there are giants there, we will tell Moses."

31

While the Canaanites were a rugged, handsome race, strengthened by generations of pleasant climate and good food, Joshua and his companions encountered no one of unusual stature as they set out the next day, traversing the highway that ran up the Jordan Valley.

Climbing the steep road toward Hebron, they passed people of many nationalities, for this was one of the three main trade routes from the east. Yet none of the folks they saw were giants.

Nor were the Hebrew travelers suspect along this international highway. Though Canaan, like every land, had heard of Israel's exploits, of its marvelous exodus from Egypt, and of its amazing defeat of Amalek, a little company like Joshua's sparked no suspicion as it passed through the region.

Hebron, the first city of any consequence the Israelites had seen since leaving the Nile, was a refreshing stop-off. Though they had to be cautious as they entered this Canaanite town, they reveled in the experience. For this place was more to them than a center of commerce or entertainment. It was the longtime home of their ancestor Abraham. And their entrance here brought Israel full circle.

Privately they delighted in the knowledge that they represented the return of the lost child, Joseph...the return of Jacob and his disenfranchised descendants. Though Israel had not yet conquered the region, they believed such conquest was inevitable.

As they headed north from the hilltop city, highest town in Palestine, they viewed the outlying fields with quiet pride. Just as in Abraham's day, the fields were dotted with sheepfolds and clumps of low-lying oaks. Somewhere out there Abraham had tended his own flocks, and one of those leafy arbors might be the Oaks of Mamre, where he had been a yearly tenant.

Then, too, one of the caves on the surrounding hills surely housed the bones of Sarah, Abraham's beloved wife. For legend had it that the patriarch had purchased such a sanctuary as her burial place.

Yes, this area was rich in history precious to the twelve Israelites. No Canaanite could have cared less for such stories, but as the young spies made their way through the territory, they thought of little else.

They would not stay long in one place. Moses had given them forty days to survey the land, and the more quickly they passed through it, the better. They were not here as tourists, and any lingering was risky.

But as the grade of the highway descended toward the northeast, they entered a most fertile little plain, and amazed by the lustrous vegetation growing along the easterly streams, they chose to camp there for the night.

On the green hillsides were many of the oaks they had seen from the highway. Quickly Joshua and the others gathered kindling from beneath the bows and proceeded to build an evening fire. In moments they had caught enough fish from the nearest brook to feed the entire company, and soon the delicious aroma of roasted trout spiraled up from the coals.

Leaning back with a sigh, Igal, of the tribe of Issachar, licked his lips, savoring the last of his dinner, and gave a contented belch. "I almost feel guilty," he laughed.

"I, too," replied Gaddiel, the Zebulunite. "When I think of our poor people, stuck back there in that desert, I wonder how we got so lucky!"

Caleb chuckled, rolling out his bed beside the fire. "Just suppose," he exclaimed, "that we are camping in the very place where old Abraham camped. Wouldn't that be something!"

Joshua nodded. "It's very possible!" he said.

No sooner had the words left his lips, than Nahbi, representative of the tribe of Naphtali, rushed up from the brook into the firelight.

"Men!" he cried. "See what I've found!"

Thrusting his fist toward the fire, he opened his palm for all to see. Lining it were four of the fattest grapes the Hebrews had ever laid eyes on, purple and luscious in the golden light.

"Where did you get those?" Joshua marveled.

"In the wadi, sir," Nahbi replied. "There is a whole vineyard only yards from here!"

Darting a glance at Caleb, Joshua rose to his feet, suddenly on alert.

"A vineyard?" he repeated. "We are on private land!"

But Nahbi shook his head. "I don't think so, sir," he replied. "It is not a tended vineyard."

Dubious, Joshua took one of the enormous grapes in his fingers, turning it over and over. "Impossible," he objected. "Such fruit could not possibly grow wild."

"But there are no fences, sir," Nahbi argued, "no trellises, no poles. The vines grow every which direction, even into the water itself!"

Passing the grape to Caleb, Joshua enthused, "This is indeed a holy land! Where but on holy soil would such riches grow free for the taking!"

32

Though the twelve Hebrews must be moving on, they marked firmly in their memories the exact location of the vineyard camp. One of Moses's requests, when he had sent them forth, was that they bring back a sample of the fruit of the land. What better example would be found than those magnificent grapes?

And so they determined that they would find the place again on their return trip, to take a cluster to Moses.

From here, their immediate destination was the city of Jericho, two days' journey to the northeast. The most important city in the entire Jordan Valley, it was a strategic fortress, commanding the eastern entrance to Canaan and the three trade routes that branched north, south, and west from the Jordan River. No investigation of the land would be worthwhile without a report on Jericho. For if Israel intended to invade the territory, they would inevitably go against that place.

Though the highway led directly from Hebron to the great walled fortress, the traveling was not easy. Hebron sat well over half-a-mile *above* sea level, and Jericho was positioned in a parched valley eight hundred feet *below* sea level. The descent toward the Jordan through the shepherd hills made for treacherous going.

When, by evening of the second day, the spies glimpsed the city, their hearts froze. If ever legends of Canaanites had stirred their souls to fear, the sight of Jericho and its formidable walls did more so.

Jericho's name had several interpretations, and it was thus called "the city of palm trees," "the place of fragrance," and "city of the moon." Though it was nearly night when the spies came upon Jericho, its silvery light illumined gleaming turrets and enhanced the foilage of towering trees. Exposed as it was in this wide, dry vale, Jericho was indeed moon-kissed, its palm-lined streets a thrill of green. And even to this distance the aroma of gardens and flowers was borne through the desert air.

But it was none of these attributes that caused the Israelites to tremble. Huddling together upon the sloping highway, they spoke in hushed tones, marveling over Jericho's impassable walls.

More like a castle than a town, the city covered only six acres, its tiny streets so jammed with houses that sunlight rarely touched them. The gardens and bowers that lent their green to its glory grew atop the flat roofs, and while the palace of the king sat perched at the crest of the mound which was the result of three thousand years of habitation, other residences were literally hung along the space that separated the city's inner and outer walls.

Creeping down the sunset highway, Joshua leaned close to Caleb. "Those walls must be as tall as six men standing on each others' shoulders!" he whispered.

"And the thickness of them!" Caleb added. "Why five men stretched full length across would not reach from side to side!"

Pausing for breath, Joshua sat down beside the road and gathered his men about him.

Surveying the crowded city, he shook his head. "To think, we were afraid of giants!" he sighed. "What we see before us is far more awesome! Like a town built by a giant's hand!"

His eleven companions sat with him in silence, paralyzed by the prospect of taking on so substantial an obstacle.

Surrounding the mound was a glacis of cracked and broken stones, a sheer drop-off which would slice an invading army's feet to shreds. And that hazardous slope led directly to a wide moat, which encompassed the entire circumference of the city.

"Sir," said Sethur, the Asherite, "even if we could scale that wall, how would we ever make it across the water? Who knows what creatures lie beneath the surface, just waiting for the taste of human flesh!"

Nodding in agreement, the others murmured fearfully, and Joshua knew their imaginations were again running wild.

"Let us deal with what we know!" he squelched them. "Not with what we do not know!"

"Very well," replied Gaddi, of the tribe of Manasseh, "but what we know is bad enough! I think we should turn back and tell Moses what we have found. What is the point of going further, when Israel will never get past Jericho?"

Astonished, Joshua confronted his kinsman. "Gaddi!" he cried. "You are, like me, a son of Joseph! I expected greater courage from you!"

Shamefaced, Gaddi looked at the ground, but his comrades rallied to his defense.

"Moses told us to bring back a report," they argued. "We know enough now without going further. We know enough to tell him that invasion is suicide!"

Flushed with anger, Joshua glared at them. "Do you all feel this way?" he snarled.

"Not I!" Caleb answered. "Brothers, where is your faith?"

Silenced by this question, the objectors squirmed, and Joshua stood up, heading down the road.

"Come!" he shouted over his shoulder. "We will camp with the caravans outside the wall, and tomorrow we will spy out the city!"

* * *

Joshua could not sleep that night. It was not the noise of the encampment that kept him awake, as caravans and bedos from the three major trade routes settled beneath the shadow of the great wall. It was the attitude manifested by his fellow spies that would not let him rest.

As his companions slumbered, he lay staring up into the star-studded sky, fretfully recalling the many times Israel had resisted the will of God.

Were it not for Caleb, even Joshua might have given up this venture by now, so weary was he of struggling with his followers' unbelief. Why was it that these young leaders, the choicest men his nation had to offer, were so easily intimidated? How fitting had been Caleb's question! Where *was* their faith, anyway?

Giving up his attempt to sleep, Joshua threw back his covers and stepped into the moonlight. All about him were travelers of many nations, waiting for morning when they would enter Jericho to do business, or, having completed their work there, to move on. This was the first time since leaving Egypt that Joshua had been in close quarters with so many Gentiles. He felt quite alone.

Most likely everyone in this campground had heard of Israel's miraculous flight from its four-hundred-year bondage. Doubtless they had all received news of its exploits in the desert, and wondered when the Hebrews would make their next move.

If the identity of Joshua's men were ever suspected, their lives would be in jeopardy. Therefore, as he paced through camp, he spoke to no one and hid his Hebrew face behind his mantle.

Ironic, he thought. If the Canaanites knew how spineless his spies really were, they would laugh at them rather than fear them.

I keep company with cowards! he sneered. *These ten "leaders" might as well be the enemy, for all the good they will do me!*

The enemy. Joshua paused over the phrase. He was commanding general of Israel. He had better concern himself with the nature of his adversary, as well as the nature of his own men.

Walking out from camp, he stood upon the bridge that spanned the moat, and he surveyed the walls up and down.

What sort of people lived behind them? he wondered. Proud people, they must be. Strong and ruthless. What other sort could build such a fortress? And merciless. They were surely a cold, heartless people, to have taken command of Canaan and to have held it against countless invaders for so long a time.

One thing he knew for certain: They were pagans, idolators. They worshiped a pantheon of false gods and goddesses, and had long ago abandoned themselves to the most sensual and depraved practices.

Cringing, he tried not dwell on the horrors that attended their religion, on the fornication and bloodlust that went with their rituals and sacrifices.

Clenching his fists, he dwelt instead on the righteous calling that was his, the destiny that would lead him to overthrow this wicked place.

Tomorrow he would take his men inside the walls. He would show them the reason for their venture, and inspire them with such zeal for their cause that they would put aside their childish qualms.

Feeling better, he knew he would sleep now. Or if not sleep, cogitate on strategies and plans. Returning across the bridge, he headed back for camp.

But just as he came again beneath the shadow of the moonlit wall, his eyes were drawn to a movement in a window, high atop the fortress.

One of the houses built along the wall was still alight, its owners apparently yet awake. And silhouetted against the window's yellow glow was a young woman, leaning on the sill.

Apparently seeking a bit of fresh air, she sat with her face upturned, the moon touching it sweetly. She ran a comb through her hair, which tumbled in long, red waves about her shoulders.

She was very far away in that high window. She did not look toward the camp, and was unaware of the solitary Hebrew and his admiring gaze.

But Joshua could see her clearly, and following her gaze toward the moon, he wondered what thoughts possessed her.

Only for a moment, however, did his eyes leave her face. For she was far more beautiful than the moon.

Unnoticed, he was free to linger over the graceful curve of her bare arm, where it peeked from beneath a scarlet gown. One dainty hand rested like a white bird upon the window sill, and as she lifted it to brush back her hair, he likewise lingered on the line of her neck and gentle fullness of her bosom.

"My lady..." he groaned, as feelings he had long denied himself rushed forth.

No one heard him. No one knew what surged through his masculine heart as he stood entranced upon the Jericho bridge.

Even he was unaware of himself, until a group of rowdy young Canaanites passed him, heading for the city just before curfew. In a moment the drawbridge that spanned the moat would be taken up, and the clatter of streets, taverns, and brothels would dwindle to a hum.

Suddenly aware again of his surroundings, and of the fact that he was in alien territory, Joshua felt the blood rush to his face.

Tearing his eyes from the woman in the window, he determined not to look that way again.

No matter how sweet her aspect, no matter how lovable her moonstruck face, she was, after all, a heathen. And no Israelite had a right to look upon her.

33

With daylight, the full color of the city was evident. While at night, the moon had played up the verdant vegetation and the clean white walls, sunshine showed another side of the pallet.

The moment Joshua awoke, the raging red of fire-trees, a plant peculiar to the area, stung his eyes. Bearing the brightest, poppy-colored flowers he had ever seen, these trees grew all about the roadways leading to Jericho. And as Joshua and his men entered the city, they found bright clusters of the scarlet blossoms in every niche of the marketplace.

The broad plaza where business was transacted was the only part of the congested city open to the sun. And in the light of day, what bold business was carried on!

Since Jericho controlled all access routes to the interior of Canaan, merchants from every land brought wares here to be sold. Goods from as far away as India, Egypt, Assyria, and Anatolia were on display. Joshua's men found that the language barrier was of little concern, as folks conducted trade by facial expression and wild gestures more than by the word of mouth.

But it was not only the produce and handcrafts of all nations that were traded here. Reminiscent of Egypt were the platforms of the slave merchants, who bought and sold human beings as though they were cattle.

Pierced to the heart, Joshua and his men watched as captives of foreign wars and young people born to slavery were auctioned off like sheep and goats. Their faces full of fear, or evincing no feeling at all, they stepped one by one upon the block, and listened as their prices were determined. Bound and shackled, they stepped down again, to be hauled away by new owners. If their eyes met the eyes of the Hebrews, they found there a sympathy new to them. But there was no chance for explanations, and no way to offer help.

As the slaves were led away, they met with the bite of cruel whips, and from their backs streamed another form of scarlet.

Yes, the streets of Jericho raged red in the daylight. From the far side of the square came the sound of drums and tambourines, as people brought sacrificial animals to be offered on the altars of Baal and his consort, Astarte. There would be no human life offered up today, for such sacrifices were made just once a year. But the gifts given daily to the priests were so numerous that the drain ditches leading off the main thoroughfare were choked with blood by noon.

All of this Joshua observed with growing disgust. It had been just such sights he had determined to show his men. But he had been unprepared for his own reaction.

While he had always been a hesitant warrior, he experienced today a rush of desire to wipe these people out. Egypt, for all its cruelty, had at least covered its shame with sophistication. Jericho's bloodlust bore not even a veneer of decency.

And it was not only the sacrificial system that carried the scarlet theme to the gutters. Hand in hand with bloody Baal walked his licentious lady, Astarte. On every corner, in broad daylight, her prostitutes flaunted their wares.

"Men," Joshua whispered, drawing his comrades about him, "can there be any doubt that Yahweh will destroy this place? Why would he promise this land to our fathers, yet allow this pollution to remain?"

Thoughtful, the men nodded, peering into the dark corners where all manner of lewdness abounded.

Walking toward the center of the square, Joshua led his men to the town fountain, a terraced pool fed by underground springs and graced with three tall geysers. Sitting on its ledge, the men cooled themselves from the heat of the hammering sun.

"I agree, sir," said Nahbi. "But those walls are insurmountable! How would our army ever gain a foothold?"

"How have we done any of the things we have done since the day Moses came to us?" Joshua argued. "Yahweh is the God of miracles!"

Looking at one another, the men recalled the many ways in which the Lord had intervened, from the plagues on Egypt to the quail and manna.

But as they considered Joshua's words, their contemplation was interrupted. A group of harlots, all dressed in red, had seen them sitting near the fountain, and had decided to approach them.

They did not know what tongue the Hebrews spoke, but sidling up, they bent over seductively and offered their services with universally understood body language.

Pulling back, Joshua denounced them, and muttered to his men, "Remember Sodom and Gomorrah? God told Abraham he would save those cities if only ten righteous persons could be found in them. But there were none!" Passing his hand over the market scene, he sighed, "I doubt even *one* could be found here!"

When he stood and turned for the city gate, about to lead his men away, the departing harlots jeered at him, hooting and laughing and calling unwanted attention to his little group.

To his relief, they were distracted by a party of would-be customers just as the crowd began to close in. But as the women left, one remained behind, studying the newcomers with uncommon kindness.

Instantly, Joshua recognized her. When she had been with the bawdy klatch of streetwalkers, he had not singled her out. But as she stood now alone, gazing upon him, his heart tripped.

She was the woman whom he had seen the night before, the beautiful young lady whose moonlit face had held him captive upon the bridge.

Just like the others, she was dressed in scarlet. While her scarlot garb had not impressed him last night, today it carried significance.

She was a harlot! His lovely lady was a prostitute of Astarte!

Dumbfounded, he backed away, his throat choked with shame that he could ever have given her a second glance.

But as he withdrew, her face colored, and she turned her sad, aqua eyes to the fountain.

"Will you have a drink of water?" she said softly.

Incredulous, Joshua glanced at his men, who observed her with wonder.

"She speaks Hebrew!" Caleb whispered, drawing near his elbow.

"Indeed!" Joshua stammered.

"How can that be?" his friend marveled.

But the others were frightened by the fact. "We have been found out!" they speculated. "She will report us!"

Anxiously they spurred their leader to depart.

But not before the young woman had drawn closer, offering them a skin of water, which she had just filled at the splashing pool.

"Come again," she bade them. "My house is your house."

With this she gently thrust the water bottle into Joshua's hot hands, and bowed quickly before him.

Then she hastened away, vanishing into the dense crowd like a ruby arrow.

"Let's go!" the men exclaimed, pulling on Joshua's cloak.

Complying, he followed them to the gate.

But now he knew less about Jericho than he had when he entered. The soft, kind face of the scarlet woman had made a muddle of his heart, setting up an obstacle far more confounding than the walls of her profligate city.

34

Before Joshua had entered Jericho, he had been un-afraid. Though his men had been squeamish since their sighting of the Anakim, or giants, at Hebron, it took Jericho to fill Joshua's heart with apprehension.

Nor was that apprehension based on the size of the walls or on the ferocity of the Canaanites living there. It was precipitated by a quandary of the heart, a bewilderment of the spirit.

His two encounters with the woman in red caused him to question the nature of his enemy. He wondered not only where such a lady had learned to speak Hebrew, but he wondered how someone so lovely, so apparently kind of spirit, could be evil.

Yes, she was a harlot. Harlots were wicked, were they not? Doubtless, she worshiped a heathen goddess—not only worshiped her, but prostituted herself in her name.

Still, he sensed in her a seeking soul. He wondered how he could go against her city when it would mean her destruction, and the destruction of others who might be like her.

When Joshua had fought the Amalekites at Rephidim, he had encountered the most vicious of warriors, men bent on bloodshed and filled with hate. It had been easy to oppose them with strength of purpose.

But Jericho was inhabited by families, by women and children, as well as men of war. How to hate them, he knew not.

Such thoughts filled his head during the remainder of the venture through Canaan.

Following the Jordan, the spies and their commander hugged the folds and creases of the mountain highway leading toward the northern limits of the land. They had been given forty days to complete their round-trip, and when they left Jericho they tried to travel at least ten miles a day, stopping only briefly to investigate various locales along the way to Rehob, the last city on the itinerary.

While Amalekites and other warlike groups were concentrated south of Jericho, the northern half of the land was dominated by Canaanites, likewise students of war, but more deeply rooted in towns than their transient neighbors. Joshua and his men found that most of the cities were walled, and though none of them was so strongly fortified as Jericho, each would be a difficult obstacle to overcome.

To their relief, they saw no more gigantic Anakim on their trip north, and might have avoided giants altogether had they not ventured toward the seacoast on their return.

Making a side jaunt to spy out the cities of the Philistine plain, they came across the tall, pre-Hellenic seapeoples who inhabited that region. Intermingled with them were remnants of the giant race, the Zamzummin. Together the bloodlines had created an exceptionally powerful populace.

It was with skittish glances over their shoulders that the Hebrews set out at last for Kadesh and the camp of Israel. If Joshua had had trouble maintaining morale during the early days of the venture, he had even more once his followers had been through Philistia. He hoped that their long-planned return to the wild vineyard outside Hebron might renew their spirits, for they must soon give an account of the land to Moses, and in their present mood, that report would be anything but encouraging.

It was a bright, sunny day once again when the men found the vineyard just north of Abraham's city. Laughing and running, the weary travelers headed for the brook where the thick vines trailed into the current, and stripping themselves they plunged in, playfully splashing one another.

Joshua seated himself on the bank and dangled his feet in the stream.

"We have seen much on this trip," Caleb noted, joining his friend by the water's edge, "but this place is the most impressive."

"More impressive than the giants?" Joshua tested him.

The Judahite shrugged. "Canaan is indeed a land of mighty people," he acknowledged. "But if we are meant to take it, we will overcome them."

"Well spoken, " Joshua praised him. "It seems I can always rely on you."

Caleb took the compliment graciously, and breathed deep of the warm air, a smile of contentment on his face. "We should give this place a name!" he suggested. "When we tell Moses about it, we should call it by name."

Pondering this a moment, he traced the vines where they grew down the shore. Lush with purple fruit, they beckoned to the hungry Hebrew.

Leaping to his feet, Caleb exclaimed, "Eshcol, Valley of Eshcol!"

The Hebrew name meant Valley of the Cluster, and repeating it joyously, Caleb ran down the bank to where a huge clump of swollen grapes hung shining in the sun.

Emerging from the brook, his companions gathered around him, and one drew a sharp knife from his belt, offering it to him.

"These will do, to show Moses just how lush this land is!" Caleb proclaimed. Taking the knife, he eagerly sawed through the thick vine, until the grapes fell with a thump to the earth. Then breaking off a length of the vine, he ran it between the stems of the cluster and lifted one end to his shoulder.

Nahbi hoisted the other end, and as though they bore between them a slain buck, they carried the grapes to Joshua.

The commander laughed as they approached, and stood to greet them. "Moses told us to bring a sample of the fruit of the land, but you bring the entire vineyard!"

Though they pulled off handfuls of the succulent grapes, ravenously cramming the sweet morsels into their mouths, the men barely made a dint in the cluster. Between the sounds of lips smacking and juice trickling, they sang together as though they drank fine wine.

But just as they had nearly forgotten all care, a sound less palatable interrupted their little party. Low and gutteral, it issued from the slope behind, and thinking it must be the growl of a wild animal, the revelers leaped to their feet, drawing their swords in a flash.

From a clump of bushes, a creature emerged, his shadow falling across their gathering like a thundercloud.

Mouths agape, the Hebrews surveyed their visitor. This was no animal. This was a human being. But he was enormous, taller by a cubit than the tallest of them!

And he was built like the Jericho walls, his trunk thick and muscular, his arms and legs rippling like iron. The scantiest of clothing served to enhance rather than conceal his powerful physique. A small leather breastshield was his torso's only covering, and beneath a short, rawhide skirt, swelled well-defined thighs. Crisscrossed up his limbs, from toes and fingers to knees and elbows, were studded straps of leather, and in one rocky fist he bore a spear taller than himself.

This he shook violently, throwing his huge head backward and roaring like a lion, shaking also his black mane of hair and beard.

Falling back in terror, Joshua's men clattered their swords together, endangering one another in hasty retreat.

"Anak!" they cried, knowing that they confronted one of the legendary giants.

"Stand still!" Joshua commanded. "We are the Lord's!"

But his companions ignored him, all but Caleb, who managed to take courage.

The colossus was now within feet of Joshua and his friend, still roaring and flashing his weapon like a lightning bolt. Looming over the Hebrew leader, he sneered at him like an ox above an ant, until Joshua felt his hot breath upon his face.

Then, to his surprise, the giant lowered his spear, not to drive it through him, but to point at the abandoned cluster of grapes.

Anger flamed in his huge eyes, and shaking his enormous head again, he bellowed like a wild boar.

"This is your land?" Joshua interpreted. "Your vineyard?"

Of course, the giant could not understand a word he spoke, but Joshua knew he got the message.

Snorting, he nudged at the cluster and waved his spear under the Hebrew's nose.

Swallowing hard, Joshua and Caleb listened as the towering challenger replied in his own tongue, flinging his hands toward the vineyard, and stamping his feet.

"Yes," Joshua said, his heart surging. "We will go. We will take no more grapes."

Joshua's tone convinced the titan he would comply. And while the Hebrews tiptoed backward, expecting him to wait until they vanished down the road, it was instead the giant who turned to go.

Watching him depart, Joshua and Caleb could scarcely believe they were still in possession of their lives. For a long while they stood silent on the shore, thinking the fellow would come back, and likely with an army.

But the sun was setting and night was coming on. As the first stars appeared in the black sky, the two Hebrews were joined by their companions, who one by one crept forth from places of hiding.

"We will not camp tonight," Joshua whispered to his men. "We will travel by cover of darkness."

Relieved to be going, the men headed with him toward the highway.

But Caleb was not so hasty.

"What about the grapes?" he called after them.

Joshua turned around, and seeing the pile of discarded fruit lying in the moonlight, he sent Nahbi back to help carry it.

"What if the giant returns?" the others objected.

"We have our orders," Joshua reminded them. "Moses wants to see the fruit of the land, and we will take it to him!"

35

Miles before Joshua and his men laid eyes on the camp of the Israelites, the sound of music and celebration reached them across the wilderness. Messengers who had been on the lookout for them heralded their return, and the people made ready to greet them, eager to hear their report and to plan the next steps toward their long-lost homeland.

It had been over four centuries since the children of Jacob had dwelt in the promised land. Anxious to regain their inheritance, the people who had been tested in Egypt and tested in the Sinai believed nothing more could stand in their way.

Yes, they had often failed the Lord. They had not always been strong of faith. But surely they had learned their lessons now. They had survived, had they not? Once they entered the land of milk and honey, they would never look back.

Joshua should have been glad to return to camp. This should have been a momentous occasion. But, despite the evident enthusiasm of Israel for his homecoming, it was with a leaden heart that he descended the last sandy hill and witnessed the enormous population spread out before him.

Ever since the encounter with the giant at Eshcol, his men had spoken only of defeat. Joshua knew that the report they would present to Moses and the people would be full of discouragement, and though he would try to inspire the opposite, their voices would outnumber his.

Therefore, when Moses sent a committee to meet him, asking him to address the congregation, the lift of his

167

chin and the resolute expression on his face served only
to cover a despondent spirit.

"Greetings, Master," he hailed the prophet, joining
him upon a slope overlooking the crowd. "Greetings,
Aaron," he said to the prophet's brother, bowing low.
"Your servants are safely returned."

At this, applause rang up from the desert floor, as
Israel showed appreciation for their twelve heroes.

Moses, relieved to see his closest friend, embraced him
fervently, and with tears welling in his eyes, he presented
him to the people.

"We are all anxious to know what you discovered in the
land of our fathers!" he announced. "We want to know
what lies before us as we reclaim our heritage!"

Again, applause and cheers filled the air, and Joshua
tried to appear zealous.

Turning to the congregation, he held up his hands,
calling for silence. "We went into the land where you sent
us," he began, "and it certainly does flow with milk and
honey!" Then calling forth Caleb and Nahbi, who bore
between them the grape-laden vine, he proclaimed,
"This is the fruit of the land!"

Amazed at the sight of the monstrous grapes, the
people gave a great shout, and instantly broke into song:

> Milk and honey,
> We shall have milk and honey.
> In the land of Father Jacob,
> In the Valley of Jehovah,
> We shall rest ourselves!

To the sound of timbrels and horns, they clapped and
danced, seeing the first tangible evidence of their racial
dream. When at last, Moses commanded silence, he
addressed the men who stood with Joshua.

"You have done well," he praised them. "Tell us, then,
about the people of the land, and their cities."

Caleb would have spoken, but before he could get a word out, his fellow spies took over.

Shamelessly they circumvented their commander's positive approach, coloring Canaan in the bleakest of terms.

"It is indeed a land of milk and honey," Shaphat said, "but the people who live there are strong, and the cities are fortified and very large!"

"Moreover," interrupted Igal, "we saw the descendants of Anak there!"

At the very mention of the name, fear pushed through the crowd, and the people murmured in horror.

"Amalek is also living in the Negev," added Palti, "and the Hittites and the Jebusites and the Amorites live in the hill country just north of us!"

No race of warriors was more greatly to be feared than those already mentioned, but as the crowd grew restless with dread, Gaddiel inserted the obvious.

"And the Canaanites live by the sea and by Jordan!"

By now, the people despaired indeed. Old men clutched their chests in horror, and women wept aloud. Little children clung to their mother's robes and able-bodied men trembled.

Seeing that Joshua had lost ground, Caleb managed to gain the front, and cried out for the crowd's attention. "Brothers and sisters!" he shouted. "Do not be disheartened by this evil report. Canaan is the land of Jacob, the land vouchsafed to us and to our children! Regardless of the challenge, we should by all means go up and take possession of it. For we shall surely overcome it!"

This seemed to prick the spirits of the people, but only for an instant. No sooner had Caleb spoken than Gaddi forced him aside. "Do not be foolish!" he growled. "We are *not* able to go up against the enemy. They are too strong for us!"

"Yes!" cried Ammiel, his eyes wide and his hands gesturing wildly. "The land through which we have gone is a land that devours its inhabitants! All the people we saw are men of great size!"

Flabbergasted by this gross exaggeration, Joshua tried to take control, stepping to the fore and calling for peace.

But it was too late. The ancient legends of the Canaanites and their neighbors were too deeply ingrained in the memories of the Hebrews. Passed down through generations, they required only such lies to make them flower into wild imaginings.

Vainly did Joshua attempt to regain the people's confidence. When Sethur added his account, the crowd was lost forever.

"There also we saw the *Nephilim!*" he cried. "And we became like grasshoppers in our own sight, as well as theirs!"

The *Nephilim?* The Anak were bad enough. But the Nephilim, a legend reserved for campfire tales and nightmares, were the most notorious monsters of Hebrew folklore.

Believed to be the descendants of the titanic race that dwelt on earth before Noah's flood, they were half-human and half-demon. Of unearthly stature, their descendants were of preternatural dimensions.

Utterly terrified, the people greeted this account with loud distress. Standing aside, Joshua looked on helplessly as the Israelites stirred themselves into a frenzy of weeping and wailing.

Directing their fear and their resentment at their great leader, they began to shout at Moses: "Why didn't we die in Egypt, or in the wilderness? Why is the Lord bringing us into this land, to fall by the sword? Our wives and children will become plunder! Wouldn't it be better for us to return to Egypt?"

Soon even the most respected men of the camp, the very ones whom Moses had selected as his governors, were taking up the cry. Conferring amongst themselves, they rushed up the slope, ready to overthrow Moses and replace him with one of the rebellious spies.

"Let us appoint a leader," they called to the people, "and return to Egypt!"

Cheers rose from venomous hearts, and as a body the people moved forward, ready to tear Moses and Aaron to shreds.

Surrounded, the two brothers were thrown to the ground, and there they lay, facedown in the dirt.

Always Joshua had been amazed at the ease with which the Israelites could be turned from the right to embrace the wrong. But somehow he had always held out hope for them, believing that in their hearts they must have a core of good. After all, were they not "the chosen people," the sons and daughters of Jacob, Isaac, and Abraham?

But this moment, as he observed their callous cruelty, their changeable spirit, he gave up that hope. In terror for his master's safety, he ran to him, throwing himself across his prostrate body, and shielding him from the blows of fists and feet.

"Back! Back!" he cried. "Do not do this evil, my brothers!"

Somehow, his voice penetrated the soulless mob. Somehow, they heard him, and dismayed at their own actions, they pulled away.

Raising himself from the ground, Joshua stood again to his feet, finding, to his amazement, that Caleb had likewise protected Aaron. Together, the two Hebrews managed to make a dent in the crowd, and sent the governors back to the desert floor.

Their faces tearstreaked, Caleb and Joshua paced back and forth before the people, pushing aside their fellow spies and commanding the attention of the crazed congregation.

Tearing the necklines of their own tunics, they threw dust over their heads until their tears trickled through a coating of dirt.

"The land which we passed through is exceedingly good!" Joshua proclaimed. "If the Lord is pleased with us, He will bring us into this land and give it to us—a land flowing with milk and honey!"

"Listen to Joshua!" Caleb joined in, his arms spread beseechingly. "Do not rebel against the Lord! And do not fear the inhabitants of the land! For they shall be our prey! Their defense has been removed from them, and the Lord is with us! Do not fear them!"

Again, it seemed the people might give heed. But it took only a hint of rebellion on the part of their leaders to kill their faith.

Where it began, no one would be able to recount. But from somewhere in the crowd a pebble was thrown, and then a rock, and another, and another. "Stone them!" someone cried. And soon the cry became a chant.

Driven like lepers from the edge of camp, Joshua, Caleb, Moses, and Aaron took flight. Bleeding and battered they took sanctuary in the rocky hills where the sons of Amalek dwelt.

For even in that hostile territory they would be safer than with their own people.

36

Throughout the next day, Moses separated himself from his fellow fugitives, cloistering himself in prayer within a nook of the barren hills. Knowing that they dare not return to camp, and not wishing to leave their master, Joshua, Caleb, and Aaron kept close together, hoping that the Lord would answer Moses's pleas for guidance.

From experience, Joshua knew that the prophet might be away for days. This was not the first time the servant had been obliged to wait while his mentor sought the word of the Lord. This time, at least, he had company. But this was little solace in such wild country, where their closest neighbors would as soon kill them as speak to them.

It was, therefore, a great relief to the three Hebrews when the prophet reappeared the next morning, assuring them that it was safe to return to camp.

"The glory of the Lord has appeared to the children of Israel," he told them. "They will not harm us, though the word I have for them is dreadful."

Moses's tone confirmed the expression on his face. His struggle with God had been arduous and the outcome disheartening. Lines of stress and sorrow etched his countenance. The man who had always before returned from days of prayer with renewed vigor and with hopeful news, was this time weighted down with grief.

But nothing more did he relay to his three companions. Whatever sad report he would bear to the camp, he would give only when the entire congregation was gathered before him.

Longing to question him, Joshua nevertheless refrained. Moses's silence was foreboding, reinforcing the sense of hopeless resignation which the young Hebrew had experienced when the Israelites set upon them all, stoning the master and driving them into the hills.

Israel had not learned the lessons Yahweh had tried to teach them. Over and over they had bowed to doubt, rebelling against the Lord and his emissaries. And from the look on Moses's face, there was now no hope for their reformation.

When the last mile had been traveled and the camp lay spread out at their feet, they found, just as Moses had predicted, no danger to themselves. The very people who had desired to kill them were today meek as lambs. Rather than calling for a new leader, they heralded Moses's appearance with tears of contrition.

Old men sat upon the ground in sackcloth, their hair and beards full of ashes. Young women and children huddled together, weeping for forgiveness, and the men who had tried to overthrow Moses met him in the wilderness, bowing and seeking his favor.

Still, not a word passed the prophet's lips, until he stood once again upon the slope where Joshua and the eleven spies had given their report.

As he raised his hands, the audience was hushed. Not even a breeze passed over the desert before the master cried like a trumpet, "'How long will these people provoke me? How long will they not believe in me, despite all the signs which I have performed in their midst?'"

Everyone knew it was the Lord's words that he spoke, and not his own. Too many times had they heard him address them thus, for them to mistake that fact.

Without hesitation, Moses continued, though the next utterance would be the most grievous of his prophetic career.

"'Surely all the men who have seen my glory and my miracles, which I performed in Egypt and in the wilderness, yet have put me to the test these ten times and have not listened to my voice ... surely they shall by *no means* see the land which I promised to their fathers, nor shall any of those who provoked me see it!'"

Scarcely comprehending the import of this pronouncement, the people stood in stony silence before the preacher. But as the words gradually penetrated their incredulous minds, Moses hit them with more.

"'How long shall I bear with this evil people,'" he shouted, "'who grumble against me? I have heard the complaints of the sons of Israel, which they murmur against me. As I live, just as you have spoken in my hearing, so I will do to you! Your corpses shall fall in this wilderness, even all your numbered men from twenty years old and upward, who have grumbled against me! Surely you shall not come into the land in which I swore to make you dwell, except Caleb, the son of Jephunneh, and Joshua, the son of Nun! And your children, whom you said would become a prey—I will bring them in, and they shall know the land which you have rejected! But as for *you*, your corpses shall fall in this wilderness. And your sons shall be shepherds for forty years in the wilderness, and they shall suffer for your unfaithfulness, until your corpses lie in the wilderness!'"

Awestruck, the people looked to one another, hoping that they had misunderstood. And when they saw only their own desperation mirrored in one another's faces, they began to plead with Moses.

Surely he would retract this edict! Had the Lord not threatened them in the past with total destruction? Surely, Yahweh could not mean what he said. Surely, he would reconsider!

But the prophet was unyielding as rock. When he raised his hands again, it was only to repeat the dreaded word.

"'I the Lord have spoken!'" he cried. "'Surely I will do this to all this evil assembly who are gathered together against me. In this wilderness they shall be destroyed, and here they shall die!'"

Like a twisting knife, the pronouncement severed soul from spirit. Even Joshua and Caleb, who alone of their generation had been spared the evil, slumped to their knees, terrified of the destiny prepared for their people.

Weeping and mourning such as never had been heard in Israel and never would be again, ascended that day to the skies. Would God not repent of this decision? Had he not sworn punishment upon them in the past, yet later changed his mind?

But, indeed, Yahweh had declared himself. Not even Moses, who had pleaded with him for two days, had been able to turn his heart.

And though the people soaked the sand with tears, the prophet could hold out no hope.

Turning with stooped shoulders, Moses left the hill, disappearing into the desert, silent as a shadow.

PART VI
The Governor's Apprentice

37

Dirt, sand, and tumbleweeds. Sometimes Joshua felt sure he would go mad from the sight of them.

Twenty years of bedo existence in the wilderness of Zin, following months in the wilderness of Sinai and the wilderness of Paran, should have accustomed him to the taste of grit between his teeth and the feel of desert wind upon his face. But they had not.

He was not a city dweller by nature. Though raised in Raamses, he was of Hebrew lineage, and the love of open spaces ran in his blood. But the land of his forefathers was not desert. It was the land of promise, the land of milk and honey, which he must wait yet *another* twenty years to enter.

Not that life within the wandering camp had been dull. Cohabitation with such a difficult people as Israel presented daily challenges. But those challenges were so bound up with endless sand and the bleak routine of the shepherd's life that he had come to despise the wilderness for more than its dreariness. He had come to despise it because his people would not learn from it. Always they resisted its testing, rather than growing stronger for it.

At least this was true of the older generation. The younger people seemed to be made of better stuff, their spirits more amenable to hardship. As Joshua observed their coming of age, he did from time to time take heart for the future of the nation.

Today, however, he was downcast. He had traveled out from camp toward the north, where eighteen years ago Israel had made one of its most foolish mistakes.

Kicking at the tawny sand as he walked, he had uncovered a vivid memento of that mistake, an Amalekite war helmet. Unearthing it, he was reminded of an incident he wished he could forget.

This helmet undoubtedly remained from the Hebrews' second battle with the sons of Amalek. The first time Israel had confronted the barbarians, Joshua had led them to victory. Their endeavors had been blessed by Yahweh, and the young general's first experience with combat had convinced everyone he should henceforth lead the Israelite army.

But the second time the Hebrews went against Amalek had been a disaster, lacking God's approval from the outset.

Because this helmet bore the symbol of the Amalekites of the Sinai, it was apparently one of the headgear stripped from the southern horde and worn by an Israelite in this second battle. It had been lost in the fracas which saw ten thousand Hebrews slain or routed and sent back to Kadesh in disgrace.

Neither the ark of the covenant, nor the pillar of cloud had left the camp to lead them north that day into battle. The morning after Moses had given his grim pronouncement, telling Israel that none of the elder generation would ever enter the promised land, a host of the people had sought him out in the hill country, resolved to circumvent the edict.

"Here we are!" they had announced, when they found their master. "We have indeed sinned, but we will go up to the place which the Lord has promised!"

Joshua had been present with Moses that day, having followed him into the wilds of the high country, along with Caleb and Aaron. He knew how headstrong the children of Jacob could be, and seeing the determination in their faces, he feared it was worthless to contradict them. But reminding them of the report his men had given, he said, "Brothers, there are Amalekites and

Canaanites in these hills. They have surely seen our encampment at Kadesh, and stand ready to defend their territory."

"But we have fought the Amalekites before!" they rebutted. "You led us to victory against them! Will you not lead us again?"

"Why are you transgressing the commandment of the Lord," Moses intervened, "when it will not succeed? Do not go up, lest you fall before your enemies! For the Lord will *not* be with you!"

But in typical fashion, the people stiffened their necks. "How can God be against us, if we are reclaiming the heritage of Jacob? Is it not ours by promise?" they objected.

Sighing, Moses could only repeat the warning: "The Amalekites and Canaanites will be there in front of you! You shall fall by the sword, for you have turned away from following the Lord! The Lord will *not* be with you!"

The following hours were a horror to recall. With utter disregard for the prophet, the people scorned him, calling him a senile old man and insisting that he was refuting the very promise which he had relayed to them. Surely the land was not meant only for their children! What right did Moses have to put such restrictions on the prophecy?

And wouldn't Joshua come with them? Wouldn't he lead them? He was one of them, was he not, one of their generation? How could he betray them now, when he had been named commanding general by the laying-on of hands and anointing?

Even now, as Joshua relived that moment, his heart pounded as it had that day. Torn between his calling as leader of the Israelite army, and the word of Moses, he had surveyed the faces of the many men he had inspired with courage, the ones who had become, under his instruction, a mighty fighting force. He remembered how they had first gathered before him on the plain of

Rephidim, the most disheveled and cowardly "troops" it had ever been a commander's misfortune to muster. Of course, he had been just as inexperienced as they, when they first took up arms together. But it had been that mutual inexperience and the learning process that had bonded him to his men and his men to him. How *could* he now deny their request, and let them go forth without him—go forth to war... and certain defeat?

Today, as he turned the helmet over and over in his hands, he gently brushed eighteen years of dust and rust from its once-shiny crest. Eyes misting, he remembered how his brave, foolish warriors had headed north, only to be driven back hours later, torn, bloody, and ashamed, more than half of their comrades slain in the briefest battle ever fought. Staggering and falling over one another, they left a trail of corpses half-a-mile wide and littering the hills as far south as Hormah.

Whose helmet was this? he wondered. Which of the thousands he had come to love had died wearing it?

Or perhaps the Hebrew soldier had been hauled away into slavery. That was just as possible. Perhaps he had labored the past eighteen years under whip and rod, just as he had done in Egypt, property of some Canaanite in some Canaanite city.

Clenching his fists, Joshua gazed north toward the folded hills of the promised land. It was alien territory, possessed by heathens. The thought of that nameless soldier in servitude within one of the enemy's walled cities crushed his heart, and the soldier within himself yearned for combat.

Would that God had freed him that long ago day to go against Canaan and all its inhabitants! This very moment Joshua would do so, given the chance.

But just as he savored the desire, the woman of Jericho flashed to mind, and he turned his gaze sadly to the ground.

How many times over the years had she haunted him? And her impact was always the same, softening him, supplanting the desire for revenge.

Tucking the helmet beneath his arm, Joshua turned back toward camp. Bewildered and ashamed of his conflicted feelings, he shook his head.

Someday, he knew, he would lead an army again, and that army would go against Jericho. Surely the Lord would tolerate no softness toward the enemy!

But in eighteen years the memory of the woman had not dimmed. Though Joshua often prayed for release, her memory was as strong today as when he had first watched her in her high window.

38

It was just past sunset when Joshua returned home. Sabbath was beginning, and a hush had fallen over the congregation, which would rest from all work until sunset of the next day.

As Joshua found his tent, ready himself to rest for the night, a scuffle at the edge of the company caught his attention. Someone was being dragged into camp. Half-a-dozen young Israelites, known for their nationalistic zeal, had apprehended the fellow on the desert and were apparently determined to bring him before the council. What his supposed crime might be, Joshua did not know, but one of the arresters carried a heavy sack full of oak twigs, perhaps evidence to be presented.

"He was found gathering wood on the Sabbath!" one of the apprehenders explained, brushing past Joshua on his way to the meeting tent.

Without further word, the accused was hauled through the gathering crowd, and Joshua followed, wondering what Moses's response would be.

Over the years since the sabbath had been instituted as a day of rest, there had been little occasion to test it. The first time people had gone forth upon a sabbath to gather manna, they had found none in the plain, and ever since then they had believed the Lord would not bless any labor attempted on the seventh day. The penalty for deviation from that premise had been expressly stated, and these young men were about to call for execution of justice.

Shaking, and white of face, the wood-gatherer stood before the meeting tent. His hands bound behind him, he was held between two of his captors, and the bag of branches was thrown to the ground before him.

"Moses!" one of the zealots cried. "Come forth! We have brought a man for trial!"

Such a strong word! Joshua thought. Trial? For collecting twigs?

Opening the tent door, Moses stepped forth, surveying the young men and their hapless captive with a furrowed brow.

"This man," the arrester went on, "was caught gathering wood on this holy evening! We think it proper that justice should be served, that Israel may know that the Lord is also holy!"

"Yes!" another added. And quoting the fourth commandment, he cried, " 'Remember the sabbath day, to keep it holy. Six days you shall labor and do all your work, but the seventh day is a sabbath of the Lord your God. You shall not do any work in it, you or your son or your daughter, your male or your female servant or your cattle or the traveler who stays with you'!" Then, yet another reminded Moses of God's edict: " 'Whoever does any work on the sabbath shall be put to death'!"

This was not the first time these zealots had called for a hearing. Unlike their elders, the men of Israel who forever strained the law, testing the patience of God Almighty, these fellows were among a growing segment of the younger generation who were bent on making Israel into a holy people. Having witnessed the devastations wrought on their fathers' disobedient generation, they had taken it upon themselves to clean up the nation.

How Moses felt about them, Joshua had never been certain. Most of the "cases" which they brought before the prophet had been of little import, and had been easily decided, though they *had* served to remind Israel of its sacred roots.

As for Joshua, his feelings regarding their endeavors were mixed. Almost vigilante in their approach, their fanaticism was worrisome. But he could not fault them overmuch, as their love of the law was a welcome contrast to the rebellions so often staged by their elders, and so often greeted by God's wrath.

For a long moment, Moses stood outside his door, observing the pale-faced suspect, and keeping silent. In his expression, however, Joshua read a conflicted heart. Sympathy for the arrested man, who had been caught in an after-hours attempt to stock his family's fuel bin for the night, and who had probably thought his indiscretion was of little consequence, tugged at Moses's kind soul. Likewise, reverence for the mind of Yahweh prevented him from summarily freeing the fellow.

When at last the prophet spoke, it was to buy time.

"You are right to take seriously the honoring of the sabbath," he told the young zealots. "Your concern for integrity is a virtue. But since this is indeed the sabbath, it is not proper to put a man on trial. Let him be put in custody, and when the sabbath is past, I will hear you."

With this, the prophet turned about and disappeared into his tent, pulling the door closed.

Brought up short, the young men looked at one another in bewilderment. Of course, Moses was right. But was he going soft regarding sin?

Muttering together, they at last turned the accused over to the meeting-house guards, and left with the dispersing crowd.

As the sun descended behind the dark desert hills, Joshua wandered to his own shelter. Amazed at his master's quick wit, he nonetheless knew Moses would struggle with this matter all night long.

He would not have traded places with him, for surely there could be no more difficult demand laid on a man's shoulders than the daily task of seeking a balance between justice and mercy.

*   *   *

Joshua crept into the dark of Moses's tabernacle, hesitating even though he had been summoned. It was an overcast day, but no burning lamp hung from the rafters of the meeting tent. And from the corner where the prophet kept his bed, the sound of soft weeping met Joshua's ears.

It was the day after sabbath. And what a day it had been! Dismal and horrifying.

It had begun with Moses's pronouncement of the judgment to be meted out upon the wood-gatherer. Though his single, unpretentious crime had been to deviate from the edict of rest, God Almighty had decreed that he must be stoned, taken outside the camp and stoned by the congregation until dead.

Save for a few radicals, it had been a half-hearted crowd that assembled to carry out the command. Even now, Joshua could feel the weight of the solitary rock he had managed to heave in the direction of the crouching victim. And as he tiptoed toward the master's dreary corner, he wiped imagined residue from his palm—wiped it for the hundredth time.

"Master," he whispered through the dark pall, "it is I, Joshua. You called for me?"

At this, the weeping ceased, and he could hear Moses sit up upon his bed.

"Joshua..." the prophet sighed, "I have never felt so alone!"

The servant sat down in respectful silence. Had he known what to say, he would not have spoken, for he sensed that the master's heaviness was beyond lifting.

As Joshua's eyes adjusted to the bleakness, what little light filtered in from the outside told him that Moses's face was raised to the ceiling, and his eyes were closed.

"Oh," the prophet groaned, "I have always longed to know the ways of the Lord, to comprehend his covenant! But his ways are hard, Joshua. What was I to do? I would have spared the man, but God does not allow us to follow our own hearts. When we follow our own hearts and our own eyes, even as the wood-gatherer did, we play the harlot, Joshua. We must remember the commandments, and be holy unto our God!"

Joshua still said nothing, knowing that his purpose just now was to be a listening ear, a grappling post for his master's struggling soul.

But there were others in the camp who were not sympathetic to Moses's plight. There were those who had hung back from the stoning, and who murmured against Moses and his coleader, Aaron.

Even as Joshua sat in the dark tent, trying to console the prophet, the sound of a growing crowd was heard outside. And soon, men began to call for Moses.

Their voices were familiar, for they were leaders of the Levites, members of the priesthood chosen years before at Sinai, and leaders of the Reubenites, foremost tribe of Jacob.

Regardless of the growing number of zealots, the type of which had brought the wood-gatherer for trial, these men were still the acknowledged elite of Israel, and their opinion carried great weight.

"Moses! Aaron!" they cried. "We have had enough of your dictatorship! Come forth and face us!"

Taking a deep breath, Moses wiped the tears from his face, and stood up. Joshua tried to restrain him, but he would face his accusers.

Following the master to the doorway, Joshua stepped with him into the gray daylight. Waiting outside were the most notable members of the Israelite nobility, 250 elected officials. And speaking for them were the Levite, Korah, and Reubenites, Dathan and Abiram.

Aaron, having already arrived on the scene, joined his brother, and together they listened in amazement to the rebels.

"You have gone far enough!" Korah cried, pointing a vicious finger in the prophet's face. "All the congregation are holy, every one of them! And the Lord is in their midst! So why do you and your brother exalt yourselves above the assembly of the Lord?"

Now, this was all that was needed for Moses's spirit to be utterly overwhelmed. For two days he had suffered with the burden of deciding the case of the wood-gatherer. He had come to the decision in great agony, and to be now accused of elevating himself above the people was more than he could bear.

Slumping to his knees, he fell to his face. And with hot tears streaming down his cheeks, he raised himself up again, throwing back his arms and crying, "Hear now, you sons of Levi, is it not enough for you that the God of Israel has separated you from the rest of the congregation of Israel, and has brought you near to himself to do the service of the tabernacle of the Lord and to stand before the congregation to minister to them? And is it not enough, Korah, and all your brothers, sons of Levi, that he has brought you near? Are you seeking for the *high* priesthood also?"

Gaining strength from the sound of his own voice, Moses arose and confronted them boldly. "You and all your company are gathered together against the Lord! But who is Aaron, that you should grumble against him?"

But Korah was not to be dissuaded. "You have exalted yourselves above the entire nation!" he argued. "Already one man has died, and what was his crime? Your power has gone to your heads! Where will your pride take us?"

At this, Aaron took Moses by the arm, lending support. But the prophet sank beneath a broken heart.

"Do you think I love my calling?" he cried, his voice passing over the crowd like rolling thunder. "The hand of the Lord is heavy on my head! I would rather die than bear it another day. You have gone far enough, you sons of Levi! Gladly will I pass my mantle to you!"

Then in strident tones, he shouted, the veins in his neck standing out like purple cords, "Tomorrow morning the Lord will show who is his, and who is holy, and will bring him near to himself! Even the one whom he will choose, he will bring near to himself!"

Then, swirling his robes about him, he turned again for the tent. And closing the door behind him, he retreated once more from the demands of his ungrateful public.

39

The next morning, a scene often staged in the encampment and familiar to every Israelite opened the day. Korah and his two hundred and fifty Levites stood before the tent of meeting chanting and holding before themselves firepans, or censers, of beaten bronze. Within the censers were live coals from off the tabernacle's brazen altar, and from the coals arose the pale smoke of incense, filling the air with heady fragrance.

Thus did Israel always open its holy rituals. But today, the ritual to follow was undetermined, for all Moses had told the men was that they must appear at dawn with their firepans, and that in some undefined way, Yahweh would single out from among them a chosen leader.

Conspicuous for their absence at the head of the congregation were Dathan and Abiram, the outspoken Reubenites who had, with Korah and his company, challenged Moses and Aaron the day before. Though the prophet had invited them to be among the candidates for the lead position, they had refused to appear, accusing Moses of plotting evil against them.

"We will not come up," they had sent word. "Is it not enough that you have brought us up out of a land flowing with milk and honey to kill us in the wilderness, but you would also lord it over us? Indeed, you have not brought us into a land flowing with milk and honey, nor have you given us an inheritance of fields and vineyards. Would you gouge out the eyes of these men? We will not come up!"

It was therefore an angry Moses who stepped forth from the meeting tent. Beside him was Aaron, bearing his own censer, and wearing the miter and vestments of the high priest. When the prophet raised his hands, Korah and his Levites ceased their droning chant, and the entire congregation waited breathlessly to see how God would reveal his chosen man.

Scarcely believing things had come to this, Joshua, who had lain awake all night praying for God's intervention, could not accept that his beloved master should be replaced. Indeed, how *could* anyone ever be found who could lead Israel as Moses had? He had given up the throne of Egypt for these people! He had delivered them from bondage! And yet, they had never appreciated him for the mighty man he was.

Standing by, watching the proceedings with a lump in his throat, Joshua clenched his fists. Israel was not good enough for such a leader! If God did choose to replace him, it would only be to spare him further years of torment.

Passing his eyes anxiously across the skies, Joshua waited for a sign. Would a shaft of divine light come to rest upon somebody's shoulder? Would a voice from heaven speak somebody's name? Would someone's censer flare with white flame, driving back the other candidates?

There might have been as many ways to ordain a new leader as there were people to imagine it. But as Moses had told Joshua, the ways of the Lord were not man's ways. And today, he would single out his chosen, not by pressing the divine finger upon him, but by eliminating all other contenders.

As the congregation waited, a great light did appear, settling over the tabernacle, and a voice did speak from heaven. But rather than an ordination, it gave a fearsome pronouncement.

"Moses! Aaron!" it trumpeted, sending a quake through the earth. "Separate yourselves from among this company, that I may consume them instantly!"

Stunned, the two brothers fell to their faces, and without a thought to their own safety, they began to plead for the lives of the very men who called for their resignation. "O God!" they petitioned. "God of the spirits of all flesh! When one man sins, will you be angry with the entire congregation?"

But Yahweh's wrath would not be curbed. "Tell the people to move back from around the dwellings of Korah, Dathan and Abiram!" came the reply.

Standing shakily, Moses and Aaron passed through the crowd, crying, "Get back now from the tents of these wicked men, and touch nothing that belongs to them, lest you be swept away in all their sin!"

The two hundred and fifty Levites followed the prophet, curious as everyone else to know what would transpire. When they came to the site of the tents of Dathan and Abiram, the tent of Korah nearby, Moses and Aaron stopped, and the families who lived there came forth, trembling.

Dathan and Abiram, standing with their wives and children, were joined by Korah and his kin, all together wondering at the prophet's fearsome countenance.

Turning and facing the congregation, Moses threw his head back, announcing, "What is about to happen is not my doing! It is not in my heart to do it! But by it you shall know that the Lord has sent me to lead you. If these men die the death of all men, or if they suffer the fate of all men, then the Lord has not sent me. But if the Lord brings about something entirely new and the ground opens its mouth and swallows them up with everything that belongs to them, and they descend alive into Sheol, then you will understand that these men have spurned the Lord!"

Falling back in terror, the crowd looked on as Moses's words precipitated one of the most ghastly scenes the nation had ever witnessed.

As though on cue, the ground did indeed open up, directly beneath the homes of the three rebels. Sucked toward the center of the earth, every possession, every soul of the three households fell into the pit. And just as quickly, the earth closed up again, separating them forever from the land of the living.

Terrified, the onlookers stumbled over one another in haste to leave the site, fearing that they, likewise, would be swallowed up. But even as they did make their escape, fire from heaven fell upon the two hundred and fifty Levites, consuming them to ashes upon the desert floor.

And as the people observed the demise of the revolutionaries, no more specific ordination was necesssary: Moses and Aaron were still in command; they were the chosen ones, for there were no contenders.

40

Should this not have been enough? Surely the people would never again question the authority of Moses and Aaron.

But never had there been a more rebellious nation than Israel.

Certainly the sins and injustices of the Gentiles were abhorrent. It was for this reason that God had called Israel out from among them. But the very fact that Israel was so called, the fact that they were the special inheritance of the Lord, made their rebellions more rancorous.

For theirs had been the oracles, the prophets and the patriarchs of truth. Their calling was ancient, going back to Noah, and Shem, and Abraham. And the doctrines of truth had been their special gift from the beginning, tested through generations of bondage, but never lost.

It was therefore most loathsome that they continually doubted the word of God. And despite the deaths of Korah and his men, yet another fourteen thousand and seven hundred died by plague before Aaron, as high priest, interceded.

As if that should not be enough to prove the priest's sanctity, the Lord worked a wonder on his rod, causing it to bud and bring forth ripe almonds, a testimony to Israel that it was a scepter and not only a staff.

Still, the people were obstinate, continually questioning and challenging the Lord's anointed prophets, until one day, Moses himself, in utter frustration, rebelled.

That was a dreadful day for Israel, a dreadful day for Joshua, a dreadful day for the world. For on that day, Moses did relinquish the right to lead the people into the promised land. And on that day, a shadow settled over his soul and over the soul of his servant that would remain for nineteen years.

It seemed an innocent enough transgression. It seemed a forgivable departure, much like the slip the wood-gatherer had made when he went forth upon the sabbath day.

But the consequence would be just as devastating as the punishment brought on that unwitting fellow's head.

It had happened when the children of Israel, in their wanderings, had once more entered the Wilderness of Zin. And it had been precipitated by a personal loss on Moses's part, the death of his beloved sister, Miriam.

Within the past years since leaving Sinai, Moses's father, Amram, and mother, Jochebed, had been taken by death. But this was his sister, kin of his own generation, the one who had watched over his river-cradle and who had safely transferred him to the arms of the Egyptian princess.

Spunky and spirited, she had been a challenge to live with, often butting heads with Zipporah. But she had been loved by all, and her passing left a great hollow in the prophet's heart.

It was this, and the ongoing disrespect manifested by his people, that led to Moses's desperate act.

There was no water in the Wilderness of Zin, at least not where the people were encamped. Always eager to point out their discontent, they descended upon their leader, accusing him once again of neglect.

Conferring with the Lord, Moses came back to the people with orders to lead them to a great rock. There he and Aaron were to speak to the rock, that it might bring forth water.

Given that opportunity to display power, Moses went too far. Bending the command of the Lord, he did not speak to the rock, but to the people, calling them rebels and daring them to observe his feat. Then lifting his rod, he *struck* the rock, not once, but twice.

Indeed, water did come forth, but only because God took pity on the people. "Because you have not believed me," he rebuked his prophet, "to treat me as holy in the sight of the sons of Israel, therefore you shall not bring this assembly into the promised land!"

And so, in a moment of pride and anger, Moses the Deliverer relinquished his chance to complete his original calling.

That had been nineteen years ago. In fact, thirty-nine years had passed since the people had escaped Egypt. Most of Moses's generation and even Joshua and Caleb's generation had by now passed away.

While Moses had not made public the Lord's pronouncement, sharing it only with his servant, its sorrowful impact had rarely lifted.

When his dear brother Aaron, his beloved spokesman, also died, Joshua feared his master's heart would never revive.

That sad event took place at a juncture in time and place that would forever mark a turning point in the lives of Israel and its famous leader. After thirty-nine years of wandering, the nation was ready to make momentous strides toward its geographical destiny. Believing that they should try to enter the promised land from the east side of Jordan, rather than through the Negev, Moses took the people to the border of Edom, the land of Esau's descendants. Good relations had been established with them years before when Jacob and his elder brother had been reconciled. Hoping that this would carry diplomatic weight, Moses sent word to the governors of Edom, asking passage through their territory on the way north.

Much to his surprise, and to the surprise of the disappointed Israelites, their notoriety had squelched all hope for such passage. Though Moses used all his ambassadoric skills, reminding the Edomites of Israel's hard years in Egypt, of the Lord's miraculous and repeated intervention, and assuring them that no harm would come to their country, they refused entrance.

"We will not go through field or vineyard," Moses pleaded. "We will not even drink water from a well. We will go along the King's Highway, not turning to the right or left, until we pass through your territory."

But there was no persuading Edom to make allowances. And when Israel remained encamped at the border, continuing to send messengers, the sons of Esau defended their boundaries, stationing a line of troops, fully armed, along the western front.

It was at this point that the Lord tested Moses more severely than he had ever done before. As they waited at the entrance to Edom, camped at the base of Mount Hor, which stood at the triangular site where the borders of Edom, Canaan, and Zin met, and which overlooked the very land of promise, Moses was reminded once and for all of the fact that he would never lead the people toward their final home.

With that reminder was also the incontrovertible fact that Aaron would likewise be prevented.

In fact, God said, Aaron would be taken to a more heavenly home.

In private conference, the Lord told Moses, "Aaron shall be gathered to his people. He shall not enter the land which I have given to the sons of Israel, because you rebelled against my command at the waters of the rock. Take Aaron and his son Eleazar up to Mount Hor, and strip Aaron of his garments and put them on his son Eleazar. So Aaron will be gathered to his people; he will die there."

It was with feet of lead that Joshua followed his master to a slope of the mountain that misty morning. With them were Aaron and his son Eleazar, a son born to the priest during the wilderness years. Moses had not told his servant what the Lord had said, but Joshua could see from the lines of grief upon the prophet's face that he had wept all night long, and that the cause for this climb up Mount Hor was not one of celebration.

Doubtless, Aaron and his son knew the priest was about to depart this life. In retrospect, Joshua would realize that their plodding walk and the way Aaron leaned upon Eleazar's arm indicated that they had spent the night saying goodbye and preparing for this final hour.

But nothing could have prepared Joshua for what he and the entire congregation of Israel were about to witness.

Once the master, his servant, the priest and his son had reached a level spot, Moses took Aaron's rod and put it in Eleazar's trembling hand. Without preface or formality of any kind, he continued to divest Aaron of his office, lifting his vestment off his shoulders, his mitre off his head, and placing them on his successor.

Then, raising his eyes to heaven, Moses cried, "Into your hands do I place my brother's spirit. Comfort his soul in your palace of eternal rest!"

Falling as softly as a baby into a father's arms, Aaron slumped into the waiting embrace of Moses. Tears streaming down his face, so that he could barely see, Moses called for Eleazar and Joshua to assist him, and tenderly they carried the priest toward the desert floor.

Astonished at this unexpected turn of events, the people stood mute as they took in the reality of Aaron's death. And as they watched him being carried away, the reality of their own emptiness overwhelmed them.

For years they had made Aaron's life miserable, questioning him, doubting him and his brother. Now he was gone, suddenly—without warning taken from them. And his going left a void for which they had no replacement.

Guilt, remorse, grief swept over the crowd as Moses and the little funeral party passed before them. And matching the tears on the prophet's face with their own tardy contrition, they began to mourn.

Loud and long would they bewail the loss of Aaron. Long and loud would they bewail their own sin. For thirty days they would stay at the foot of the mountain, weeping for the one they had abused.

And for thirty days Joshua would stay by Moses's side, his own soul good as dead, and fearful of Yahweh's next move.

41

The next days would forever be a blur in Joshua's memory. He went through the motions of life, but he felt no life within him.

If he felt anything, it was continual fear—fear that Yahweh was an unappeasable tyrant, who could at any moment afflict him or take from him someone he dearly loved.

After thirty-nine years of doing his best to serve God, he knew him less now than when he had started.

Incredibly, it was at this lowest point that he was called upon to lead Israel in battle. Though it had been four decades since he commanded an army, he was still considered Israel's military genius. His victory over the Amalekites at Rephidim, a generation ago, had become legend. And though few of the men who now made up the infantry and cavalry had served in that famous war, they had been raised to honor Joshua as the general who had given the people a military heart.

Therefore, when Edom refused Israel passage through its land, and when they were forced to turn toward the Negev, Joshua was called upon to lead them forth. The Canaanites would be awaiting them, and war was inevitable.

In looking back on that battle, Joshua would wonder how victory had come. He would recall the smell of blood, the cries of friends and enemies, the clash of blade and shield. But he would recall little else.

Depressed of spirit, he was borne through that fray on invisible wings, a strength beyond himself taking him and his men to triumph. And when they were finished, the cities of the Negev were theirs.

But Joshua was unaware of the divine hand. Having mastered protocol through his years under Moses's administration, he received the honors due a victorious, returning general in good form. But he felt none of the glory heaped upon him, and endured the applause only because he had to.

For the Israelites, this was a time of celebration, the first foray near the borders of the promised land in which they had triumphed. But for Joshua, it was a hollow victory, as he had not yet overcome the ambivalence of his faith.

He did not trust this victory. There had been times in the past when he thought he saw the working of God on behalf of Israel. Yet too often miracles had been followed by disappointments, and God's favor now seemed fickle.

Tonight, while the council of elders gathered in the meeting tent, enthusiastically discussing the nation's next moves and plotting how best to overcome pagan neighbors who stood between them and the promised land, Joshua stayed in his own shelter.

He had lost all heart for schemes and strategems. Why the Lord had singled him out from among his generation to go on living, he did not know.

Oh, of course, Caleb had been "privileged," with himself, to remain. He wondered, as he sat in the dim light of his rafter lamp, how his companion-since-youth felt about the honor.

Caleb had been thinking about Joshua at the same moment, seeking him at the council meeting. When he realized that his friend was not in attendance, he came calling for him.

"How can we plot advances into Canaan without our general?" he asked, finding Joshua seated in the dimly lit room. "We need you at the meeting."

"They will do well without me," he replied.

Sitting down, Caleb observed Joshua's glum countenance. "Do I detect in you the doldrums that follow great conquest?" he guessed.

Joshua shrugged. "Perhaps," he sighed.

"But," Caleb recalled, "you have not been yourself for a long time ... since ... the death of Aaron. What troubles you, friend?"

If there was one person on earth in whom Joshua could confide his weaknesses, it was Caleb. Even so, he was ashamed to admit he was afraid.

"Your faith has always been great," he answered, "far greater than mine. I will never know why Yahweh chose me, and not you, to lead the army."

At this, Caleb shook his head, his brow furrowed. "What is it, Joshua?" he prodded. "You are not only a military hero. You are the man who nobly led twelve spies to survey Canaan. You are the man who has served Moses almost forty years, his closest confidant. You are the man on whom God has laid his hand, and who will surely take the place of leadership one day! What has become of your spirit?"

Suddenly, all the pent-up emotion of the past weeks surged through Joshua like a current. And in a torrent it came forth.

"*I?*" he cried, jumping to his feet. "*I* take Moses's place? I would sooner die than betray him like that!"

Confounded, Caleb watched Joshua's frantic reaction. "Betray?" he stammered. "To succeed Moses would be betrayal?"

"Yes!" Joshua shouted. "Why should I be privileged to lead Israel into the promised land, when my beloved master has been stripped of the honor? I would sooner die than take that honor to myself!"

There. It had been said. But in the saying, Joshua had indeed betrayed Moses. For the prophet had told him of the Lord's restriction in confidence. No one else in Israel knew that he would not be allowed to take Jacob's children into Canaan.

Amazed, Caleb tried to interpret his friend's raving. "What do you mean?" he asked. "How has Moses been stripped of the honor?"

Pale-faced, Joshua sat down again, holding his head in his hands. "I have kept that secret for nineteen years!" he moaned. "I should not have told you! Promise that my words will not go past this room."

When Caleb sat mute, Joshua reached out an angry hand and grabbed him by the knee. "Promise!" he growled.

"Of course," Caleb winced. "You know your secrets are safe with me."

Withdrawing his hand, Joshua groaned heavily. "Nineteen years ago, my master told me of the Lord's punishment on him and on his brother, Aaron. Do you remember when he struck the rock in the wilderness to bring forth water? Because he and Aaron were presumptuous, they were forever prevented from entering Canaan!"

Eyes wide, Caleb leaned forward. "What?" he marveled. "Were they disobedient?"

Again, Joshua shrugged. "Apparently God had instructed them to speak to the rock. But instead, they took the glory for themselves, using the rod wrongly."

Even this much was hard for the loyal servant to admit. He himself had come to the assessment only after much spiritual wrestling.

"But," he went on, his face etched with resentment, "is not the Lord's way much too hard? I can understand his destruction of Korah and the rebels. But for one small infraction, two of the best and noblest men on earth are put to shame . . . one already seeing death rather than the holy land!"

With a shudder, Caleb considered these words. Suddenly, Joshua's disillusionment, his agony of spirit, came clear. Who would not have felt as he did, in his place?

Standing, Caleb leaned over his friend respectfully. "These are hard things to understand," he agreed.

Downcast, Joshua looked at the floor, and Caleb placed a hand on his stooped shoulder.

"It is at times like this that we must remember the miracles of God," he offered. "Surely Yahweh loves Moses more than any of us could ever love him. Surely God knows what is best, and in time will lift up your master higher than ever."

Joshua closed his eyes, feeling the sting of tears upon his lashes. "I hope you are right," he whispered. "If you are wrong, there is no hope for any of us."

42

A sweet breeze blew inland from the Gulf of Aqaba, where Israel was camped. Over nearly forty years of wandering, the great company had come to rest here on occasion. When they did, Joshua was always put in mind of the conversation with Moses just before the twelve spies were sent north.

That had been a time of anticipation and excitement for the much younger Joshua. And on the occasion of that talk, Moses had wished for him, not only success on the spying venture, but a future of personal fulfillment.

"May your life be full when we reach Canaan," Moses had said. "May you find life and love, as I did."

Today, Joshua sat in the same place, atop the same dune that commanded a view of the gulf and of the vast northward stretches. As he contemplated the past four decades, he smirked.

Little good the prophet's wish had done! Joshua was now well past middle age, eighty-four to be exact, and they had not reached Canaan. While he was not elderly for his generation, neither was he in the prime of life, and personal fulfillment still eluded him.

Below, on the valley floor, was spread the enormous nation of Israel. More than half of the present population had been born after the flight from Egypt. They had known, in all their lifetime, nothing but wandering and sand. They had seen none of the miracles that had freed their forefathers from Pharaoh's hand. They had not been present at the crossing of the Reed Sea, and had not been part of the victorious war against Amalek. They had not heard the voice of God echo from Mount Sinai, and the covenant of the ten commandments was given to them secondhand.

Realizing this, Joshua ran a veined hand through his hair. Mingled with the dark locks were streaks of silver, and his salt-and-pepper beard was more patriarchal in length than he had worn it years ago.

He was old, he and Caleb and Moses. His father and his grandfather had departed this life long ago, as had most of the men and women who had first heard the liberating voice of Moses ring forth in Raamses square.

But though he wore a patriarch's beard, he was not a patriarch. He had no children of his own, no wife, no family.

Four decades of futile nomadism had brought none of the fulfillment Moses had desired for him. And for a long time he had tasted little more than the gall of life.

A week ago, Moses had announced that the people were to head for the Aqaba, and then turn east, making a circuitous path around Edom. Determined that they should enter Canaan from that side of Jordan, Moses could find no other way to go, seeing that the Edomites had refused them passage up the King's Highway.

This should have been a time of excitement for Israel. They were at last moving on, however obliquely, toward their promised land. In typical fashion, however, the people had thus far spent the journey complaining. They hated the trip through the hot sand. They hated the lack of fresh water, and the dreary manna they had been forced to eat for almost forty years.

As often as possible, Joshua left camp, longing to be free of their continual harping.

He wondered how Moses could go on, day after day, enduring the reproaches of the malcontents. As he rested on the sandy knoll, he ran Caleb's words through his mind for the hundredth time. In a few weeks, barring unforeseen impediments, the nation would be ready to make its first foray into Canaan. If God was indeed planning to restore Moses to a position of honor, he had better do so soon.

As he tried to imagine just how this might transpire, however, his ruminations were interrupted by screams rising from the camp.

Standing up, Joshua headed down the dune toward the sound of the cries.

What met his eyes was scarcely believable. As though the earth itself had grown weary of the griping Israelites, it brought forth from its surface thousands upon thousands of poisonous vipers. Slithering up from nests beneath the sand, and flaring the hoods upon their necks, they struck like flying arrows at the legs and feet of the astonished people.

On every side, men, women and children fell victim to their burning venom, writhing and contorting upon the ground, their faces and limbs swollen and purple, until they expired in feverish torment.

Like helpless infants, those who had avoided the stinging bites or who managed to survive the poisonous fangs wept aloud for deliverance.

"Moses! Moses!" they cried, forgetting the complaints they had against him. "Help us! Or we die!"

Skirting the worst sites of the infestation, Joshua made his way toward the tent of meeting. Despite the grasping hands that clawed at him, begging Moses's servant to lend aid, he managed to reach the front of the encampment.

But to his dismay, when he arrived at the tent, Moses was not to be found.

"Over there," one of the tent guards said, seeing that he sought the prophet. Pointing toward the altar of sacrifice, he directed him to Moses.

There the prophet stood, engrossed in a strange activity, watching the bubbling contents of a cauldron atop the altar.

"Stir, men, stir!" he ordered, as the smiths threw armloads of copper vessels and brass implements into the molten soup. Reaching into the smelter with long poles, the men mixed the shining vessels into the golden stew, until the forms of cups, plates and utensils succumed to the heat, and the soup thickened.

It had been a very long time since the man of God had been so animated, so spurred to action.

"Master!" Joshua hailed him. "What is happening? The people, Master...they are dying!"

But Moses did not look at his servant. Transfixed by the work of the craftsmen, he was absorbed in seeing to it that a peculiar bronze casting was made to order.

"I know," was all he said. "It is the sting of sin that kills my people!"

Oh, no! Joshua thought. Years of stress and disappointment had at last overwhelmed his master's mind. Moses was out of touch with reality, the victim of hopelessness and defeat.

Taking the prophet by the arm, Joshua tried to lead him away from his futile distraction. "They need you, Master!" he pleaded. "Can't you do something?"

But at his touch, Moses turned to him, energy sparking through his black eyes such as Joshua had not seen in twenty years.

"My people perish from the sting of sin!" the prophet repeated. "But the Lord has promised to take their sins upon himself! Go, Joshua! Fetch the standard of the tribe of Judah, the one they bear into battle. Bring it here!"

Utterly bewildered, Joshua nonetheless set out to do as the master said. Running back through the crowd, darting this way and that to avoid the flashing bite of a million serpents, he at last came to the place where the people of Judah camped.

Why Moses had singled them out, and why he wished to have their standard, he had no inkling. But calling for Caleb, their chief representative, he gave him the prophet's command.

Quickly Caleb and a young Judahite, Salmon, brought the standard to him. "We will carry it," they offered, hoisting the pole to their shoulders.

Joshua rolled up the green flag, which bore the symbol of the tribe of Judah, a powerful, striding lion. Securing it to the pole, he headed back to the tent of meeting.

The return trip was not so hasty. Bearing the long standard between them, Caleb and Salmon found it very difficult to weave through the frantic crowd while keeping an eye out for the lethal vipers.

But by the time they reached Moses, the brazen figure he had ordered was cooling in its mold, and while it was still soft, the blacksmiths lifted it from the long pan.

"A brass serpent?" Caleb marveled. "But why..."

"Here," Moses instructed his smiths. "Wrap it around the top of the standard!"

Holding the metal snake with hot tongs, the men complied. Gently unfurling the flag of Judah, they proceeded to artfully coil the brazen viper about the pole.

"Come!" Moses cried, directing Salmon and Caleb to follow him. Taking the pole in his own strong hands, he plodded to the top of a slope overlooking the desperate camp.

There he erected the standard, calling on his two companions to assist him. Steadying its base against the ground, the two Judahites held the top-heavy pole upright, as Moses shouted to the people, "The Lord is our salvation! This very day he takes upon himself the sins of his people—even the very form of their sins he takes upon himself! Look, my children, and live!"

Though they did not understand Moses's words, in despair the Israelites gazed upon the shining image. And as they did, the sound of their weeping was gradually exchanged for shouts of joy.

Everywhere throughout the crowd, people who had been bitten were healed, the venom neutralized and the fever cooled. Mothers held babies aloft, praising God for rescuing them. And men embraced each other, dancing and singing for happiness.

Many others fell to their knees, worshiping and thanking God for his saving hand.

Joshua was among those. And as he knelt at Moses's feet, lifting his hands in praise toward the sky, it was not only the miracle of the brazen serpent he applauded, but the miracle of healing he witnessed in his master's soul.

Caleb's words had come true. The man of God had regained his honored position.

For the first time in nineteen years, Moses stood tall and confident once again, the light of faith and renewed vigor shining from his face.

PART VII
The Giant-Killer

43

As the sun glazed the eastern sky with the pink tints of morning, Joshua stirred restlessly in his saddle. Strange thoughts ran through his mind as he awaited the full light of dawn—thoughts of his youth in Egypt, when he and Caleb had ridden their master's horses through the streets of Raamses, their boyish imaginations full of conquest and glory.

It was hard to believe that today, a lifetime later, he and Caleb once again sat atop husky mounts, eager for the clash of weapons and the cries of battle.

It was also hard to believe that Joshua, who had experienced four decades of debilitating and aimless wandering, who had come of age through great hardship and who now stood within glimpse of his own sunset, should feel so young, so energetic.

But the entire nation had been renewed since the encounter with the serpents, and their sense of covenant with God Almighty had taken on fresh meaning.

Ever since that day, they had marched on toward the east, and had then turned north, with a vigor reminiscent of their flight from Egypt. Except that this time they were not fleeing an enemy. They were on the offense, heading through pagan territory and ready to do battle with any people who stood between them and the land promised to Jacob.

This morning, Joshua and his able assistant, Caleb, sat atop a crest of wilderness between the River Nahaliel and the River Arnon, in the desolate land of the Amorites. Behind them on the wadi-riddled plain spread the Israelite millions, their well-groomed army arrayed in orderly files, and the rest of the nation waiting anxiously beyond them.

Ahead was the Amorite fortress of Jahaz, sprawled like a sleeping lion upon a sheet of sand.

"King Sihon is a clever fellow," Caleb whispered, his voice blending with the constant, arid breeze. "The fort appears to be unmanned."

"It may well be unmanned," Joshua replied. "Sihon may have called his militia back to Heshbon, when he heard we were coming on."

When Caleb evinced disappointment, Joshua was quick to add, "But keep your eyes to the northern horizon. Soon enough you will see Amorites, more than can be numbered!"

Months ago, when the Edomites had refused Moses entrance through their territory, the prophet had turned away from their border, and had lingered south of Canaan. There Joshua had led the successful battle against the natives of the Negev. But neither he nor his master had had much heart for the takeover.

Now, things were different. The Amorite king, Sihon, had also refused permission for the Israelites to pass through his region. But this time Moses had not taken the tuck-head. His army's reputation preceding him, and the inspiring memory of the brazen serpent behind him, he did without incident lead his people straight through Edom and Moab, and then boldly proceeded straight up the King's Highway into Amorite territory. If King Sihon wished to contravene his progress, he would have to meet him in full force.

As rumor had it, Sihon *would* oppose Israel. Though no Amorite was in sight, messengers between the two nations had transferred word to Moses and his general that the king would meet them on the plain of Jahaz.

His pulse pounding with anticipation, Joshua glanced behind him to the troops arranged within the Arnon canyon. The fortress of Jahaz was strategically located between the two rivers to command a view of the south-land. The nation of Israel waited on the field beyond the Arnon, but the army itself was well-hidden in the enormous wadi. Sihon would not see them until they chose to rush forward.

Scouts had informed Joshua and his commanders that there were no Amorites similarly hidden in the Nahaliel canyon beyond Fort Jahaz. Therefore, they knew they would have good advance notice of the oncoming horde, having a clear view across the northward plain.

Still, it was an anxious interval for the Israelite general. He had never led an army in such rugged landscape. The first war against Amalek had been on flat desert, and the war in the Negev was amongst rolling hills. This, by contrast, was precipitous country, and Sihon, knowledgeable of his own terrain, could have many tricks in mind.

But there was no turning back. For the first time since leaving Egypt, Joshua was about to engage in a face-off with neighbors of the promised land that would decide progress toward its borders.

Just as the rose of dawn gave way to full-blown daylight, the anticipated army of Sihon appeared along the northern horizon.

Spine-tingling was the sight, and Joshua's breath caught in his throat.

So vast was the Amorite host that it seemed to spread from Jordan to the borders of Ammon, straight across the desert stage. And as it came on, it did so in waves, one enormous contingency following another, until the landscape was swallowed up with horses and men.

The sound of their marching filled the wilderness like thunder, until they drew within a mere mile of Jahaz.

At first glimpse of them, Joshua and Caleb dismounted, leading their horses behind the lip of the wadi, and lying flat upon their stomachs. Sihon would see neither troop nor officer of Israel until Joshua gave command.

Doubtless, Sihon and his men thought that Moses had retreated. After crossing miles of uninvaded territory, the Amorites began to run rather than walk, laughing and hooting as they surveyed the unimpeded landscape and the unarmed nation that sat motionless on the southern plain.

In the forefront of the waiting nation, between the army and the general populace, Moses was stationed, flanked by Eleazar and the Levite priests. As always, the ark of the covenant was well-guarded at the head of the congregation, but today, the cloudy pillar, which normally hovered at the head of the traveling nation, had moved back away from the hidden troops. Apparently Yahweh himself was in league with the silent hosts, and would not give away the secret of their presence.

Closing his eyes, Joshua said a silent prayer, trusting that the cloud's retreat did not indicate the removal of God's hand.

Then, when the time was right, when to hesitate might jeopardize the element of surprise, he gave a shout.

Mounting their horses, he and Caleb rushed up the wadi bank, and with an unleashed roar, his army followed, leaping onto the plain of Jahaz like panthers roused from a lair.

Stunned by this unexpected appearance, Sihon and his troops were momentarily disoriented. Spilling around the base of the fortress, they suddenly stopped their march and began to fall over one another in retreat.

But this reversal did not last long. Regaining themselves, they echoed the shout of Israel, and pushed forward, meeting Joshua and his legions hand-to-hand on the Jahaz floor.

Still, they were unprepared for the countless number of men who continued to flood up the wadi bank. Vigorously, Joshua and Caleb led the way, pushing back the enemy, slashing and driving with their swords, until the fortress of Jahaz was even with the front lines of their own army.

At some point in the fray, when his sword was sheened with blood, and his hand slipped on the crimson hilt, Joshua looked above and saw that the pillar had moved forward.

"Caleb!" he shouted to his valorous comrade. "God is with us!"

No longer aloof, the cloud had joined the Israelite forces, and like the rod of Moses, which had lifted the spirits of God's army in the clash of the Amalakites, the pillar maintained its position over the invaders.

"On!" Joshua cried, flashing his scarlet sword in the air. "On to Heshbon!"

Yes—he would take the capital, ten miles to the north! He would not stop on the plain or along the King's Highway until he had overwhelmed the very seat of Amorite power.

All that day and into the night, all the next day and into the next night, Israel would push forth, crushing the troops of Sihon and all his machines of war. Behind them, on the broad road and across miles of desert sand, fallen chariots and slain horses, broken camels and dismembered men would tell the story of Joshua's power.

The land of the Amorites would never be the same.

Nor would Joshua.

He was on his way to the promised land, and behind him he would leave a trail of glory and conquest the likes of which no neighboring nation, or nation of the world, had ever seen.

44

Deliciously weary, Joshua stumbled toward his tent and propped himself against one of the poles. Below him, on the terraced plains of Moab, a festive celebration was in full swing, and he had enjoyed it along with all his victorious troops.

But he had had a bit too much wine, and having been the object of adulation all evening, he wished now to be alone.

The party, and Joshua's fatigue, were the result of one more successful military escapade.

After the battle with Sihon, the Israelites set up headquarters in this green-rimmed swale in the land of the Amorites. From there they had gone forth to subdue the kingdom of Bashan to the north, and it was from this foray that Joshua had returned today.

As a result of that war, the Israelites occupied all the land from the River Arnon, by the Salt Sea, north to the border of Syria, at Damascus. All this they owed to Joshua, and the hand of the Lord upon him.

But being a living legend was exhausting. Joshua was glad for the caressing breeze that blew up from the Jordan River, and for the soothing scent of gum-arabic acacias that thrived in groves along the foothills of Mount Nebo. Should he live out his days in this place, he might be content. Except that its commanding view of Canaan's threshold kept him yearning for the coveted land of promise.

Sliding to the ground, Joshua sat with his back against the pole, tilting his head and breathing deep of the heady air while listening for the rush of the river far below.

Gradually the rhythms of wind and water lulled him asleep. But in an instant he was again awake, jolted by the dream-induced sight of a dreadful giant careening on horseback toward him.

Sitting upright, he wiped cold sweat from his brow. Upon his right palm was still the feel of the spear which he had borne all the way back from Bashan. He had not trusted the weapon to any servant, nor had he trusted it to the sheathe which was part of his saddle. He had carried it by hand all the miles home, because it was proof of the most daring feat of his life.

He had killed a giant! The giant's spear was his souvenir.

Glancing to his side, he saw that the weapon still rested near him upon the ground, and with trembling fingers he stroked it.

"The spear of Og?" Moses greeted him.

Surprised at the prophet's sudden appearance, Joshua jumped to his feet. "Yes, sir," he replied, snapping to attention.

Amazed at the size of the weapon, Moses squatted on the ground and studied it closely. "It is made of iron," he marveled. "I thought only the Philistines had iron."

"I thought so, too," Joshua said, kneeling beside him. "But they say that King Og and his sons are the sole survivors of the race of Rephaim. Perhaps he inherited the spear from his forefathers."

Moses stroked his beard, recalling the legend of the giant race. "Long ago they were a part of Philistia," he agreed. "It is said Og's bedstead is made of iron, as well, and that it is over thirteen feet long!"

Joshua drew his cloak to his chest, all-too-clearly remembering his opponent's gigantic stature.

Over and over, throughout this evening, Joshua's men had told of their commander's exploit, rehearsing the story around the campfires of the celebrating Israelites, telling and retelling how he had met King Og on the misty plain of Bashan, how at dawn of their first warring morning, the black-bearded colossus had thundered forth from the bowels of his stony castle, storming toward the general with fire in his eyes and lightning in his titanic spear.

Like the smoke of a furnace was the pall of his coming, matched as he was on every side by comrades of formidable cunning, all dressed in black armor and heralded by the snorting and stamping of their steeds.

But Joshua, though dwarfed by comparison, had faced him squarely, the story went. And when the King of Bashan charged at him, thrusting his spear toward his chest, Joshua had not dodged it, but had caught it in his own bare hands, and riding it to the ground had turned it about, driving the giant through with his own weapon.

How much of the tale was true, and how much exaggeration, not even Joshua could be certain. But the finale was all that mattered, and the finale was real enough.

Indeed, he *had* speared the giant, and in a deafening fall, his armor crashing with him to the desert floor, Og had met his death.

With that fall, the Bashanites had turned and fled, the Israelites giving chase through the dustclouds of their retreat.

When the war was over, not one remnant of Og was left. His sons and all his family were demolished, and his land overtaken.

All of this Moses had heard from the mouths of Joshua's men. And when he saw, from the shaken look on the general's face, that he had indeed come triumphant through another great test, he placed an arm about his shoulders.

As the two knelt together, before the captive spear, and in the quiet of the breeze which blew up from Jordan, Moses looked deep into his friend's eyes. "My years upon this earth have been many," the prophet said, "and I have not always pleased the Lord. But long ago, when I took you for my servant, I made a wise choice."

Honored by this endorsement, Joshua was nonetheless troubled by his master's wistful tone. "Thank you, sir," he whispered.

But Moses did not hear him. His eyes were closed, and holding Joshua's hand in a firm grip, he was praying aloud.

"O God," he groaned, "may the Lord, the God of the spirits of all flesh, appoint a man over the congregation, who will go out and come in before them, and who will lead them out and bring them in, that the congregation of the Lord may not be like sheep which have no shepherd!"

Now, this made Joshua even more uneasy. But he dare not interrupt his master's meditation. So when Moses left off speaking with the Lord, and looked at him again, the warrior stammered, "Sir, *you* are their shepherd. They need no other."

But Moses disregarded this. "Joshua," he said, "your eyes have seen all that the Lord your God has done to King Sihon and King Og. So the Lord shall do to all the kingdoms into which you are about to go. Do not fear them, for the Lord your God is the one fighting for you."

With a sigh, Joshua looked at the spear. "Yes, sir," he weakly replied. *But can't you go with me, as well?* he longed to cry out.

There would be no answer to this unspoken question. Moses was already making ready to depart for the evening.

Standing, the prophet headed into the darkness toward his own tent.

But calling over his shoulder, he gave one more word. "Meet me at the edge of camp at dawn," he called. "The Lord has told me to climb Mount Nebo, and you are to go with me. Together we are going to view the promised land!"

45

No one came calling for Joshua, to wake him at dawn. The sound of massive movement in camp roused him, and pulling back his tent flap he found that the entire congregation was heading toward the east, in the direction of Mount Nebo, where Moses and he were to make their climb.

Pulling on his cloak, Joshua skirted the crowd and ran for the foothills, finding, to his further surprise, that the tent of meeting had been relocated there in the night.

Apparently an announcement had been made after he left the celebration last night, to the effect that some great event would transpire at Nebo, and Joshua looked desperately for Moses, hoping for an explanation.

When he found him, Master Moses was already halfway up the mountain, and was accompanied by Eleazar, the high priest. Running breathlessly after them, Joshua at last caught up, and took Moses by the arm. "What is happening?" he inquired. "Why didn't you tell me..."

But Moses only gave him a look of grateful relief. "Thank you for coming," he replied, his steps picking up vigor.

Apparently nothing more would be revealed just now, as to the purpose of this gathering.

Helplessly, Joshua glanced over his shoulder. Indeed, the view from this mountain was spectacular, more and more so the higher they climbed.

But as Joshua gazed across Jordan, he stopped short, his breath catching in his throat.

Far out on the distant plain, on the west side of the river, the glimmer of white walls could be seen, topped with turrets and gleaming towers.

"Jericho!" he marveled. "Master, it is directly across from us!"

As quickly as he made this observation, however, his spirit sank within him. He had always known that if he were to lead the hosts of Israel into Canaan, he would have to go against that mighty fortress. Like always, it was not only the strength of the enemy, but the memory of the woman in red, that caused his pulse to trip.

Turning about, he tried to put her from mind. Perhaps she did not even live there any longer.

But he could not fool himself with that notion. She had been a young woman when he saw her, much younger than himself. Doubtless, she still kept her home upon the wall, and lived . . . for Astarte.

So, he sighed to himself, plodding behind Moses, *this is the reason for this venture. The master wants to lay before me the plot to overthrow Jericho.*

Just how small-minded such thinking was, he did not begin to realize until Moses, reaching a flat spot visible to the vast company, stopped and addressed the entire nation.

With a face of zeal and glory, he spread his arms wide, and cried, "Hear, O Israel! The Lord our God is one! And you shall love the Lord your God with all your heart and with all your soul and with all your might! And these words, which I command you today, shall be in your heart, and you shall teach them diligently to your sons and shall talk of them when you sit in your house and when you walk by the way and when you lie down and when you rise up! And you shall bind them as a sign on your hand and they shall be bands about your forehead. And you shall write them on the doorposts of your house and on your gates!"

Awestruck, the people listened, sensing that Moses was about to commission them for their future.

Without a pause he went on: "When your son asks you in time to come, 'What do the testimonies and the statutes and the judgments which the Lord commanded you mean?' you shall say to your son, 'We were slaves to Pharaoh in Egypt, and the Lord brought us from Egypt with a mighty hand. The Lord showed great and terrible signs and wonders before our eyes against Pharaoh and all his household. And he brought us out from there in order to bring us in, to give us the land which he swore to our fathers.' So the Lord commanded us to observe all these statutes, to fear the Lord our God for our good always, that he might keep us alive. And it will be our righteousness if we are careful to observe all this commandment before the Lord our God, just as he commanded us!"

Rehearsing the ten commandments, as well a multitude of lesser ordinances, Moses cried, "Remember all the way which the Lord your God has led you in the wilderness these forty years, that he might humble you, testing you, to know what was in your heart! Remember how he fed you with manna, that you might understand that man does not live by bread alone, but by everything that proceeds out of the mouth of the Lord!"

Standing perfectly still beside his beloved master, Joshua felt his own soul quiver. How could he have been so petty as to think this occasion was one of attention for himself? With each passionate word the prophet spoke, it was increasingly obvious that this was his parting speech, that he was about to relinquish his leadership over the people for whom he had given his life.

His eyes riveted on his master's face, his ears tingling with each syllable, Joshua choked back tears, longing to embrace the prophet, to keep him for himself.

But Moses was not finished.

"Hear, O Israel!" he cried again. "You are about to cross over the Jordan to go in to dispossess nations greater and mightier than you, great cities fortified to heaven, and a people great and tall! Know, then, it is not because of your righteousness that the Lord your God is giving you this good land, for you are a stubborn people! You have been rebellious against the Lord from the day I knew you!"

How fatherly were these words, how tender, yet how true! Tears welled in the people's eyes, as they recalled the many times they had turned against this precious man, and against the God of their fathers. Yet he was loving in spite of this, both the prophet and the Lord himself.

"Now, Israel," he went on, "what does the Lord your God require of you, but to fear the Lord your God, to walk in all his ways and love him, and to serve the Lord your God with all your heart and with all your soul, and to keep his commandments and his statutes which I am commanding you today for your good?

"He is your praise and he is your God, who has done these great and awesome things for you. Your fathers went down to Egypt seventy persons in all, and now the Lord your God has made you as numerous as the stars in the sky!

"See, I have set before you today life and prosperity, death and adversity. So choose life in order that you may live, you and your descendants, by loving the Lord your God, by obeying his voice, and by holding fast to him. For this *is* your life and the length of your days, that you may live in the land which the Lord swore to your fathers, to Abraham, Isaac, and Jacob!"

Now, suddenly, the prophet's voice broke, and falling back, he gripped his chest. Reaching for him, Eleazar and Joshua helped him to stand upright, and a great gasp escaped the crowd.

Wishing to deny the obvious, Joshua closed his eyes, and his throat grew tight, as though a cord were wrapped around it. "Lord," he thought, "spare him! Spare my master! I cannot live without him!"

And as if in answer to that thought, Moses spoke again, opening his arms to embrace each one of the millions who stood before him. "I am one hundred and twenty years old today!" he cried. "I am no longer able to come and go, and the Lord has said to me, 'You shall not cross this Jordan.'"

At this revelation of the long-kept secret, the people gasped in horror.

But Moses calmed them. "It is the Lord your God who will cross ahead of you. He will destroy these nations before you, and you shall dispossess them. Joshua is the one who will cross ahead of you," he announced, "just as the Lord has spoken!"

Unprepared for this, Joshua felt his knees buckle, and as Moses turned to him, placing his hands upon his shoulders, the prophet declared, "Be strong and courageous, Joshua! For you shall go with all these people into the land which the Lord has sworn to their fathers, and you shall give it to them as an inheritance!"

Now, the servant did not realize it, but he was weeping; large, hot tears coursing down his cheeks. He would have stopped his ears, if it had kept Moses from leaving him.

But there was no circumventing prophecy. And as the master concluded, he plumbed the depths of Joshua's soul.

"The Lord is the one who goes ahead of you," he asserted. "He will be with you. He will not fail you or forsake you. Do not fear, or be dismayed!"

Then, with Joshua hardly knowing it, Moses took him by the hand and led him toward the door of the meeting tent. As they arrived there, the cloudy pillar, which had hovered over the mountain, descended and stood before them, turning this way and that, as though to ward off danger.

Now Eleazar prayed over them, laying his hands first on the head of Moses, then on the head of the servant. And Joshua felt a warmth, as a vibrant stream, course through his body. When Moses likewise placed hands on his head, Joshua felt a tremor pass through him like a quake at Sinai.

"Be strong and courageous!" a voice trumpeted from the cloud. "For you shall bring the sons of Israel into the land which I swore to them, and I will be with you!"

46

Like a dead man, Joshua lay facedown upon the silent mount, his cloak crisp with dew, and his limbs frozen in place where he had lain weeping through the night.

As the light of early dawn found him, he awoke stiff and sore, tears crusted on his cheeks.

The instant he awoke, he wished dearly that he might sleep again, that he might put from mind his master's departure.

Pulling himself erect, he knelt on the ground and peered up the gray morning slope, hoping against hope that Moses might come back again.

But he knew the prophet was gone, forever taken from him, and that although he had similarly disappeared many a time upon Sinai, only to return if Joshua waited long enough, this time it would not be so.

After the glorious speech, in which Moses had commissioned the children of Israel, and after the laying-on of hands, ordaining the general as his successor, the prophet had turned his back to the multitude, and using his sacred staff as a walking stick, had ascended the mountain height. Knowing he must not follow, Joshua had fought the desire. Had it not been for Eleazar's touch upon his shoulder, he might have taken off in a dead run up the mountain trail.

Slowly did Moses climb, but his gaze was lifted high, and there was no hesitation in his aged step. He was going to meet his own Master, the Lord of Heaven. And there was no sorrow in his gait.

His brother, Aaron, had also died upon a mountain. But that had been a terrifying moment, taking place as it did before the eyes of the people, and falling as he did into the arms of son and brother.

It was clear from Moses's demeanor that his death would be a private affair, greeted only by the hosts of heaven. And the arms that caught him would lift him high, away from the gaze of men.

All this Joshua knew, as he watched his beloved's departure. But it did not ease the ache of his heart or fill the vacuum of his soul.

When Moses was no longer visible, having entered the distant folds of the mount, and after the people had remained for a long while upon the plain, the crowd at last dispersed. But Joshua would not turn back. Though Eleazar spoke gently, trying to draw him away, he would not leave the mountain.

Afternoon passed, and dark fell, before Joshua even sat down upon the ground. For hours he had stood, straining his vision up the slope. And only in great fatigue did he at last rest a little.

He did not know when he fell asleep. But all night long he was riven by desperate dreams, crying out like an abandoned child, searching like a wandering son, for his misplaced father.

Now the sun was on the zenith of the mountain, and Joshua knew he could not stay here forever. Hunched with grief, he arose and turned his face to the Jordan breeze, letting it dry the tears that still remained upon his cheeks.

How, he wondered, was he to carry on? How was he to abide life, let alone lead millions of contrary people toward a prophetic destiny?

Afraid to set one foot in front of the other, he stood rooted to the place where he had spent the night. But as he let the breeze pass over him, it seemed to bring solace to his heart.

And in the breeze was a voice. Though it was almost imperceptible, it somehow reached through the turmoil of his soul, and held him for a rapturous moment in the grip of love.

"Moses my servant is dead," it said. "Now, rise up, cross the Jordan with all my people, to the land which I am giving to the sons of Israel. Every place on which the sole of your foot treads, I have given to you, just as I spoke to Moses."

Joshua's chest heaved as the breath of God himself coursed through his lungs, and he fell back, amazed by the courage the words imparted.

"From the wilderness and Lebanon, even as far as the great river, Euphrates, all the land of the Hittites, and to the great sea toward the going down of the sun, will be yours," the voice promised. "No man will be able to stand before you all the days of your life. As I have been with Moses, I will be with you. I will not fail you or forsake you."

How wonderful were those words. If only Joshua might see the one who spoke them!

"Be strong and courageous," the voice came again, echoing the instruction of Moses. "Have I not commanded you? Be strong and courageous! Do not be terrified or discouraged, for the Lord your God is with you wherever you go."

Then, like the breeze that tapered toward noon, the words also died away.

For a while, the successor to Moses waited for further orders, and when none came, he scanned the mountain, not looking, this time, for the departed prophet, but for the face of Yahweh.

His search was vain, but he sensed that he was not alone. Energized, he stepped forward, walking and then running toward camp.

The time had come to move out, and he could not wait to tell the people so.

47

The woman of Jericho sat in her high window, brushing out her long red hair, as was her custom every evening of her life. She was no longer a young woman, but she was still beautiful, perhaps more so than the day Joshua had seen her. For her loveliness had ripened with age, and her womanly qualities were more defined by the wisdom that time had lent to her face.

She did not gaze upon the moon this night, as she had that evening long ago, when, unbeknownst to her, a Hebrew general had admired her. Instead, her eyes traveled across the hills, toward the Jordan River, beyond which the Israelites were camped.

Joshua did not know that she thought of him as often, over the years, as he had thought of her. She had not seen his lingering gaze from her nighttime window, but she had spoken to him, and to his men, in the street next day. And though she did not know his name, or the importance of his office, she had never forgotten the handsome Hebrew with the dark hair and the scrupulous eyes.

It still pained her, all these years later, to remember the look of disapproval that had flashed across his face when his eyes took her in that day. Surely, he was a holy man, like the mighty Moses whose fame had spread from Egypt to Canaan, and to all parts of the world.

Surely, by his standards and the standards of Israel, her profession was lewd and unpardonable.

Still, she often thought of him, wondering what his position might be among the millions who had terrified the nations round about. He was obviously a leader; at least among the small group of men who had entered Jericho, he was the spokesman.

She remembered how he had denounced her group of women at the fountain, and she wondered if he would have looked more kindly on her had she not been marked as a harlot.

He became ever more present in her reveries when the traveling hosts of Israel entered the regions east of Jordan, subduing and occupying the land from Edom to Syria. Perhaps he served under the great general, Joshua, whose military feats were heralded far and wide, equaling the miracles of Moses for legendary value.

Whoever, he was the oft-returning vision of her fantasies. No matter how many men Rahab had known, the one she had seen but once dominated her romantic dreams.

No presence so great as Israel could stay in any one place without its every move being reported among the neighboring lands. Just today, in the Jericho streets, it was reported that the invaders were regrouping, making preparations to push on. Speculations ran wild as to the company's next plans.

Word also had it that Moses had disappeared, that perhaps he had died, and that leadership had been passed to Joshua.

If this was true, Israel's next move would doubtless be to make a definitive advance against Canaan.

No Canaanite, however unschooled, was ignorant of the fact that Israel had long ago been uprooted from the land of its fathers. And no citizen of the world failed to marvel at the flight of the enslaved from four hundred years' bondage in Egypt.

It was widely held that every race and every nation had an overseeing god. Apparently the god of the Hebrews had taken matters in hand to return the people to their homeland. It remained now to be seen whether the god of Israel would prevail.

Rahab shivered with the desert breeze, and drew a scarlet shawl over her shoulders. Israel had thrown terror into the hearts of all people round about, but she, more than most, believed the gods of Canaan would fare ill in any encounter with Yahweh.

It was not only the fate of Egypt that told her this. Everyone knew the story of that defeat, yet most Canaanites held fast to the hope that Baal and Astarte were mightier. Rahab, however, had been influenced from childhood to respect the God of the Hebrews.

Indeed, her personal background was a jumble of environments and mixed training. Her earliest memories were of a caring home, wherein mother and father, simple fabric makers, raised their children to be responsible tradesmen and women. The home was always abustle, in those days, with industrious activity, the coming and going of customers from the front-room shop, and chatty dinners around the evening fire.

Predominant in those memories was the figure of a jolly cook, a Hebrew slave, whom her father had purchased and brought home from Egypt.

Ada was a large woman, as wide as she was high, and she filled the house, from the moment she entered, with songs and happy stories. Most of those songs and stories were of the Hebrews and their history, full of legend and miracles. And as Rahab spent a good deal of time in the kitchen, playing at Ada's skirts and later helping with the chores, she grew up learning to speak Hebrew as fluently as her native tongue.

Along with the language was also imparted a reverence for the God of Jacob, and a wonder at the workings of Yahweh on behalf of those ancient people.

This was a reverence that never entirely passed away, despite the fact that, in time, Rahab's life was radically changed.

The death of her beloved papa, and the introduction of a stepfather, brought with it an new lifestyle, one which would forever sweep away the innocence of her early years, and release a tide of activity that left her helpless in its wake.

Her stepfather maintained the family fabric business, but finding that it did not produce sufficient riches to satisfy his appetites, he began to use his wife's daughters for other purposes.

Selling them for a night or an hour to his male customers, he turned the family home into a den of fleshly indulgence. And when he relocated the residence to the city wall, making it an inn for travelers, the "business" flourished.

Of course, the Hebrew cook had to go. According to the father, she was an undermining influence. After all, he claimed, his daughters' work was a religious activity, done in honor of Astarte, deity of erotic pleasure. While most gods consorted with the love goddess, the god of Israel was much too confining, and the demands he made were not only unrealistic, but contrary to the worship of Baal.

Therefore, when Rahab was only a girl, Ada's influence was removed. And being the oldest sister of the household, Rahab carried the greatest burden of fulfilling her father's goals.

The day Joshua and his men had seen her in the street, she accompanied her sisters and several of the paid women who had come to live in the house. Over the intervening years, she had become head mistress of the brothel.

Despite her attempts to serve the goddess, she had never forgotten Ada, or the stories heard at her knee. Nor had she forgotten the language of the Hebrews, and the chantlike songs that her beloved friend had taught her.

Out of devotion to her family, she tried to suppress the longing they gave rise to. But in her private moments, they returned to haunt her, wooing her heart with wistful phrases and kissing her brow at night like sweet, sad lips.

Placing her brush upon the windowsill, she leaned out toward the east. It was harvesttime in the Jericho Valley. Everywhere the scent of scythed hay and the smoke of stubble fires rose to fill the air. Somewhere beyond the fields the Jordan River swelled, overflowing its banks. And further yet was the camp of Israel.

What did the handsome Hebrew do this evening? she wondered. Would she ever be blessed to see him again?

As she pressed her palms against the sill, rising and leaning out as far as possible, she could see harvesters bedding down for the night outside the city walls. Within the hour, the gates of Jericho would be closed to all traffic, and wealthier people hurried to find lodging inside.

Among the folks entering from the highway, and crossing the great drawbridge, two men especially caught her eye.

In their clothing and general appearance, there was nothing unusual. But as they walked, they seemed to study the walls and the roadway with special care. Now and then, they stopped, conferring together, but scanning the moat, the bridge, and the steep glacis that surrounded the town.

One of them, the elder of the two, especially intrigued Rahab. Something about him was familiar, and when a breeze caught the hood of his mantle, pulling it back from his bearded face, she gasped.

Surely this was one of the men who had, those many years before, entered Jericho! Of course, age had touched him, as it had her, but if he was not the man of her dreams, he might have been his brother, so much did they look alike.

Vainly, she tried to catch a direct look at his eyes. If she could clearly see them, she would know, for no one had such eyes as the man of her fantasies.

But it was too late. The men were moving on, entering the gate, and joining with the multitude who sought sanctuary for the night.

Quickly, Rahab bundled her shawl about her, and headed for the door. If she could descend the stairs of the wall-side house before the men reached the city square, she might see them directly.

Whether or not she had found her long-lost dream, these were surely Israelites. That being so, they were here to spy out the city.

And if they were spies, they were forerunners to an invasion!

48

It was not unusual for Rahab to stand on a street-corner. She had spent a good deal of her life doing so. But the streets of Jericho were not safe at night, especially for a woman. And it was unusual for her to go out after dark.

Nevertheless, it was not fear of danger that made Rahab's heart pound as she stood in the shadows at the foot of her stairs, watching pedestrians pass through the gate.

She stood on tiptoe, waiting for the two Hebrews. If she could spot them, she would try to speak with them. It was this that made her anxious, for if she approached them, they would think she propositioned them. And she had no such intention.

There was no time for strategy. Already they entered the town, observing everything about them with exceptional interest.

Collecting her courage, Rahab stepped in front of them.

"Sirs," she said, just loudly enough to be heard in the moving crowd, "if you seek lodging, I know of a place."

Over the years Rahab had approached hundreds of men with the same suggestion. She did not often blush when she did so. But tonight, her face burned, and her hands trembled.

A mixture of feelings was hers, as her eyes met the eyes of the elder Hebrew. She was embarrassed to intrude herself upon a representative of Yahweh. But she was also disappointed, for she knew instantly that he was not the long-remembered man who had captured her heart.

When she spoke to them, however, the men paid no mind to her feelings, side-stepping her as though she were a leper.

"This is a foul city, Salmon," the elder addressed the younger, as they hastened away. "When I came here with Joshua, such women approached us, and he rebuked them."

At these words, Rahab clutched her shawl to her heart. Remembering how the man of her dreams had denounced her sisters, she reeled at the implication. *Oh, by the gods!* she thought. Could it be that the one she had loved from afar these many years was the Israelite leader himself! Was her beloved *Joshua*?

Falling back against the stairway railing, she drew a sharp breath. Should she go after the men, and try to persuade them to join her? Surely they would need protection in this vile place.

But no. Friends of Joshua would never set foot in a house like hers.

Stoop-shouldered, she turned for home. Tears clouded her eyes as she realized that the very man she had dreamed of was none other than the great general, the holy leader of the chosen people. How he would have laughed, had he known that such a woman longed for his approval!

Lost in dejection, she was halfway up the stairs, before a voice halted her.

"My lady," it called, "psssst . . . my lady . . ."

Looking toward the street, she saw that the Hebrews had returned, and stood directly beneath her door, motioning to her.

It was the younger one who hailed her, and she knew they risked detection, calling to her in Hebrew. Hurrying down the stairs, she met them on the landing, and the elder surveyed her up and down.

"Woman," he said, "it occurs to us that when you addressed us in the street, you spoke the Israelite tongue."

Then looking nervously about him, he leaned close and asked, "Are you friend, or foe?"

* * *

Like an anxious housewife, Rahab arranged and rear-ranged the stalks of flax that lined her rooftop garden. Still engaged in the fabric trade, her family stored the supplies for linen-making on the flat roof, drying the bundled flax in the sun.

"You will be safe here," she said to the two men, as she spread pallets between the stalks, making their beds. "That is, you will be safe if no one heard us in the street."

Standing up, she looked at her new lodgers with a furrowed brow. "You must keep your voices low, for we have . . . guests . . . that come and go all night, in the rooms below."

Caleb, the elder Hebrew, cleared his throat. "We will do well, madam. Your generosity is more than we could ask."

Salmon, the younger, smiled broadly. It was apparent that he was infatuated by her beauty, and though he felt awkward in this place, he was eager to please the hostess.

"Do not trouble yourself," he said. "May the Lord bless you for your kindness."

At the reference to Yahweh, Rahab's face colored, and she rubbed her hands together nervously.

"You are servants of Joshua," she sighed. "Did he send you to this city?"

"He did," Caleb answered. "Joshua is now governor of our people."

Rahab blinked back tears. "So I have heard," she replied. "And a fine man he is . . ."

That she was in awe of the general was obvious. But the two men could not interpret the quaver in her voice when she spoke of him.

For a tense moment, she surveyed their faces. And then, beseeching them, she pleaded, "I know that the Lord has given you this land. Your terror has fallen on us, and the inhabitants of the land have melted away before you! We have heard how the Lord parted the Reed Sea when you came out of Egypt, and how you utterly destroyed the kings of the Amorites, Sihon, and Og. When we heard it, our hearts melted and no courage remained in any man because of you!"

Caleb and Salmon looked at one another, wondering if they should try to console her, so desperate was her tone.

But she went on, as though to hesitate would mean destruction.

"The Lord your God, he is God in heaven above and on earth beneath!" she groaned. "Please swear to me by the Lord, because I have dealt kindly with you, that you will also deal kindly with my father's household! Pledge to me that you will spare my family, my father, my mother, my brothers and my sisters, and save us from death!"

Burying her face in her hands, she wept, the relief of her own testimony sweeping over her, as well as dread of God's holy hand.

But her confession warmed the hearts of her two visitors. Stepping up to her, they embraced her, and Caleb lifted her face in his hands.

"My dear woman," he pledged, "we will give our very lives if any ill befalls you. So long as you keep our secret safe, it shall come about that when the Lord gives us the land, we will deal kindly and faithfully with you and yours."

49

Rahab rested upon her bed, but did not sleep. She had given her servants the word that she would take no clients this evening, yet she lay awake listening to every knock upon the front door, and every voice in the halls of the wall-side inn.

The house where she had served Astarte since girlhood was a popular stopping-place for men of all nations, not only because its women were practiced in their art, but because of its convenient location near the city gate. Rahab was accustomed to the sound of perpetual comings and goings, day and night, within her house. But tonight she listened for a different kind of caller, for militia or castle guards seeking the two spies.

Sometime toward midnight, she must have dozed, for when a loud rap came at her chamber door, she jolted.

"What is it?" she cried. "Did I not say I wish to be alone this evening?"

Again the knocking came, as though the door would be forced open. Leaping from her bed, she drew on her scarlet robe, and yawning as though she had been wakened from a sound sleep, she peered out into the hall.

"What is it?" she snarled, pretending offense when she saw two palace police. "Can't a lady get any rest?"

"Israelites are in the city!" one of them growled back. "Spies, here to search out the land! They were seen entering your brothel. Bring them forth!"

Buying time, Rahab shut the door, and called through it, "I don't know what you are talking about. Give me a moment to dress, and I will be with you."

Running a shaky hand through her red tresses, Rahab

tried to think of a way to cover her tracks. She had, in fact, thought of nothing else all night. Now she must perform.

When the police once more pounded on her door, she stepped into the torchlit hall, and with admirable coolness, confronted them.

"Now, gentlemen," she crooned, "you surely know that men come and go from my place of business day and night. How can you expect me to learn about them all? I know of no Hebrews entertained here this evening."

One of the guards leaned over her, leering into her aqua eyes. "You were reported seen with them, speaking with them in the street and leading them, personally, up your stairs," he said through gritted teeth. "Do you deny this?"

Rahab paused and rubbed her chin, as though trying to remember. "Oh," she gasped, "those two? Why, do you mean to tell me that they were...Oh, it can't be! Israelites? Under my very roof?"

Looking aghast, she glanced up to the roof she spoke of, silently praying for the men who were not *under* it, but *atop* it, this very moment.

Then, focusing again on the guards, she said most persuasively, "I had no idea! I thought they spoke with a peculiar accent. But they seemed innocent enough. Yes, they came to me, but I did not know where they were from. Had I known...why..."

Impatient, the guards pushed past her, ready to rifle the house, but she pulled on their sleeves and continued, "Yes, they were here, but they did not stay long. And when it was time for the city gate to be shut, the men went out. I do not know where they went. But if you go after them, you might catch them on the plain!"

As she spoke, the guards intruded upon several of the brothel rooms, even going so far as to throw back bedcovers, interrupting one lewd scene after another in their quest.

"Perhaps she is telling the truth," one of them growled, as they approached the stairs leading to the roof.

Rahab jumped at this. "Listen!" she cried. "Do you want them to get away? Head for the plain! Pursue them quickly, and you will overtake them!"

By now, the entire house was aware of the search. Men and women in various stages of undress lined the hallways, inquiring into the matter.

Sheathing their swords, which they had carried boldly into the house, the guards turned to go. And when they exited, Rahab soothed her upset patrons.

"Rest easy," she said, turning on a practiced smile. "The police were seeking some vagabonds. But I assured them we take only upper-class clientele here. Go now... my friends... go back to sleep."

* * *

Hurrying up the rooftop stairs, Rahab crept through the flax rows, calling anxiously for Caleb and Salmon.

"Dear men," Rahab stammered, coming upon them, "I suppose you heard the ruckus below?"

"We did," Caleb replied, pulling on his cloak.

"Yes," said Salmon, rolling up his pallet.

"But," Rahab objected, seeing that they made ready to leave, "you are safe now. They will be looking for you everywhere else but here. You cannot mean to go!"

"We will not endanger you further," Caleb insisted. "You are a kind woman, and we do you a disfavor being here."

Fearing for their welfare, the Canaanite woman begged them to stay. But it seemed they were bent on self-destruction, and not even her tears could change their minds.

"Oh," she cried, tugging on their cloaks, "you do me no disfavor! You honor my house! You... bless it!" And holding out her hands to them, she wept, "What will Joshua think of me, if some evil now befalls you?"

Amazed at her persistence, the men might have succumbed to her pleas. But knowing they only jeopardized her safety as well as theirs by further delay, they headed for the rooftop door.

Yet again, she cried to them, "Very well! If you must go, hear me! Slip down by way of the wall. All the city guards will be searching houses and streets, and even the plain beyond. But they will not watch for you upon the wall. You can go down swiftly, and slip through the dark toward the river!"

Curious, Salmon asked, "But how are we to do this? The wall is too high."

Already, Rahab had removed her outer garment, the scarlet robe in which she received her clients. With deft hands she was tearing it seam from seam and length from length, into long strands of blood-red cloth.

"Quick!" she ordered. "Tie these into knots. It is good, strong material! It will make a sturdy rope!"

With a shrug, the two Israelites glanced at one another, and almost laughing, they took up the long shreds, doing just as she instructed.

In moments they had a fine, long tatter of rope. And this Rahab took to the roof's edge.

"Go to the hill country," she directed, "lest those who pursue you happen upon you. Hide yourselves there for three days, until they give up the chase. After that, you may go your way!"

Could any man question such a commanding woman? Why, not even Joshua himself would have withstood her.

But Caleb was still in charge, and was quick to let her know so. "Remember the promise we made to you?" he said, as he threw the rope over an aperture in the ledge. "We shall be free from it unless, when we come into this land, you tie this cord of scarlet in this very opening. And gather your family in the house—your father and your mother and your brothers and all your household."

"Yes," Rahab agreed, securing the top end of the rope to a beam.

"If anyone goes out of the house, into the street," Caleb said firmly, "his blood shall be on his own head, and we shall be guiltless. But if anyone who stays with you is harmed, his blood shall be on our hands!"

"Yes, yes," she nodded. "Now, the two of you be gone!"

Together the men started toward the ledge. But in tandem they returned, embracing her fondly.

Then, composing himself, Caleb cleared his throat.

"Remember," he said in as manly a tone as he could muster, "if you tell this business of ours...we shall be free from the oath."

"So be it," Rahab confirmed, wiping her eyes.

And as the two spies climbed down the wall, she called softly after them, "Bless Joshua for me! Tell him the woman of Jericho prays for him."

50

Up and down the east bank of Jordan, Joshua traipsed on horseback, straining his eyes toward the sunset.

His spies, one of whom was his best friend, had been gone for four days. They were due to return this evening, according to the plan laid out before they left.

The general did not know that they had been in hiding. He did not know that they had almost been discovered their first night in Jericho, or that their "spying of the land" had taken place with the militia of that city scouting the west bank behind them.

When they appeared, true to schedule, the evening of the fourth day, their commander led his horse into the ford to meet them.

"Caleb!" he cried. "Salmon! How did you fare?"

Waving their arms in the air, they greeted him, and Caleb shouted, "Surely the Lord has given all the land into our hands! And all the inhabitants have melted in fear before us!"

* * *

It was a joyous reunion that took place in the general's camp that night. All the leading men of Israel joined about the fire of the meeting tent, which, since the death of Moses, had come to be Joshua's abode.

Eager to hear the story of the spies' adventure, and their military assessment of the region, they sat transfixed as Salmon and Caleb spoke instead of nearly being discovered, of being on the run, and of the woman on the wall who had saved their lives.

The moment they mentioned the "woman in red," Joshua's heart stuttered. No man in the room could have guessed his feelings, or would ever have dreamed that she had been the subject of his thoughts countless times over the past four decades.

"She spoke Hebrew!" Caleb emphasized. And then turning to Joshua, he enthused, "Do you remember that we encountered such a woman in the city square, when we entered Jericho long ago? I am certain as I can be that this is the same lady!"

He need not have suggested this. The general had ascertained as much the moment she was first described.

Nodding weakly, Joshua nudged him to go on. "She is a ... prostitute ... is she not?" he muttered.

Caleb and Salmon looked sideways at one another, fearing a rebuke.

"Well ... yes ..." Caleb admitted. "But she seemed to be a friend, and she gave us shelter ... nothing more. Master, she is a good woman ... for a Canaanite. And I hope we did not overstep our authority when we promised her, by oath, that we would spare her and her family when we take the city."

When the men about the fire whispered in private snickers, the two spies looked at the floor, color rising to their faces.

For a long moment, Joshua was silent, disguising his sense of gratitude, as though the matter deserved careful consideration. "Very well," he replied cryptically. And changing the subject, he asked, "What of the land? Will we have success?"

He knew the answer to that question. Caleb had proclaimed it when they had met upon the Jordan shore.

"Indeed, sir," he repeated, "the land is as good as ours already! The people tremble at news of our every move— not only the people of Jericho, but those of the hill country and the plain, the Jebusites, the Hittites, the Hivites ... all of them."

"But what of the walls?" someone challenged. "The land lies open before us, and the smaller towns may be easily taken. But Jericho is the most strongly fortified city in Canaan. How do you suggest we move in?"

"Yes," another jibed, "since you stayed upon the wall, you had a good chance to become familiar with it!"

This allusion to the harlot's house was meant in good spirit, but Joshua bristled at it.

"Enough!" he objected. "Our men did no wrong in entering there. And it seems the woman was kind of heart. Judge her by this alone, and thank Yahweh she was there."

PART VIII
Joshua: God's Warrior

51

It was a misty morning on the banks of the Jordan when the people of Israel began their entrance into the promised land. In the gray of that dawn, Joshua watched as the dream of nearly five centuries was fulfilled, as the people, compassed behind and before with miracles, took their first steps into the homeland.

According to his instructions, the ark of the covenant was borne to the waters first. The instant the priests' feet touched the swollen rapids, the river parted before the eyes of Israel, just as the Reed Sea had parted, and the people crossed over on dry land.

Sitting on horseback, where the tumbling waters gathered in a heap, Joshua watched as the long-sung hope of Israel came to pass, as the longing of enslaved generations was satisfied.

The priests who bore the ark stood still on the river bed, in the very center of the pathway, until all of the Israelites crossed over. And as the people ventured into Canaan, they danced and they sang and they worshiped, for they knew they were the most blessed of the generations who had desired this.

It took several hours for the enormous nation to pass beneath the water-wall. All that time, Joshua prayed for the armed men who led the way, forty thousand warriors ready for combat. Directly behind them went the coffin of Joseph, guarded on every side, and ready for burial, at last, in the land of Jacob.

When everyone had crossed, twelve representatives, one for each tribe, bore on their shoulders twelve great rocks, chosen from the river bed for a memorial to be erected on the western shore.

Spurring his horse, Joshua at last ventured, himself, into the stony bed, and when he had reached the other side, he called to the priests, "Come up from the Jordan!"

Once they had done so, the ark secure upon its poles, the people stood back, awed as the great wall of water tumbled down and a mountain of entrapped rapids swelled through the bed, splashing over the banks and rushing toward the Salt Sea.

Riding to a hill that commanded a view of the Jericho plain, Joshua addressed his people, his throat tight with emotion. "The twelve stones which your leaders have borne from the Jordan are to be a memorial of this great day!" he cried. "Engrave upon each the name of a tribe of Israel, and erect on this shore a monument to the saving hand of the Lord! When your children ask, in time to come, 'What are these stones?' then you shall tell them, 'Israel crossed over this Jordan on dry ground.' For the Lord your God dried up the waters of the Jordan before you until you had crossed, just as the Lord your God did to the Reed Sea, that all the people of the earth may know that the hand of the Lord is mighty, so that you may fear the Lord your God, forever!"

As the nation looked on, the twelve representatives rolled the stones into a high pillar, facing the engraved words outward, so that every morning and every evening of the generations to come, the names would catch the sun and remind the world of Israel's promise-keeping God.

* * *

The days following the Jordan crossing were an active time, not a time to take ease, but a time of preparation and planning. Though the dream of ages had come to pass, there were many trials to be endured, many victories to be achieved, before the people truly *possessed* their heritage.

How Joshua wished Moses were here to talk to!

Much had happened in the few months since the homecoming. The general had commanded that all Hebrew males born since the flight from Egypt be circumcised; the first Passover in the new land had been observed; for the first time in forty years, the Israelites had eaten of the produce of the earth (the rich harvest of Canaan); the manna had ceased; and the pillar of fire and cloud disappeared.

Nothing remained to be done before the long-anticipated assault on Jericho. But how could Joshua make such a bold move without knowing that Moses cheered him from the sidelines?

Sometimes it still seemed terribly unfair that the great prophet had been prevented from enjoying the goal of all his work—that he had died on the east side of Jordan before his dream was realized.

Yet when Joshua remembered the glory of his countenance as he took his final steps up Mount Nebo, disappearing forever into the mists of heaven, he wondered if the prophet had indeed missed anything.

Today, as was his custom, Joshua ventured a way out from camp, to be alone, to meditate on the upcoming days, and to seek help for the responsibilities he shouldered. Tethering his horse to a nearby clump of sage, he sat atop a rock on the Jericho plain and scanned the lush terrain. Fields of chartreuse heather were interrupted everywhere by furrows ready for planting, and the rolling hills leading toward the distant city were thick with budding orchards and tender vineyards.

Truly, this was the promised land, longed after for centuries, the land flowing with milk and honey.

Dominating the landscape was the towered city itself, forebodingly quiet. Here and there a guard could be seen, pacing the walls and gazing toward the east, toward the camp of Israel. There was no coming and going from the gate, no commerce across the moat or in the streets.

The gate was, in fact, closed, and had been since the Israelites were reported entering the land.

Indeed, the city was tightly shut up for fear of the people of Yahweh. But as Joshua surveyed the silent turrets, the sandstone walls, tawny in the evening light, the city put him in mind of a lion, apparently dozing, but ready to pounce.

How much bloodshed, how much devastation would be required for Israel to conquer that mighty fortress? And the question which had plagued the strategy meeting the night the spies returned never ceased to haunt him. Just how was Israel to overcome those walls?

No matter how huge Israel's army, no matter how skilled its bowmen, Israel faced in Jericho its greatest challenge.

The time had come to face that challenge. There could be no delay. Consumed with this reality, the general tried to imagine what wisdom his mentor would have shared.

But he could only recall the smile that had lit the prophet's face the day he ascended Nebo, and he wondered what secret lay behind it.

As Joshua relived that day, he remembered other times when the prophet's face shone with unearthly light. Though sorrow had hounded Moses many years of his life, he had been closer to God than any man, and he seemed to see a future beyond even the conquest of Canaan.

In fact, now that Joshua faced his gravest test, it seemed but one step on a great, tall ladder—a ladder that stretched across the cosmos. And while he had come here to plot maneuvers, it occured to him that all the battles of Israel, every loss and win, all of Israel's worship, her institutions and rituals, were mere shadows of something higher, something deeper than themselves.

The days since the crossing had been full of such shadows: the Passover, the circumcision, the manna, the guiding pillar, the ark which contained the ten commandments, and indeed, the crossing itself. Yet Joshua had no clear understanding of what their deeper meaning might be.

Moses knew. But Moses was not here, and without his instruction, Joshua met a blank wall in his understanding, a wall as high and difficult to scale as the fortress laid out upon the plain.

Laughing sardonically, Joshua shook his head. What was he doing here? How had he come to lead this nation? He had been a prophet's servant, but he was no prophet himself! Because it had been imposed upon him, he had taken the helmet of military leadership. But a man of war was not the same as a prophet!

He regretted that he had not taken fuller advantage of his time with his master. Especially he wished he had asked Moses to expound upon the brass serpent and the healing it represented. For Moses, that emblem, erected by Salmon and Caleb on the standard of Judah, had turned years of heaviness to joy in an afternoon.

"The Lord is our salvation!" Moses had declared, holding the standard high. "This very day he takes upon himself the sins of his people—even the very form of their sins he takes upon himself! Look, my children, and live!"

In desperation the dying people obeyed Moses's command, and they received healing. But none of them understood the symbol, not even the servant of the prophet himself.

Feeling like a spiritual infant, Joshua gazed across the plain to the city of Israel's enemies. Shrugging, he tried to pin his thoughts to the moment. Jericho might be a symbol, but it was also very real. And Joshua might not be a prophet, but he was a soldier. He must be responsible for the duty placed before him.

Had the Lord not spoken to him the day Moses departed? Joshua had not been alone upon Mount Nebo;

the Lord had come to him, promising guidance and insight.

Looking at his hands as they lay open in his lap, Joshua saw the callouses which his spear had worn. Running his hands down his arms, he felt the strong muscles and ligaments that had wielded his sword in combat, and glancing at his thighs, he saw the well-worked sinews that had gripped the flanks of his warhorse.

Joshua was not a prophet, but he was a man of war. And he did not carry a sacred staff, but he bore the spear of the Lord.

This was his calling. This was his duty. And it would serve him well to leave other matters to God.

Ahead, the walls of Jericho deepened to twilight rose. He would find a way to conquer them, he told himself. The Lord had a way, and soon enough he would reveal it. If that was all the prophecy Joshua understood, it was enough.

Standing, he turned for camp. He did not know when the answer would come, but he would be back here tomorrow night, and every night until it did.

Mounting his horse, Joshua drove his spurs into its sides. But suddenly the animal stopped short, snorting at a presence upon the trail.

Through the gloaming, Joshua made out a figure straight ahead, a man dressed in armor, a sword drawn in his hand.

The general's heart leaped, but wheeling in his saddle, he detected no other soldiers in the heather. And charging toward the stranger, he flashed his own sword.

Incredibly, the man stood unmoving on the trail, and Joshua crouched down as he approached, waving his weapon in warning and giving a menacing shout.

"Who are you?" he demanded. "Are you for us or for our adversaries?"

"No," the man replied, his chin raised dauntlessly. "I am the captain of the host of the Lord!"

Gaping, Joshua replaced his sword in its sheath, and with a faltering step, he climbed down from his horse, bowing with his face to the ground.

"What has my lord to say to me?" he cried, stretching his hands along the earth.

"Take off your sandals from your feet!" the mysterious figure replied. "For the place on which you are standing is holy!"

Quickly, Joshua obeyed. Unbuckling his shoes, he flung them aside. Then sitting back, he raised his face to the angel and awaited instructions.

Lifting his sword toward the distant city, the figure said, "See, I have given Jericho into your hand, with its king and its men of valor. You and all the men of war shall march around the city, circling it once. You shall do this for six days, circling it once each day. And seven priests shall carry seven ram's horn trumpets before the ark. Then on the seventh day, you shall march around the city seven times, and the priests shall blow the trumpets. And it shall be that when they make a long blast with the rams' horns, and when you hear the sound of the trumpets, all the people shall shout with a great shout. And the wall of the city will fall down flat, and the people will go up directly to take it."

52

Rahab gripped the sill of her high window, leaning out wide-eyed. The city which had been her home all her life had been quiet as a tomb for days, but just moments ago the shout of a guard had been heard upon the walls, and then another and another, sending an alarm through the streets.

It was the shout every citizen of Jericho had dreaded, the notice of the watchmen that Israel was on the move.

For weeks, ever since word had come of the peoples' Jordan crossing, and of the parting of the waters, no one had left the city. The gate had been pulled shut that night, the drawbridge taken up. It was planting time, but no one went forth to sow the fields. No one went out to prune the orchards and vineyards of the city. All commerce had been cut off, as the king barred entrance to foreigners.

Shut in, the people of Jericho kept close to their homes, speaking in low voices and extinguishing their lights early each evening. The towers of the city were bolted, the doors barred, and all lived in fear of the Israelites' next move.

As for Rahab, the moment she heard of the river-crossing, she had run to her rooftop, securing the scarlet cord to the breach in the ledge, and letting it trail down the wall outside. Such had been the agreement between herself and the spies, that they would be free from their oath of protection if they did not see the cord when they entered the land.

There the scarlet rag remained, a symbol no longer of her profession, but of her dependence on the God of Israel. And her family remained in the house with her, not because they believed as she did, but because they had no other hope.

At the sound of the shout upon the wall, Rahab had gone to her window, throwing back the shutters which had been closed for days. Just now she craned her neck as far to the east as possible, knowing that the army of Joshua approached. All her relations gathered about her, jostling for a view out the same narrow opening.

"See!" Rahab cried, pointing across the desert. "Toward the river! There they are!"

Forcing the others aside, her stepfather joined her at the sill, his hardened face animated by fear.

With the glow of the morning sky behind them, the troops of Israel made a black smudge against the horizon, growing like a cloud of locusts as they moved across the earth, wave after wave of them emerging from the wadis and the fields of the west bank and gobbling up the landscape.

The points of their spears, higher than their heads, flashed in the dawn light, and the sound of their marching grew like the drone of a gigantic swarm.

In the streets below, could now be heard the scramble of the king's forces, as they armed themselves, and prepared for battle. Soon the vibration of chariot wheels was discerned along the top of the wall, and the clopping of horses' hooves as the cavalry joined them. Divisions of Jericho's army would be stationed behind the gate and in every quarter of the city. But they were also trained to fight from the towers, and their surefooted horses were used to maneuvering between the broad battlements.

At first sight of the oncoming horde, the machines of war, movable nets and banks of spear-throwers, were put in position.

But as the people of Jericho peered out from their windows and walls, they saw no such instruments of battle flanking the army of Israel. While the oncoming warriors wore helmets and vestplates, while they bore before them shields and bucklers and carried spears and swords, they were not preceded by battering rams or catapults.

What did precede them was one lone rider, tall and straight upon his horse, but keeping his sword in its sheath.

At the sight of him, Rahab steadied herself against a pounding heart. "Joshua!" she whispered.

Her father did not hear. Nor did her sisters or mother. But they all knew that the dashing figure could be none other, and they exclaimed amongst themselves when they saw him.

"How does he expect to fight, when he has no means to scale the walls?" the stepfather jibed.

But Rahab replied, "They say the God of Israel does the fighting. Shall we mock *him*?"

Snorting, the father turned away, and the others clustered around Rahab, gawking at the dashing general who drew near enough to be clearly described.

"Oh," the sisters marveled, "he is handsome! Is he not, Rahab?"

The woman did not answer, captivated by the ruddy Hebrew as she had been nearly forty years ago.

"How many men does he have?" the brothers gasped, pressing their faces to the opening. "Is there no end to them?"

Indeed, as the city looked on, peering through its closed gates and high windows, it seemed there was no end to the stream of people arising from the Jordan. Two great divisions were interrupted by a small company of men in long robes, bearing a golden box upon poles, and holding beneath their arms ram's horn trumpets.

Then the Canaanites realized it was not just the army of Israel that advanced upon them, but the entire nation. At the fore were the armed men, tens of thousands of them. But taking up the rear, behind the men with the box, were the unarmed hosts, the women and children, the cooks and the tentmakers, the old and the young, the sick and the well, tramping en masse across the desert.

At first the realization was confounding. But then the city began to laugh.

Did Joshua think to intimidate Jericho with numbers alone, when millions of his people were not even soldiers? And where *were* his battering rams, his ladders and catapults? Did he think to demoralize a walled city by the sight of a golden box and seven skinny priests?

As the city scoffed, however, its streets and its battlements resounding with laughter, Joshua came on, reining his horse across the heath until he stood within sprinting distance of the moat.

Directly before him was the place where the drawbridge usually touched down, the bridge from which he had once gazed upon a distant window. Taking his charger to the edge of the moat, he scanned the city wall, until his eyes lit upon a scarlet cord, and tracing it, he found the house of the woman in red.

Raising his right hand, he halted his army and all the nation behind. As the dust of their journey settled around them, he sought the woman of his dreams.

Yes—there she was, leaning out as she had done that long-ago day. This time she did not gaze at the moon, or at the rising sun. She looked instead upon the warrior, the servant of Moses, who had shunned her years before.

And this time, as her eyes met his, he did not disapprove. Smiling, he crossed his arm over his armored breast, saluting her.

Then, with a shout, he hailed his army and his people. "March!" he cried.

Wondering just how the Israelites intended to invade the fortress, the army of Jericho manned its stations. Ten thousand archers stood poised in the parapets, twenty thousand men crouched behind gilded shields, sweaty hands clutching scabbards, hatchets, and razor-fine swords.

If they anticipated a charge across the murky moat, across the jagged, knife-edged glacis—if they expected a thousand ladders against the perpendicular walls and the clawing and grappling of climbers—if they shielded themselves against the sting of arrows and the flight of spears, they need not have done so.

Joshua had other plans.

"March!" he cried again.

And the priests of Israel raised their trumpets to their lips, playing a loud, blasting drone, not once, but over and over, each man's blast overlapping the others' so that they made a perpetual cry.

With them tramped a silent army, their eyes fixed to the top of the wall, and their faces stony.

And behind the army came the nation—men, women, and children, silent as death, their eyes, too, turned toward the turrets and the windows, their expressions grave.

"What is he doing?" Rahab's family marveled.

And the city marveled as well, until, as minutes turned to hours, the Israelites still marched, circling the city in one slow sweep.

By that time, the archers of Jericho had lowered their spears, the soldiers along the wall had seated themselves, as for a show. And word circulated through the city that Joshua was a clown.

By midmorning, every soul of Israel had made one full circuit around the fortress. And as they had come, so they left, crossing the desert toward the Jordan like a dissipating cloud.

Hilarity filled the city streets, as the people congratulated themselves on victory won without a fight.

"When Joshua saw the size of our walls, he lost heart!" they hooted.

But there was a hollow tone in their laughter. Rahab discerned it, and she told her family to stay put within the house.

53

Six million feet which had for forty years tramped through the wilderness, marched for the seventh day around the impregnable fortress of their enemy. Voices which had for decades been lifted in complaint and discontent were silent, obedient to the command of their leader, Joshua. And hearts that had, for generations, doubted that God truly cared, swelled with gratitude and expectation.

Could Israel doubt that the walls of Jericho would collapse, just as Joshua promised? Only recently, the nation had witnessed the parting of the Jordan, and that had been preceded by one victory after another against the kings of the east.

Surely Yahweh was about to reveal himself in another miracle! It remained only for the people to follow his instructions, spoken through their general.

For the past six mornings, those instructions had required one circuit per day about the city. But this day there would be seven full swings about the fortress.

The first few days when they had circled Jericho, the citizens had scoffed. But by the fifth and sixth days, their haunting tread, their steadfast, stony gazes, the bleating of the priests' trumpets and the vibrations of their persistent march had so jangled the nerves of the city dwellers, that even the most mocking soul grew anxious.

Today, when the tramping did not cease with the first circuit, when the Israelites did not vanish again toward the river after one pass, the distress of Jericho increased.

Something, they sensed, was about to happen—something dreadful.

Still, despite the vibrations that shook the city's foundations, despite the eerie wail of the ram's horn trumpets, the Canaanites consoled one another. What, after all, could Joshua do against their invincible walls?

And so they huddled together, wondering how many times the clownish general and his flock of fools would torment them today. Twice? Thrice? Four times?

On and on the marching went, until, for the first time, the city quaked.

Did it only seem that the shutters hung crooked, or that the doors did not swing evenly? Had those large cracks always been in the rafters or the header boards?

When plaster began to flake from the siding, when tiles slipped from the roofs, the people began to congregate in the city square and in the bazaars, hoping for safety in open places.

And on the fifth passage, the citizens called out for their king: "Come forth, O king, from your castle! Come forth nobles and governors, from your sturdy palaces! The streets are cracking, the storm drains are breaking, the monuments and the gates are shattering!"

Then, that which they most greatly feared came upon them. On the sixth passage of Israel, the invincible security of Jericho, the boast and pride of the works of their hands, *the very walls themselves* began to crumble!

They did not fall, they quivered. They did not tumble, but hairline fractures appeared along their joints, and then flakes and chunks plummeted to the streets.

At the witness of this, the king and his governors did come forth from their dark chambers. Standing unceremoniously upon their balconies, they watched, aghast as the commoners at the riddling of the city.

Upon the plain beyond, Joshua and his people also saw the growing damage. The walls appeared to lean a bit, and the jagged shale of the steep glacis was sliding into the moat. Here and there a soldier atop the parapets slipped on a chunk of sandstone, and the warhorses along the wall teetered and skidded, whinnying in fear.

Steadfastly, Joshua kept his face to the wide path before him, the path that had been worn by his nation's six million feet. He was leading his people on the seventh pass around the city, the seventh pass of the seventh sortie, and the thirteenth pass of the "war."

Remembering the promise of the captain of the Lord of Hosts, to be with him in this venture, he closed his eyes and lifted his head to heaven. Then, taking a deep breath, he turned about in his saddle, facing the men of the first division and all the people behind.

Raising his hand, he gave the order for the final trumpet blast. And as the priests blew the long wail upon their bleating horns, he cried, "Shout! For the Lord has given you the city! The city is cursed and all that is in it belongs to the Lord! Only Rahab and all who are in her house shall live!"

With this, such a sound as had never ascended from the earth and never would again, arose from the desert round about Jericho, as three million voices shouted to the skies above.

In an instant, the invincible walls tumbled, crushing the inhabitants, throwing the turreted army to the earth, skiddering down the glacis and burying the moat, toppling outward across the plain and collapsing inward upon the palaces and streets.

The dust of shattered buildings and broken roads ascended to the heavens like a colossal mushroom, and the survivors cried for one another amidst the rubble.

But their cries were overwhelmed by the ongoing shout of Israel, the laughter and the praise of the invading host who ascended from the plain, rushing over the disemboweled city like locusts over a giant's corpse.

Only one fragment of the wall remained intact, the

tiny sliver beside the fallen gate, upon which was perched the house of Rahab. From its rooftop still waved the scarlet cord, and within, the family remained alive.

54

Joshua waited on horseback as the people of Israel spilled past him, shouting and dancing and making their way toward the vanquished city. As the millions crawled over the fallen walls, ready to take the booty, they pushed through the rubbled streets, completing the task of destruction.

Men and women, young and old, oxen, sheep, and donkeys they killed with the sword; and any remaining husk of a building they demolished.

Bearing sacks full of silver, gold, bronze, and iron upon their shoulders they emerged from the cataclysm, depositing the booty in a stash which would go into the priests' treasury. This they would do for the next several hours, returning over and over, hauling out whatever was of value to the nation, until the city was utterly stripped.

As Joshua observed all this from the field, Caleb and Salmon joined him. "Did I not say the Lord has given us the land?" Caleb cried, running up to the general. Spreading his arms wide and turning round and round, he laughed, "All the inhabitants of Canaan will melt away before us!"

"Yes," Joshua replied with a broad smile, thinking that Caleb looked as young as he had the day they left Egypt. "So you said! But let us not forget the promise to the lady who saved you."

"Indeed not!" Caleb enthused.

And Salmon jumped to comply. "Shall we fetch her?" he offered.

Joshua glanced toward the tiny pinnacle of wall that still stood, teetering beside the crumbled gate. A lump rose to his throat as he traced the scarlet cord toward the shuttered window.

"Yes," he answered. "Fetch her."

* * *

Evening was coming on over the fallen city of Jericho. The legendary fortress was no more, its only marker a titanic mound. And into the darkening sky flames leapt from its midst, as the children of Israel set it ablaze.

By morning it would be a nothing more than a funeral pyre.

But there were a handful of souls left alive who had called it home, and these Joshua watched as they emerged from the rubble.

Approaching him upon the plain, they were at first nothing more than silhouettes, hunched and tiny against the orange stage. But as they became more distinct, he saw that a woman led the way, supported by Caleb and Salmon, her family trailing behind.

Now Joshua had led mighty armies, he had conquered kingdoms. He, who had begun as a hesitant warrior, had become accustomed to the feel of weapons in his hand, and to the weight of armor upon his breast.

He was a mighty general, unafraid of anything.

But as the woman became distinct before him, walking toward him on the plain, his hands trembled and his pulse fluttered.

He was used to the drama of war, but unused to dramas of the heart. He had often thought of this lady, tracing her face in his mind. But he had never had to trace the lines of his own feelings.

A man in a man's world, he had been able to put her aside when he wished, taking her out at night, when he slept beside his fire, or placing her upon the saddle behind him when he daydreamed along the trail. She could be whatever he wished at those times, say what he wished, and leave when he wished. For she did not live in flesh and blood before him.

Now, this very moment, that was changed. And so the fearless one trembled, the valiant one slipped from his saddle, clinging to it upon knees of jelly.

Bright-eyed Caleb and Salmon did not know what a war their general fought as they presented Rahab to him.

Bowing respectfully, they gently ushered her forth.

"The woman who saved our lives, sir," they said. "If you greet her, she will understand, for she speaks our language."

But Joshua did not hear them. He did not see them, nor did he see the star-struck family clustered at her back.

All he saw was Rahab, dressed not in scarlet, but white linen. Upon the linen and upon her radiant face were traces of smoke and ash. But beyond this she was perfect, her crimson hair a halo, and her aqua eyes transparent as a virgin's.

He could not know that she thought him also perfect, the savior of her people, the captain of her heart. But as she gazed upon him, he read volumes in her worshipful eyes.

Before he could say a word, she fell to her knees before him, grasping his feet and kissing them. Then pulling back, she surveyed his handsome face, and clung to his hand.

"Master!" she wept. "You have kept your promise!"

Overcome, Joshua choked back tears. "Dear lady!" he groaned, lifting her to her feet. "You once told me your house was my house. Now your house and your city have fallen. But you are welcome to live with us. *Our* house is *your* house, for as long as you wish to stay."

EPILOGUE

The Lord your God is He who has been fighting for you.

—Joshua 23:3 NASB

Joshua sat outside his tent in the camp of Gilgal, where the children of Israel had dwelt since entering the land almost seven years before. From inside his shelter, a new tent erected alongside the tent of meeting, came the sounds of soft singing and childish chatter. And those sounds blended on the air with the aroma of good home cooking.

Though the woman who bustled about the cookfire was not Hebrew, the songs she sang were of the Hebrew tongue and to the Hebrew God. They were songs she had learned at the knee of a slave, the family maid who had taught her the love of Yahweh when she was a child.

Now she had children of her own, the offspring of her love for a Hebrew man. Though such fulfillment had come to this couple later than to most, it was all the sweeter for it. And it was all the sweeter because of the miracle it represented.

For the union of Joshua and Rahab symbolized more poignantly than most the grace of God.

Men generally stayed away from the house when their wives were cooking. But Joshua had gone without the comfort of wife and children, and had endured the blandness of solitary meals all his life. It was now his chief joy to linger over Rahab's shoulder when she puttered in the tent.

Moments ago she had shooed him away. But just now, he drew the tent flap back again, and seeing her bent over the fire, a baby on one hip and another playing at her feet, he could not resist the urge to sneak inside.

Standing, he tiptoed in, lingering in the shadows just

beyond the door. No matter how many times he had let his eyes feast upon the beauty of his wife, she never failed to please him. Right now, she was unaware of his presence. Had she known he looked on, she would have brushed the hair back from her face, she would have disentangled the baby's sticky fingers from her long red curls. But Joshua loved the effect, just as it was.

Drawn like a moth to a pulsating ember, he crossed the room, and bent over her, breathing on her neck.

With a soft giggle, Rahab turned to him, and Joshua lifted the babe from her arms, placing him on the floor to play with his brother.

Then taking the ladle from her hand, he dropped it in the pot and encircled her small waist with his arms.

For a long while he gazed into her aqua eyes, recalling how his master, Moses, had desired for him fulfillment and happiness once they entered Canaan.

Only days later Joshua had seen this woman for the first time. Though forty years had intervened between that glimpse and their union, thoughts of Rahab had kept the spark of hope alive through many trials, and ultimately the prophet's desire had been fulfilled.

"I love you," Joshua whispered, drawing her to his chest.

To these simple words, so often spoken, Rahab thrilled, for they represented the approval she had so long craved.

Reaching up, she ran a soft hand down Joshua's bearded cheek, and he grasped it in his own, pressing the palm to his lips.

As he did, his kiss traveled to her mouth, and a surge of ecstasy passed through him like always.

But the baby was crying now, and its brother tugged on mother's skirt.

To the door came visitors, and Joshua reluctantly released Rahab from his embrace.

"Papa," yet another son called, "Caleb and Salmon are here to see you."

The general stepped outside, greeting his tousle-headed firstborn, and joining his Judahite friends about the outside fire.

"Sit," he offered, prodding the embers with a stick. "Will you stay for supper?"

Glad to do so, the two companions, one as old as Joshua and the other much younger, reclined upon the ground. Joshua pulled his eldest son onto his lap, and Caleb chuckled, patting the little boy on the knee.

"Has your papa ever told you the story of the day the sun stood still?" he asked, stirring the fire with a stick of his own.

"Many times!" Joshua interjected.

"Tell me again, Papa!" the lad begged. "It is a good story!"

Shaking his head, Joshua sighed, "Oh, son, not now..."

But already Caleb was rehearsing the account. "The kings of the Amorites came out against your papa," he recalled, "after the defeat of Jericho. And all the people of the hill country assembled against him! 'Do not fear them,'" Caleb quoted, throwing his chest out and mimicking Joshua, "'for I have given them into your hands! Not one of them shall stand before you!'"

At this, the boy's eyes grew wide, as though he had not heard it a hundred times, and he looked up at his father proudly.

"So your papa and the hosts of Israel came upon them suddenly, by marching all night from Gilgal and surprising them! And we struck them as far as the cities of Azekah and Makkedah. And it came about as they fled from before us, that the Lord threw large stones from heaven upon them, and they died. More of them died from the hailstones than those we had killed with the sword!"

The lad stirred excitedly in his father's lap, and Joshua smiled, remembering that day well.

"Then your papa spoke to the Lord before the entire congregation," Caleb went on, "and he prayed,

'O sun, stand still at Gibeon,
And, O moon, in the valley of Aijalon!'

"So," Caleb said, leaning forward and pointing a finger at the boy's nose, "do you know what happened then?"

"Yes!" the boy laughed. And then he chanted, joined by Caleb and Salmon and his father:

The sun stood still,
And the moon stopped,
Until the people avenged themselves on their
    enemies!
And the sun stopped in the middle of the sky,
And did not hasten to go down for about a
    whole day!
And there was no day like that,
Before it or after it,
When the Lord listened to the voice of a man!
For the Lord fought for Israel!"

Thrilling to the oft-recited tale, the three men and the boy laughed together, and Joshua held his son tight to his chest.

But supper was about ready. Rahab called through the door that she needed help, and Joshua, gazing across the fire, saw the light leap in Salmon's eyes at the sound of her voice.

Nodding toward the tent, Joshua said, "Would you mind?" And Salmon eagerly complied, jumping to do Rahab's bidding.

Sending the boy into the house, as well, Joshua stared into the flames of the campfire, and Caleb studied his mellow face.

"I have been greatly blessed," Joshua said wistfully.

"Yes...you have," Caleb agreed. "And there are many more blessings yet to come."

Joshua nodded. "Rahab is a young woman," he mused. "She deserves the best."

"And she has it!" Caleb declared.

Joshua knew he had the loyalest of friends in Caleb. He also knew that Caleb read his heart. Leaning near the fire, he looked soberly into the Judahite's face.

"I am not so young," he reminded him.

"Nor I," Caleb deflected.

But Joshua would not abide sidetracking. "If the time comes..." he said, "when she is alone..." At this, he cleared his throat, his eyes misting, "...if the time comes... Salmon is a good man."

Caleb looked at the tent, listening to the friendly voices inside. Then, casting his gaze to the ground, he nodded.

For a long while, silence hung between them. But at last, Caleb shook himself and clapped Joshua on the back.

"My general," he said, "there is much yet to be done! The land must be colonized, the government established! We were in our forties when Moses sent us to spy out Canaan. We are now twice that age, yet look at *me*! I am still as strong today as I was the day Moses sent me! As my strength was then, so my strength is now, for war and for going out and coming in!"

Then, grabbing Joshua by the knee, he declared, "So is yours! You are as strong today as ever!"

The general smiled openly, leaning back with a laugh.

"You are good medicine!" he chuckled. "My dear friend, Caleb, you have always been a joy to my soul."

"And you to mine," Caleb affirmed. "We have neither of us been prophets. But we have done well in the role we play!"

Huddling together, the two men prodded the fire with their sticks. As they did so, the sticks became swords in their hands, and they dreamed together, as they had as children, of wars yet to be won and worlds to be conquered.

So many were the battles won by Joshua, and so numerous the territories conquered, no single book could do them justice. They are recorded in the chronicles of the Jews.

And he had yet more years of vigor and productivity. Eight prophets were descended from him and Rahab, so say the Jews. And when he left her to Salmon, a descendant of Judah, she bore the line of Christ.

So Joshua, the reluctant soldier, had become the warrior of God. And when he spoke to the people, he always reminded them, "One man can put to flight a thousand, for the Lord our God is he who fights for us... just as he promised."

The Powerful and
Moving Saga of

Moses: The Deliverer

Through the skillful pen of Ellen Gunderson Traylor, Moses comes alive as the brilliant young prince of Pharaoh's court torn between his love for his Jewish kinsmen and his dedication to Egypt. The course of his life takes a radical turn when he slays an Egyptian lord to protect a Hebrew slave. Now he must flee Egypt and leave behind the wealth, power and prestige that were his.

How God molds the character of Moses and guides him into the ways of righteousness is a powerful story of human nature and divine love. In this riveting drama, you will be moved again by the undeniable truth that God can shape the life of *any* man or woman into a life of greatness for His glory.

HARVEST HOUSE PUBLISHERS

For The Best In Inspirational Fiction

BIBLICAL NOVELS

Esther, *Traylor*
Joseph, *Traylor*
Moses, *Traylor*
Joshua, *Traylor*

June Masters Bacher
PIONEER ROMANCE NOVELS

Series 1
1. Love Is a Gentle Stranger
2. Love's Silent Song
3. Diary of a Loving Heart
4. Love Leads Home
5. Love Follows the Heart
6. Love's Enduring Hope

Series 2
1. Journey To Love
2. Dreams Beyond Tomorrow
3. Seasons of Love
5. My Heart's Desire
6. The Heart Remembers
7. From This Time Forth
   (Coming Fall 1991)

Series 3
1. Love's Soft Whisper
2. Love's Beautiful Dream
3. When Hearts Awaken
4. Another Spring
5. When Morning Comes Again
6. Gently Love Beckons

RUTH LIVINGSTON HILL CLASSICS

Bright Conquest
The Homecoming
The Jeweled Sword
Morning Is for Joy
This Side of Tomorrow
The South Wind Blew Softly

PIONEER ROMANCE NOVELS

Sweetbriar, *Wilbee*
The Sweetbriar Bride, *Wilbee*
Sweetbriar Spring, *Wilbee*

ROMANCE NOVELS

The Heart that Lingers, *Bacher*
With All My Heart, *Bacher*
Another Love, *Brown*
If Love Be Ours, *Brown*
Lady of Penross Manor, *Brown*
Echoes from the Past, *Bacher*

FIRESIDE ROMANCE NOVELS

A Place Called Home, *Wick*
A Song for Silas, *Wick*
The Long Road Home, *Wick*
A Gathering of Memories, *Wick*
  (Coming Fall 1991)

**Available at your
local Christian bookstore**

Dear Reader:

We would appreciate hearing from you regarding this Harvest House fiction book. It will enable us to continue to give you the best in Christian publishing.

1. What most influenced you to purchase *Joshua*?
   - [ ] Author
   - [ ] Subject matter
   - [ ] Backcover copy
   - [ ] Recommendations
   - [ ] Cover/Title
   - [ ] _____

2. Where did you purchase this book?
   - [ ] Christian bookstore
   - [ ] General bookstore
   - [ ] Department store
   - [ ] Grocery store
   - [ ] Other

3. Your overall rating of this book:
   - [ ] Excellent [ ] Very good [ ] Good [ ] Fair [ ] Poor

4. How likely would you be to purchase other books by this author?
   - [ ] Very likely
   - [ ] Somewhat likely
   - [ ] Not very likely
   - [ ] Not at all

5. What types of books most interest you?
   (check all that apply)
   - [ ] Women's Books
   - [ ] Marriage Books
   - [ ] Current Issues
   - [ ] Self Help/Psychology
   - [ ] Bible Studies
   - [ ] Fiction
   - [ ] Biographies
   - [ ] Children's Books
   - [ ] Youth Books
   - [ ] Other _____

6. Please check the box next to your age group.
   - [ ] Under 18
   - [ ] 18-24
   - [ ] 25-34
   - [ ] 35-44
   - [ ] 45-54
   - [ ] 55 and over

Mail to: Editorial Director
Harvest House Publishers
1075 Arrowsmith
Eugene, OR 97402

Name _____

Address _____

City _____ State _____ Zip _____

**Thank you for helping us to
help you in future publications!**